WARRIOR FIRE

ANGEL FIRE, BOOK 4

MARIE JOHNSTON

LE PUBLISHING

Sandeen has done the impossible: he's busted out of the underworld and now roams Earth in his own half-demon, half-angel form. His obsidian horns and black wings make it hard to blend in, but he hasn't survived this long without being crafty. Just so happens, he knows about an empty cabin in the middle of Montana. Solitude. Peace. No need to worry about getting shanked in his sleep. Until a persistent warrior angel hunts him down.

Harlowe's world has turned upside down. Her best friend betrayed their realm and lost her wings, then blew up Harlowe's past with a mind-blowing secret. So when a hauntingly handsome half demon gets away from her team, Harlowe throws herself into her job: hunting that half demon down. Forget his downy-soft wings and the horns her palms itch to caress. His inability to stay out of trouble is sure to put him back on her radar.

The mission succeeds—right up until Sandeen kidnaps Harlowe. Softening toward him could cost her everything. Keeping her alive could mean the end of his hard-earned freedom. But as the lines between them blur, the only thing clear is that Harlowe's not the only one hunting Sandeen. The fate of three realms depends on them learning how to tell friend from foe—and it's not as simple as wings versus horns any longer.

CHAPTER 1

A black bird flew into the air only to land on another evergreen tree a few down from where it had originally perched.

Sandeen eyed the bird from the front stoop of the little Montana cabin he was hiding out in and dipped his head. Smart creatures. Humans saw them as pests or ignored them completely. Demons did the same—except when considering whether to eat them.

Not him. He hadn't survived the underworld by underestimating what he faced. Sylphs were worse pests than crows would ever be, but the little demons had their uses. On Earth, they slipped unseen through the realm, interfering with humans' lives until negative feelings in those humans coalesced into damaging thoughts that opened the human up to becoming a host for a higher-level demon.

In the underworld, sylphs were like cats. Ugly, stinky cats that no one wanted to let into their home. Sylphs shat where they ate and then they ate that too. But they had their uses. For a few tasty morsels they didn't have to scrounge for, the little gossipmongers spilled their hearts out.

A second crow cawed. The first crow answered.

Sandeen flicked his gaze from the first bird to his right, then swiveled to look at the other bird. Each crow perched close to the top of their respective evergreen.

Interesting.

When Boone had lived here, he'd probably read the land a different way. Sandeen had seen the trapping lines the human had used to catch his food, but he had no clue how to use them. Wi-Fi for the win. He'd skimmed off someone else's service until he'd gotten his own put together. Now he could order his own food and supplies delivered to the middle of Nowhere, Montana.

In the old days, all of ten months ago, he would've just found a host with a full fridge. But then he'd have to stay in that host to stay in the earthly realm.

No longer.

Sandeen ruffled his wings. Both birds stared at him, cocking their heads one way, then the other. The first bird cawed.

"Thanks." His voice was scratchy. He hadn't spoken to anyone for months. He didn't speak bird, but he liked to imagine that the crows hung around him thanks to his own glossy black wings.

It was probably bullshit. It wasn't like a couple of antelope were going to hang around because of Sandeen's obsidian horns. The birds were something to talk to, to keep his voice box from going rusty. To make him think he had a place in this realm where, as far as humans were concerned, he was an abomination. He was also evil as far as angels in the realm of Numen were concerned. Yet he refused to return to the underworld, the realm of Daemon.

They'd have to drag his dead body through the Gloom first.

The second crow cawed and flew to another tree a little closer to Sandeen. The bird cocked his head at him.

Indeed. Sandeen dipped his head.

He looked down at his clothing. Boone had left quite a few things behind when he'd sold this place to what he thought was a single man who wanted a hunting cabin. The deal had been done online, thanks to a discreet identity Sandeen had constructed, along with a healthy savings account filled with money he'd pilfered from several hosts over the years.

It paid to be prepared.

The brown hiking boots would be fine. His heavy-duty blue jeans didn't blend into his surroundings, but his wings threw all kinds of shadows around him. Paired with the black hoodie he'd cut the back out of to make room for his wings, he blended well.

Taking another sip of the coffee and grimacing—would he ever get used to this drink?—he opened the cabin door behind him. The hinges stayed quiet thanks to the WD-40 he'd found in the shed. Boone had taken many of his tools but left some essentials behind.

Sandeen set his cup down on the counter. A large knife rested on the island. He hooked it on his pants. Boone had also taken all his hunting rifles and shotguns. Sandeen could've used those, but blades would have to do. He didn't want to risk buying a gun with his fake identity. No need to flirt with trouble.

He passed a ball cap but ignored it. Getting it over his horns was one thing, but his hair had grown thick and shaggy. Since he'd been alone for months, he'd quit trying to trim it. Same with shaving.

In the underworld, he'd been fastidious about his hair,

facial hair included. Anything that could be used as a handhold for an enemy was kept short. And in the underworld, every demon was an enemy—including his sire.

Other high-level demons like his sire had underestimated his softly feathered wings for years. Sandeen had let them. Same with his horns.

Sandeen slipped outside and squinted into the sky. The crows had moved closer. The bird on the left tilted its head as it peered into the canopy of the trees. Sandeen flared his wings out and curled them around his body. Their silky darkness cast the same shadows as the trees until he was nothing more than a moving shadow.

He sidled left of the second bird. Hopefully whatever had interested the crows so much wouldn't have the same advantage as him. Toeing his way through the underbrush, he took his time. Movement in the trees caught his attention.

Ah, so it was as he'd feared. He was being hunted. And, as he'd suspected, it wasn't his fellow Daemon.

Oh, they were looking for him. But they had no idea this cabin existed and lacked the technical savvy to track his electronic trail, if they could even determine where it started.

But angelic warriors wouldn't be so daunted. He'd known they would hunt him. He'd given them the nudge they'd needed to help their fallen friend and her human lover, Boone. But he'd also had to show his hand to do it. They wouldn't let him go so easily.

The second crow flew closer to his cabin, its head cocked in the same direction as the first. Just one warrior. And judging by the long, lithe body and long blond braid, Sandeen knew exactly who hunted him.

His quiet life was about to be upended. There was no

way the warrior would leave without knowing who, exactly, resided here. He should be irate. He should be raging at the unfairness. He should be planning how to kill his opponent.

Yet a smile stretched his lips. He'd faced this warrior before, but always while he was in a host. This time, it would be just him. And just her.

TINGLES SPREAD like promises across Harlowe's skin. Not the usual reaction she got when she hunted her targets. She paused as a crow cawed above. She shot it a dirty look. If she didn't have her own wings morphed behind her back, she'd flap them in its face.

Nosy birds.

She was in the middle of the mountains in Montana. She'd been near here before, when Sierra had contacted them.

Harlowe's heart wrenched. Sierra. So many feelings.

Betrayal. Loss. Jealousy. The lies behind the death of Harlowe's mother. The lies behind the life of Sierra.

Her teammate. Her best friend. Her *sister*. Harlowe had lost Sierra when she'd been blackmailed into betraying their team. It wasn't until after Sierra had lost her wings that they'd learned why she'd been blackmailed—she was half demon. Worse, Sierra'd had a fling with another fallen angel and gotten pregnant.

Sierra had been as good as dead to Harlowe, as per the rules of their realm regarding fallen angels, but also due to the betrayal. And Harlowe had lost Sierra again when she'd learned of Sierra's parentage: She and Harlowe shared a mother. But Sierra's father? A demon. It was a combination that should have been an impossibility. Like the creature that Harlowe was tracking down—the frustrating male known as Sandeen.

The half angel—or was that half demon?—had figured out how to roam the earth in his own skin. With his glossy wings hanging out. His presence threatened the security of their kind. If humans learned that angels and demons were more than characters in stories, it'd be chaos. Demons would find a way to abuse the knowledge, cultivate a following, and, well, they'd seen how that turned out with the fallen Jameson. The very bad fallen who had fathered Sierra's baby. Jameson was dead now, but thanks to events he'd set in motion, Harlowe's team had barely avoided more of her kind getting killed, along with a nightclub full of humans.

The crow cawed again and Harlowe rolled her eyes. Were those birds trying to fuck up her mission?

She paused under the branches of a tall tree, squatting until she was concealed by prickly green needles. Her standard warrior wear—black tactical pants, black boots, and a black long-sleeved shirt—was not ideal in the green and brown environment.

A bead of sweat rolled down her back. Summer in the mountains wasn't as hot as she'd feared, but she'd started her hike a few miles away. If the sneaky demon had taken up residence in Boone's old cabin, she couldn't just drive up and check it out.

Anticipation swirled through her belly. Could this be the day she finally tracked that bastard down? He'd been a thorn in her side since she'd first run across him at the club Jameson had run, Fall From Grace. The club had indeed fallen from grace, but Sandeen had slipped through their fingers before then. In his own form. Something no demon should have the ability to do.

Her kind would lose their wings if they revealed their

presence to humans. And the aggravating male thought he could wander around Earth as a grotesque demon?

She bit the inside of her cheek, squinting through the branches at the cabin. Lying wasn't supposed to come naturally to angels. Her mind rebelled at labeling Sandeen "grotesque."

Startling blue eyes. Square chiseled jaw. Black horns that filled her with more curiosity than revulsion, and feathery wings so unlike the wings of every other demon she'd ever come across. Other high-level Daemon, archmasters like Sandeen, had leathery wings with claws that could slit her throat as easily as stab her. Sandeen's made her think of lazy mornings lounging in bed, tangling limbs as they—

Gah. Harlowe remained crouched as she wove her way closer to the cabin. That male had to be stopped. He had to be eradicated.

Nausea twisted her stomach. The thought of killing him sent a sense of wrongness through her. Whatever happened to him, Sierra ought to share the same fate. Both were part demon, after all. Harlowe was angry at her ex–best friend for keeping secrets, but did her sister deserve more than what had already happened to her? To lose the peace she'd found with her new baby and human mate?

Shame circled through Harlowe as the crows wailed overhead. Harlowe wasn't that coldhearted. But she was good at her job and that was why she was tracking the demon.

There was no movement at the cabin, but the tingles were back, tracing down her spine and heating her blood. That only happened when *he* was close.

Gritting her teeth, she crept closer. The place was small, a simple square with windows. A small, single-stall garage that was little more than a shed sat on the edge of the clearing. She could use that for cover to spy on the house.

Could the demon be out hunting? What'd he eat? How'd he dress? Did he stay secluded with those wings and horns? Did he shout at the UPS guy through the door as all his food and supplies were delivered?

Did he eat the UPS guy?

The demon would answer. She'd make sure of it.

Trees ringed the cabin as if the tiny home had been airlifted into a clearing just large enough for it and the small garage.

Skirting behind the cabin, she reached the back of the garage. Pine needles and bits of branches snagged in her hair as she ducked and wove through the foliage, but she ignored them. Camouflage.

She went still. The birds she couldn't shake flew overhead, from one edge of the clearing to the other. They cawed back and forth.

She was supposed to love all of God's creatures, but these birds were annoying the shit out of her.

There was no other sound. The cabin was quiet.

Was he sleeping? Was the demon even here, or was it just another wild-goose chase like they'd all been for the last ten months?

She'd scoured Las Vegas for the demon. After several run-ins with demons who were also hunting him, she'd given up on Vegas. She'd gone to all the large cities around the world, places dense with humans and trouble, where demons could do their worst. New York City. London. Dubai. Then she'd started with the opposite. Remote. Hidden. Like Boone's old cabin. It made perfect sense. Right under the noses of her warrior team, familiar for the demon, and the last place the demons hunting Sandeen would look. Too many angels knew about the cabin.

She drew a dagger from her belt. The cool metal centered her and the heft of the blade focused her mind. She was here for one reason.

Send the demon back to hell. Fallen blood on Numen steel was keeping him in this realm. So she'd take the steel and carve off whatever part of himself he'd stained with the blood.

Creeping to the wall of the garage, she was about to peer around the corner when tendrils of heat curled around her body until she wanted to groan and sink into the source. The scents of pine and cedar wafted across her nose.

"Hello, Lowe," said a deep, mesmerizing voice from behind her.

She tensed, tightening her hold around the blade. She was in the middle of a spin, planning to sink the dagger into the demon's carotid, when pain bloomed through her skull and everything went black.

CHAPTER 2

A low groan amplified the pain in Harlowe's head. What the hell?

The demon. He'd known she was there and he'd knocked her out. The headache faded quickly as her body healed itself.

How was he always one step ahead?

Cunning demon.

She kept her eyes shut and took stock of her surroundings. She was sitting up, but not on a hard chair. A surprisingly soft surface was under her butt. Her arms were bound in front of her and her feet were bound together. Her boots were off, likely to make binding her ankles more secure. The comforting weight of her weapons was gone. The ever-present vial of angel fire on the chain around her neck was gone as well.

Something warm but rough stroked across her face. "You can open your eyes, angel. I know you're awake."

Tingles sizzled across her body. He'd touched her. She tried to summon rage, tried *really* hard, but her body lit up like the Rockefeller Center Christmas tree. All her nerve endings flared to life as if they wanted to let the demon know how much he affected her.

Her eyelids popped open and her glare landed directly on him.

The fledgling anger she'd nursed wavered. His big body was folded into a hard chair. He'd grown a beard. Instead of mischievous, he looked dark and dangerous. His hair was longer than when she'd last seen him. Thick and wavy, it'd be perfect to push her hands through. Was it as silky as it looked? And the hint of smooth horns. Warm or cool to her touch? Would they heat up if she stroked him?

Revulsion filled her. Horns were not sexy!

But those *wings*. She had a harder time convincing herself there was nothing desirable about his wings. A demon was a demon. But his wings were magnificent, even by Numen standards. Covered in glossy black feathers, his wings arched high behind him and draped down to the floor. His back muscles must be chiseled to hold them off the ground.

She ground her jaws together. There had to be a spot on his body she could glower at without wondering about touch, texture, or taste.

The only thing that made her feel a little better about the way he affected her dormant hormones was that she knew his secret. That had to be the reason he made her go haywire. He was half angel. She had the urge to protect him as much as destroy him.

His bright eyes danced. "Good afternoon, sleepyhead."

Afternoon? She glanced around. The cabin was one room. A small island separated the kitchen from the living area and the bedroom was just a bed in the corner. A door in the wall between the bed and the living area must be the bathroom. She looked out the window. The thick curtains were pulled apart to show the sky outside. Brilliant blue. Like the demon's eyes. She'd started hunting him at dawn. It hadn't taken that long to hike to the cabin. How long had she been out?

"It's only four o'clock." The demon chuckled. "But you must've needed the rest. I didn't give you that hard a knock."

Lines fanned out from his eyes as he smiled. She sensed no malice. True humor danced in his eyes and her body answered with a belly flip.

Demon. Regardless of his secret, he was still a demon. He used people, and her one duty in life was to keep demons like him from hurting humans. From destroying mothers and fathers and robbing kids of their parents and their best friends.

Sierra isn't dead. Neither is Father.

She slammed down on those thoughts.

He peered at her. "How's your head?" Tapping his forehead, he grimaced. "It was the only way, I'm afraid. You'd have put up a fight until one of us got hurt."

"Until *you* got hurt," she sneered.

Those eyes danced again. "Ah, ah, angel. You haven't taken me on in this form. It won't be as easy as when I was in a human I didn't want to hurt." He leaned closer and his pine scent curled around her. What had happened to the brimstone stench? "But I think *you* wanted to make those humans suffer a little bit. They let a demon inside them, after all."

She narrowed her eyes. "I'm not falling for your mind games." But guilt returned. She shook it off.

The demon was tricky. Killing humans went against everything her kind stood for, and she would never intentionally hurt them. But sometimes it was necessary to throw a punch or two if the demon possessing the host was attacking her.

He leaned back in his chair. "How's Alma?"

The switch in topic made her mind spin. She almost said *fine, feisty as ever,* but she stared at him instead.

Annoyance crossed his rugged face. He wasn't dirty like the last time she'd seen him. Before, when he had possessed a host, she had viewed him no differently than any other archmaster or less powerful symaster. He'd been like a 3D hologram. Then he'd shocked them all when he'd shown them that it was possible to walk in the human realm in his real form. He'd been dressed in nasty rags, his skin full of grit and smeared with mud or dried blood. She had no idea what Daemon was like to live in, but if she imagined smelly and dirty, he'd fit the image.

Today, he was real. In all his robust, healthy flesh. The only image he fit was a mountain-man-slash-avenging-angel.

When the demon didn't challenge her lack of a response, she said sweetly, "Why don't you possess her and find out for yourself?"

Alma would love it. The elderly lady had hosted the demon while he'd tracked down Sierra and then helped her and Boone escape demons sent by an evil human. She continued to refer to him as *my demon.*

"I would, but it might risk my stay in this realm. I'm not willing to do that."

Harlowe rolled her eyes. "You're telling me that your possessing days are over?"

"Ever possessed anyone, angel?" the demon asked, his quiet voice resonating with churning emotion his expression hid. "Ever shared in their worst feelings, their darkest emotions, or their curdling self-hatred?"

"Isn't that what gets your kind off?"

Resignation flickered through his expression. "It's supposed to." He folded his arms across his massive chest. A black hoodie had been tossed on the bed. The black T-shirt he wore molded against his muscles but hung loose at the sides. Had he cut the back out to fit his wings? Probably. He didn't have access to special clothing made to accommodate wings like she had in her realm.

"Are you telling me that it bothered you to possess humans? To use them and ruin their lives?" The possibility that his answer would be yes hung in her mind. She knew what he was, but she wasn't giving him the benefit of the doubt. He was a lying demon.

"Would you believe me if I told you the truth, Lowe?"

She hated when he used the nickname only he ever called her. "Angel" was more generic, if still unsettling, in his deep timbre. "No."

He spread his hands, like *there you go*. "I can't let you go and risk you ruining my good time. But you won't believe that I just want to be left alone for eternity."

"For eternity?"

He lifted a shoulder. "Better than life in Daemon."

"Gerzon is still alive. They're looking for you." Hunting for him, like she had been. "So is Zanda."

The demon blanched at the second name.

"An old girlfriend?" Harlowe stomped down the jealousy that flared to life.

He winced. "I guess you could call it that."

"I call it disgusting."

"I would agree, though Zanda was better than most."

Harlowe curled her lip. When she'd helped free Sierra from Andy's clutches at the club, she'd fought Zanda. The demon had gotten away as soon as Harlowe had tossed her out of her host and into the Mist. Coward.

"She'll probably want to kill me though," the demon

said. "I can usually sweet-talk my way out of it, but this time there aren't enough orgasms in all three realms."

Heat swamped her body. The demon looked like he would be good at giving orgasms. "Your kind actually feels pleasure?" He was a creature that hurt people. He'd been bred and raised to hurt others. Why was that so hard to remember?

"We feel pleasure as acutely as your kind, probably more so. It's a rarity in our world. Agony and terror are our daily life, so the pursuit of pleasure is desperate and often turns twisted."

"It's not an excuse for hurting others."

"When it's all you know, you don't need an excuse." He slapped his hands on his powerful thighs. Most demons had leathery skin, bloated, rancid flesh, and a putrid stench. This demon looked like he'd walked out of a photo shoot for *Lumbersexual Monthly*. "So here's how we're going to do this. You're chained to the floor." He gestured to a large metal loop sticking out of the floorboards. A long chain ran from the loop, almost reaching her chair.

Her gaze popped to the bindings at her feet. They were rope, but knotted to chains—in the most complicated knots she'd seen in her life. And they were glossy, like they'd been bonded to the metal. How had she not noticed the details of her own situation? The demon had been all-consuming, but informative in a way. She'd never had the chance to chat with a being from Daemon. They weren't exactly talkers. Just killers.

"You'll be able to sleep on the couch and make it to the bathroom."

Confusion blocked any panic that should've risen as soon as she'd noticed her predicament. "Why?" Why keep her alive? Why hold her prisoner? Why give her a soft place to sleep when he had a garage to shove her in and forget about?

He lifted a muscled shoulder. "Because you're pretty. Looking at you gives me pleasure." He leaned closer, his hot breath wafting over her face. Minty. Did he brush his teeth like a domesticated demon? His proximity exponentially increased those damn tingles. "After all, angel, I'm still a demon."

HE HAD no idea why he'd chained her up. It was crazy. It risked everything he'd worked for.

Harlowe was a warrior. She was one of the few beings trained to fight him. Being tied up in a cabin in the middle of Montana would only slow her down, not stop her.

And she was more than pretty. Beautiful. Violet eyes, statuesque, with a powerful build and a healthy glow. She smelled like sunshine after a rainstorm.

He'd grown up with the stench of brimstone, blood, and feces. Rot. Death. Harlowe's scent was life. Her bright eyes were the color of wildflowers and her hair was the color of a cloudy day on Earth. The underworld was cloudy, but that was a noxious fog that made his skin burn.

The heartless demon he'd been raised to be would have beheaded her on the spot. It was the best way to ensure his freedom. No witnesses. She'd foolishly come alone. Her team would never know what had happened.

Instead, he was keeping her like a prize—one that would bury a blade in his heart and saw his head off. Since he doubted Boone had held women captive in the cabin, the chain was probably left over from another owner or had been used as a tow chain. He'd anchored the bolt in the floor. It ran through the boards and was secured to a metal plate on the other side.

He wished he'd had time to fashion a better chain, one that was strong, yet more delicate, like the warrior herself. The pretty angel would be surprised at his blacksmithing abilities. All of her comrades would be too. The entire realm of Numen would be shocked to learn exactly why Daemon were intimately acquainted with the forging of metal.

Harlowe wiggled in her seat. Boone, with all his snares, had left no shortage of rope. Sandeen had used plenty around her wrists and ankles.

"Demon, you're going to regret this."

"Probably."

The slack in the chain was barely enough to allow her full body onto the couch. He wasn't going to give her a choice. Because after a lifetime sleeping on a rock slab, he was sleeping in the bed. The bathroom might be tricky with her bound hands, but he'd leave that up to her to figure out.

She tried kicking him. "You bastard."

"All demons are."

"I'm going to kill you. You won't see it coming. You won't have time to take that little bloodstained blade you use to walk around as yourself—"

He straightened and pulled the bowie knife from his belt. She paled and he grinned. "Hate to ruin the surprise, but I don't need your steel to walk around like this."

He laid the knife on the floor, out of her reach of course. He held his arms out and slowly spun around, then stooped and lifted the legs of his pants so she could see that he wasn't hiding any weapons above his boots. He didn't seem to need tattoos either, but that explanation could wait. She was smart enough to figure out that the vial around his neck was fallen angel's blood and that as long as he had that, he could freely walk the earth.

"Figures," she said, her mouth pursed like she'd sucked on a lemon wedge.

"Anyway, Lowe, you understand that I have to leave you tied up. I'll keep your hands in front, unless you're a naughty angel." He tried to keep the suggestive smile off his face. He really did.

"Quit calling me Lowe."

He tilted his head. "You like 'angel' better?" Taunting Harlowe had always been the best game he'd ever played. She didn't want anything from him; she wanted him dead. Yet she'd had plenty of opportunities to destroy him. And here he was. Was that what made it fun?

" 'The warrior who will end your worthless life' is a better name," she gritted out.

"Worthless" hit a vulnerable spot inside of him that he'd been protecting for years. Daemon didn't care if they had any worth. Why was he afflicted with the inconvenient emotion? "My life may be worthless, but I was given it regardless. I intend to spend the rest of it a free male."

"You aren't free. You're on the run."

He clenched his jaw. The warrior could fight with words as effectively as her fists. "I'd rather worry about getting eaten by bears than getting gutted by my sire."

"Why would your— Never mind. You're a demon. That's enough explanation."

She wasn't wrong, yet he couldn't leave it at that. "He liked to watch me try to protect myself as I healed. A test, he called it." He couldn't stand still under her scrutiny, so he checked the knots again. They were just as secure as they'd always been.

She stared at him, working her jaw like she hated her curiosity taking over. "Are you serious?"

"Serious as sin, angel."

"Why would he—" She shook her head and he practically read the word scrolling across her mind. *Demon.*

He yanked at her chain and stepped back. She twitched as if restraining herself from lunging at him, knowing damn well it wouldn't do any good. She had no way to free herself or incapacitate him.

After he'd knocked her out, he'd stripped her of her weapons and her vial of angel fire. He'd been tempted to dump it and let it burn itself out in the yard, but it was a precious substance. Daemon didn't have angel fire. Daemon had steel.

Now he had both.

He'd taken her weapons to the shed while she was passed out. The knock to her head had been severe, but it had to be for an immortal who healed quickly.

She tugged and jerked on the chain but it didn't budge. She might be immortal and a trained Numen warrior, but she wasn't breaking that chain.

She glared at him, her face red, her eyes radiating rage. "You can't keep me prisoner. It won't work."

"There's a pillow, sheet, and blanket at the end. The chain will reach to the toilet. Shutting the door might be an issue."

"You'd like to see that, wouldn't you, demon?" she snarled.

"Trust me, I've seen females defecate, fornicate, and procreate. None of it turns me on. The miracle of birth is not for demons. Trust me."

She stopped, staring at him like he'd spoken a different language.

He continued his verbal tour. "You'll find towels, but I must admit that I have no idea how a shower will work for you. Promise I won't look though." He couldn't remember making a promise he'd kept.

"I will kill you."

He grinned and her gaze dropped to his fangs. They weren't long, but they were more than prominent canines. "Lowe. I'd be disappointed if you didn't try."

A yellow, congealed mess steamed on the plate the demon held toward her. "What the hell is that?" she asked.

The demon scowled. "Eggs."

"Did you wait for them to hatch into little chicks and then mash them up?" Numen had eggs. Numen acquired whatever angels wanted and set up markets. She could buy white eggs, brown eggs, even blue eggs. Chicken eggs. Duck eggs. Fish eggs.

None of them looked like this.

"They're scrambled. Perhaps you've heard of the method?"

She glanced at him but couldn't tell if he was joking. What did demons do for food in the underworld? "Seriously. What is this?"

"Eggs. Scrambled."

She sat on the edge of the couch. He'd arranged the small living area so the couch was right by the bathroom. The bed had been shoved against the wall. She could kick at the edge, but if he slept on the far side, she couldn't reach him.

While he cooked, she'd tried picking the lock. The craftsmanship was surprisingly delicate for such a bulky piece of metal, but it was sturdy. The seams in the welds were strong. She couldn't bust them, nor could she untie the knots. Had he glued them together? The lock on the chains had a key that she hadn't seen the demon pocket or put anywhere else. The bolt in the floor wasn't budging either. And there was no lock, no break in the metal, for her to tamper with.

She was caught. The only way she was leaving was if she dragged the cabin with her.

And she had to pee.

The things he'd said about his world were bleak. *Defecate, fornicate, and procreate.* No one had seen her use the bathroom. Ever. She enjoyed a good round of sex, though minus an audience. And she had no mate to procreate with. She wasn't going to pin her hopes on one male, then find out he wasn't her destined mate.

It just seemed like a waste of time.

"I can't eat this. I might be immortal, but I can still get salmonella."

"Who's Sam and Ella?"

"Food poisoning, demon."

The corner of his mouth kicked up. Damn demon was messing with her. She caught a wink of fang. A jolt of awareness hit her like it had when he'd grinned. The fangs were worse than the horns. She'd been bitten with fangs and gouged with both. But she'd never stopped to look at them before, during, or after a fight. That must be why she was fascinated. Had to be.

"I've never heard of an angel getting a stomachache. I think you'll be fine. They're good."

Gelatinous portions of the heap mocked her. "They're not cooked."

"They are too. Didn't you see me at the stove?" He shoved a hand toward the kitchen.

"Did you turn it on?"

He rolled his eyes, but she caught a flash of hurt. He couldn't be sensitive over a crappy meal.

"Look. I get you probably don't have appliances in your realm, and I'm sure you fleeced your host to buy food they couldn't afford, but this isn't edible. Half of it is raw." She peered closer. "Is that a hunk of butter?" Had he really not turned the stove on?

"My hosts cooked."

She lifted a brow. Hunger fisted her stomach. She hadn't eaten all day and she'd had to heal from a major head injury. But she still had her head. There was that.

He could've easily beheaded her. He could've used her own vial of angel fire on her. The two most reliable ways to kill an angel dead. Why hadn't he?

Shouldn't he want to debase her? He was living a demon's dream, walking around the human realm in his own body with a captive angel.

Yet she'd awoken fully dressed and completely healed. Now he was trying to feed her.

She didn't forget that the only help he'd given her team had ultimately been for his benefit. She was alive and well for a reason. He planned to use her. It was what he did.

Didn't mean she had to eat half-cooked eggs with chunks of butter. "From what I was taught, demons learn from their hosts."

He crossed his arms and nodded, waiting to see what her play was. For now, she kept it simple: edible food.

"If you have to drive," she continued, "you can do it because your host knows how." He didn't respond, so she must be on the right track. It wasn't like she was giving away trade secrets. In fact, she was validating what her kind thought they knew about his. "So if you never cooked in a host, you don't really know how to."

"I've seen it done."

"What do you eat in Daemon?" She sounded incredulous, but her curiosity ran rampant.

"Other demons. The smaller ones, usually."

She fought a gag. "Do you cook them?"

"Depends." He stuffed a hand in his hair, running his hand over his horn. "Why do you think we spend so much time in the human realm? Eating on Earth is full of pleasure. Good tastes. Good smells. We're only in possession of the host, but it's not like we can't starve to death. That kind of secondhand sustenance can keep us going for a while."

His information was disturbing. She killed demons to save humans from the demons using them. But to think she'd yanked them out of hosts and into the Mist and fought them to the death over the joy of eating chocolate chip cookies was . . . odd. Could they save human lives by shipping real food to the underworld?

She leveled the demon with her most commanding look. "Turn the stove back on to medium high heat."

He stared at her for a moment, then pivoted on his hiking boot.

"Take the plate with you."

He paused. The flutter of his wings was eerily silent. Was that a trick of his upbringing? Then he lifted her plate and went into the kitchen. He did as she instructed.

A demon couldn't get a ton of groceries delivered in the middle of the mountains. She wouldn't waste food. "Do you see the bits of butter on my plate and yours?"

He peered at both and nodded.

"Put those in the pan and let them melt." Again, he followed her lead without question.

She'd trained arrogant pricks brand new to the Numen warrior academy and they hadn't listened as well as the demon. Not a one.

As she rattled off instructions, she tried not to remember giggling with Sierra as they'd cooked during nights off in various safe houses over the years. Harlowe had learned to cook out of necessity. Her father hadn't been interested in full meals. He'd gotten no pleasure from good food. He hadn't found pleasure in much of anything after her mother had died.

Harlowe had grown up on eggs and toast. Then she'd met Sierra, who'd shown her how to use plain eggs and bread to make French toast, toad in the hole, bread pudding, meals Sierra had learned from her warrior father, who'd spent plenty of time on Earth.

In any other situation, Harlowe might take comfort in passing on knowledge she hadn't been able to learn from a parent to another being who hadn't had parents to help him either. But he was a demon, Sierra was gone, and Harlowe wanted to eat. That was all.

Boone had left behind all his seasonings. The demon ran through the names, using the ones she approved of. Soon the cabin smelled like a greasy diner and her stomach was going wild.

She managed to keep from straining against her chains to grab the plate he offered her out of his hands.

Something made her pause and watch him take his first bite. His eyes rolled back and he groaned. He shoveled another bite in, not stopping until the plate was clear.

Harlowe clutched hers. The delight he took in eating simple scrambled eggs . . . He'd grown up eating other demons and getting gutted by his father.

No, she couldn't soften.

But she could, and she knew damn well why, while he had no idea.

She stuffed eggs into her mouth and reacted the same way the demon had. Awkward. She glanced at him. He'd noticed.

Was that pride in his gaze?

"It's the seasoning salt," she said. "It's the secret ingredient."

"I thought butter made everything better. Alma said that a few times while watching her cooking shows."

"Alma loves Las Vegas." She didn't know why she'd given him that. Maybe because he'd risked humiliation to feed her? "Her bones don't ache as bad in the warmer weather and she found a senior group to join."

Wistfulness flickered through the demon's expression, but he shuttered his gaze and cleared his throat. "Good. If she's feeling better and she's happy, then she won't get possessed as easily."

Did the demon really care about the old lady? He'd been protective of her during their time in the safe house in Las Vegas, but it had been for his own benefit. Yet it didn't benefit him to have one fewer human to possess if he lost the ability to roam in his own form.

Which spurred several questions she'd had earlier when he'd revealed that he didn't need Numen steel stained with fallen blood to stay on Earth. How was he still in his own form? She'd heard rumors that Numen steel didn't originate in the angelic realm. Was there substance to those whisperings?

Maybe it was still the effect of Sierra's blood from when he'd used it to leave the safe house in Vegas. Or maybe he'd harvested more fallen blood elsewhere. That vial around his neck *had* to be fallen blood. Did the blood of a fallen angel keep both the Gloom—which separated Daemon and Earth—and the Mist—which separated Numen and Earth—from allowing him to cross, thus trapping him on Earth?

Or was it his heritage? No, he would've escaped to Earth before if that was the sole reason. Then again, she recalled how Jameson had been able to enter Numen again to save his son Jagger. What was the saying? Intention is nine-tenths of the law?

No, that was possession. *The road to hell is paved with good intentions.* Reverse it and maybe that was the road to Earth from the underworld.

What they were learning was that this was a complicated issue and there were multiple variables involved. She'd have that to report to Director Vale, at least. Something to show for being tied up and eating the demon's food.

In her short time with him, she'd learned about life in Daemon. She was his captive, and for now, that wasn't going to change. It made sense to gather as much intel as she could. When she didn't report back in a few days, her team would go looking for her. They'd follow the same line of thinking Harlowe had and check the cabin.

Had he killed the person who'd bought it from Boone?

Her gut said no, but she had to know for certain. She had to find out everything she could about the demon. It'd mean the difference between life and death for him, and she was starting to care about the outcome.

She was too compliant.

Sandeen hunched over the screen, combing through

food blogs. Mostly, he was spacing out, thinking about his captive.

The first night, he'd expected his prisoner to rage against her chains. To try to kill him. To maim him at the very least.

After she'd eaten the eggs, she'd primly laid out her blankets on the couch. When he'd gone outside to look for signs of other warriors hunting him down or demons getting close to his trail, she must've used the bathroom.

The first night, she'd slept hard. He'd dozed with one eye open, expecting an attack any second. Yesterday, she'd walked him through making oatmeal and ordered him to add sugar and canned fruit he found in the cupboards.

Like the eggs, it'd been transformative. Eating in a host had been as close to heaven as he thought he'd get. But eating decent food with his own taste buds was damn near orgasmic. Better than an orgasm, since the majority of his experience with sex had been in his realm—and thus accompanied by a lot of pain.

For lunch, she'd made him dig through the freezer that Boone had left stocked like a housewarming gift. He'd found plenty of pheasant meat. Since he'd confiscated her phone, she demanded he be the one to comb through recipes online and compare them to what he had in the cabin. Eventually, she'd tinkered with a recipe and walked him through cooking it, sitting on the couch and watching him like a hawk, throwing out directions.

He'd made comments about how he might as well play along since there was nothing else to do, when in reality, it'd been the best day of his life. He'd cooked. He'd conversed with another being with minimal bickering and zero physical fighting. He'd pleased an angel with the food he'd prepared. It was a heady experience that they were repeating today.

But he wasn't an idiot. She was docile for a reason. Was her team on their way? She knew about Gerzon and Zanda searching for him, yet she was kicked back on his couch with her feet dangling over the armrest.

He landed on a skillet chicken recipe. A bird was a bird. They were interchangeable, right? "I've got one that uses rice and something called cream of mushroom soup." He'd seen that in the cupboard and had all sorts of questions about creaming celery and mushrooms.

"That'll work."

He went to grab the package of meat wrapped in white paper that he'd found in the freezer.

"Wash your hands."

She demanded he do that every time he stepped foot in the kitchen and several times throughout the process of cooking.

"I'm not nearly as dirty as I used to be, angel."

She swung her legs, her hands anchored behind her head. "I have no clue what you're doing for a bathroom and I might not be affected by food poisoning, but I don't need your nut juice all over my food."

His lips twitched. "I go outside." Otherwise, she'd use that slack on her chain to tackle him while he was combing his unruly hair. Brushing wasn't easy to do around horns, but he tried not to look like he was born and raised in the underworld.

"Exactly."

He smirked. "It's not like we have plumbing in the underworld."

Her foot went still. "You don't?"

"What does Numen have? Angelic plumbers?" He was only half kidding. What did they do?

"We just go and it, you know, disappears."

"To where?"

"Wherever stuff from the bathroom goes," she said slowly.

"You truly have plumbing?"

She sat up, her feet hitting the floor. "Like toilets? Yeah. We're not heathens."

He ignored the dig. It wasn't like he could claim to be anything else. "And how does all that work? Plumbing lines that run through the clouds?"

"It works like the rest of the realm. We mimic human environments, and our natural energy just makes things run. It's just how it works. Same with electronics."

His eyes widened. "You can use a phone in Numen?"

"Yes," she said cautiously. Was she going to shut down when he was only just learning how unfairly balanced the realms were? "You can't do any of that in Daemon?"

He couldn't see a point in not telling her. "Our natural energy is used to keep ourselves alive. Nothing grows in the realm. It's stone and dirt and toxic fog and rotting waste."

"Do you think Daemon deserves better?"

"No." He couldn't imagine giving demons comfort. It was a benefit to the other realms that demons killed and feasted on themselves. But still. A toilet. His place didn't even have a hole in the ground. "It doesn't stop us from wanting better."

"And that's what you're here for? Better?" Her brows were drawn together.

Was he speaking to a warrior or a curious angel? "Isn't that what all Daemon are? Selfish heathens that want all of your creature comforts for themselves?" He went back to cooking, but the burn of her eyes traced across his shoulders.

"What creature comfort are you selfishly after? Specifically?" He didn't answer immediately and she continued, "I mean, in this cabin, in the middle of nowhere. You know, the one with all the creature comforts."

His lips twitched again. Smiles were a weapon. His kind smiled when they were eviscerating an enemy—or an ally. They smiled when they were in hosts to blend in. Glee was reserved for the extra malicious. Harlowe was making him smile *genuinely* when she probably wanted to gut him.

"Lowe, it's not as much about what's here as what's not here." Pain. Fear. Stench.

He made supper with minimal help from her. The atmosphere in the cabin was clogged with her curiosity. She wanted to ask more, practically vibrated with the need to. He didn't appease her. Making her want more from him than his head on a pike had become his new hobby. A spark of delight that he marveled over.

He dished up her plate. He barely trusted her with a fork, but this meal would only need spoons anyway.

Her violet gaze tracked him the short distance from the kitchen to the couch.

He handed the plate over. "One day, you'll have to tell me the mystery of how they get cream from mushrooms."

That divot between her brows appeared as she searched his face. "It's not literal."

He shrugged. "Ah, well. That's not as fun, is it?"

They ate in silence, her on the end of the couch and him at the island. He was about to stuff the last bite into his mouth when a shadow moved across the window. Prickles skittered down his spine.

He'd been in the cabin long enough to know what birds flying across the window were like. The sounds. The rustle of trees and the chittering of birds and other animals. This shadow was different.

He put his spoon down and took his plate to the sink. When he turned, Harlowe studied him from the corner of her eye. To anyone else, she would look hunched over her food. But he knew her better.

She'd felt it too. Damn.

The window was the obvious choice. He used his long strides to go to the door, whip it open and charge outside. He darted around the cabin. A sylph slinked along the base of the cabin. Its yellow eyes widened as Sandeen leaped toward it.

He wasn't sure he could touch a sylph in this form. They were invisible, like ghosts that could affect the world around them in minor ways. Enough to irritate the shit out of a human, to create a bad mood that continued to degrade until the human was vulnerable to possession.

The sylph danced backward, its clawed feet making no noise. Sandeen's hands closed around air and the sylph laughed, his eyes brimming with greed. He'd get rewarded as the first creature to find Sandeen. Other than his angel.

Sandeen jumped up and extended a wing. He whipped it at the sylph and sent it cartwheeling backward until it disappeared into the Gloom.

Shit. It wouldn't be long now. The town near the cabin would be inundated with sylphs and possessions.

Shattering sounded from inside the cabin. Harlowe. He raced through the door. Harlowe was standing, the plate he'd given her broken at the base of the island and an ugly sylph dancing through the shards, untouched.

Sandeen flung another wing out. The sylph ducked but the air from Sandeen's wings somehow knocked the little beast over. It disappeared like the first one. The shock of feeling something in this realm had sent them both scurrying.

His chest heaved as he looked over Harlowe. She was unhurt, but she glowed with rage, her eyes blazing like radioactive amethysts.

"We have to go," he said and crossed to her.

He kneeled at her feet and worked on the band around her ankle. While he'd been outside, anyone could've gotten in. A demon would have to be in a host, and Harlowe could defend herself, but he didn't want to take the chance. A sylph sighting was only the beginning.

Didn't mean he'd give her the weapons she might come after him with.

She remained still, like she couldn't believe he was freeing her. As soon as her bindings fell away, she exploded into action. He'd expected it.

Batting her fists away, he caught one, then the other. She tried to kick, but he backed her into the wall by the bathroom. He secured her wrists in his hands and slammed them against the wall above her head.

"Listen, angel. Believe it or not, I don't want to hurt you, but I will. I'm not their prisoner, and I'm not yours."

Her chest heaved against his. One breath more and his body was all too aware of the stroke of her breasts as they rose and fell. She sucked in a lungful of air, her gaze widening as she stared into his eyes.

He probably looked feral. His peaceful mountain existence had come to an end. He was pissed, and on top of that, physical need raged through him like a cyclone with her long, lean body plastered between him and the wall.

"I get it," he said quietly, his gaze stroking down her cheeks to her long neck, stopping before he got a hard-on so painful he couldn't run. "You have a job to do. You're probably holding a little grudge about me capturing you. But if you come after me, I'm going to end up hurting you."

"With your bad cooking?"

He winced. "Low blow, angel." He tipped his head toward the pile of ceramic shards on the floor. "Don't think I didn't notice that you ate everything."

His face was inches from hers. Her breath puffed across his skin, better than any summer breeze. His wings were flared behind him like an obsidian wall. For a few precious moments, it was just them.

The purple of her irises captivated him. "Demon, you have nowhere to go. They found you way out here. They'll find you anywhere. Come with me. You'll at least have a chance with Numen."

"Since when has your realm let a demon go with his head intact?" Even when her kind made deals with the devil, they reneged.

Something traveled through her gaze that he couldn't identify, followed by guilt. Did she agree with him?

Regardless, he couldn't ignore her words. He had another place he could go, a place only his awful sire knew about and had hopefully forgotten, but shit would have to get pretty dire before Sandeen went there.

It was inevitable his kind had found him. He'd been in Green Valley before, looking for Sierra. He'd hoped Gerzon and Zanda had perished when Sierra had killed the human Andy, but his luck hadn't been that good. Because of Andy, the other two demons knew about Sandeen's recent business on Earth. Gerzon was a dumb brute, but Zanda wasn't. She would hunt him down, flay him alive, then fuck him a few times before she killed him. If she killed him. He came from a realm of natural liars, but they seemed to take getting lied to personally.

"Coming with me is your best option," she insisted.

He tightened his hold around her wrists. Her rigid body trembled, but she didn't budge. He liked her physical strength. He'd inhabited several human women, the last being elderly Alma. Humans broke so easily. Not Harlowe. "Angel, I didn't lose all my brain cells when I flapped my wings. No, thanks."

"We can't kill you." Her cheek pinched like she was biting the inside of it. Had she said something wrong?

We can't kill you. Can't.

He'd have to figure it out later.

"Well then, as much as I'd love to become your sex slave, I'll have to pass."

Bright spots of pink bloomed on her cheeks. His angel was blushing.

A slow grin spread across his face. He couldn't stop it or hide his fangs in time. A smile just to smile. Who knew?

Her gaze brushed across each fang and her blush deepened.

He didn't mean to, but he pressed closer. "See something you like, angel?"

She shoved against him, but he didn't move. His wings vibrated with the effort. She was deliciously strong.

Her gaze jumped to the wall of feathers behind him. Her lips parted and he felt every moment of her gaze on his wings like little butterfly kisses.

"See something you like, angel?" he repeated.

"You're a disgusting creature."

Females didn't react like that to disgusting creatures. Could the angel be attracted to him?

A bird cawed outside. He whipped his head toward the door. That was one of the crows, the same warning they'd given him when Harlowe had hunted him.

"Sorry, Lowe. I've got to go." He released her, pushing away so hard she stumbled like he'd wanted her to. While she was off-balance, he ran out the door and stopped in the shed to grab her weapons. Then he dashed into the trees. He needed to get away from her as quickly as possible before he did something stupid like try to kiss her. That'd either get him kneed in the crotch or busted by demons.

Besides, creatures like him didn't get females like her and it was its own hell to entertain the thought.

His delay in the shed had given her enough time to get her boots on. Dammit. She'd caught up with him and stayed on his heels. "Where are you going?"

"Away."

"You can't run forever, demon."

"It's better than the alternative." He wove through and around trees, ducking under sweeping canopies of needles, his wings tucked behind him.

She ran with him, following his steps, not hindered by her own wings. Demons couldn't morph their wings into their back. Just another obstacle that kept them trapped in Daemon.

"Where can you go?" she puffed as they ran. "Do you know of another fully stocked mountain cabin? One that you can get to without being seen? Because those wings of yours are kind of noticeable."

He glanced over his shoulder. He hadn't expected ditching her to be easy, but she wasn't struggling to keep up. She jogged like the rough terrain was nothing more than a nuisance. He knew this path. It was a planned escape route, chosen for the sharp rises coming up in several yards. He might lose demons possessing humans who weren't used to running through the mountains. He wasn't losing the warrior.

He stopped and spun. She couldn't stop before she crashed into his chest, but she tried, pulling up short so fast she careened backward. He clamped his hands around her biceps.

"Tell me exactly why you're following me."

She yanked an arm out of his grasp. He released her other side.

He closed the distance between them until they were

almost as close as they'd been against the wall. This didn't make sense. She wasn't trying to stop him; she was making sure she didn't lose him. "Tell me why you can't kill me."

"You know too much."

"Like hell. I'm a demon. You said can't. You *can't* kill me. Why?"

Indecision filled her gaze. She was speaking the truth. She couldn't kill him, which meant she wasn't allowed to. Again, he was a demon. That alone ought to be enough.

"Tell me," he growled. Was that why she hadn't tried to escape? Numen had other plans for him? Plans that would get him killed in a million worse ways than if Zanda got ahold of him?

Harlowe swallowed hard. "Don't you know?"

He shook his head. He knew a lot more than what angels had grown up being told. So what did the pretty angel know that he didn't?

Her gaze lifted to his horns, then touched on his wings. After sprinting through the trees, his horns were visible. The sun set later this time of year. He needed to get distance between him and that cabin now that he'd been seen.

"Don't I know what, warrior?"

Her breathing slowed and her shoulders hunched. She didn't want to tell him what she was going to say next. "You knew what Sierra is. How could you not have figured it out?"

Sierra was a fallen angel. A detail tickled his mind. Something obvious that was welling up like a gas bubble from a cesspool. He knew the stench was coming and could almost smell it, but he had to watch, slowly, waiting for the inevitable.

"You're like her. You're half angel."

CHAPTER 4

Sandeen staggered back, his expression twisted, disbelief and horror racing over his features. Harlowe stayed rooted where she was.

He came to a stop, staring at her like she was the one with shiny horns sticking up from her head. His hand floated up to touch the vial around his neck, then rub his chest. His brows drew together. Then he spun on the heel of his boot and took off at a jog.

"Sandeen." She started after him.

He didn't respond. Just kept jogging. The terrain grew rougher. The trees spaced out, but only because the incline grew steeper. Was there a drop-off on the other side? How would they descend?

His long strides were hard for even her to keep up with.

Her irritation levels soared as steeply as the ground. "Demon, what the hell?"

That got him to stop. But when he turned, his blue eyes were shadowed. Hard. Conflicted.

She slammed her hands on her hips and tried not to sound like she was gasping for air. "I tell you you're half angel and you keep going like it's nothing." She cocked her head. Had he known? Were the emotions he showed now only because her kind knew too?

"But I'm not an angel, though, am I?" His hard glare slid away. He ground his teeth together and his blue eyes were windows within. Staggering emotion roiled inside of him. She wouldn't have thought him capable of this depth of feeling if she hadn't been his prisoner for the last few days.

He wasn't like anyone she'd ever come across.

"There's nothing *angelic* about my life." He stalked closer, sliding down the incline a few steps before he stopped several feet away. "My sire is one hundred percent demon, Lowe. Cruel. Intelligent. Brutal. He's one of the worst. Can I believe he captured an angel and forced me out of her and then didn't tell me? Absolutely." His empty laugh echoed through the forest. "Makes a whole lot of sense when I think about it. All those tests," he gritted out.

"What tests?"

"Be grateful that you never have to know, *angel*." He spun again, the muscles of his legs bunching as he climbed. Fading sunlight glinted across his wings.

She clambered after him. He was bitter. Resentful. The news that he was half angel wasn't an enlightenment. It was just . . . another burden. One of many cruel facts in his life.

He also didn't seem gleeful about the prospect of getting into Numen. He might not have reached the conclusion yet that it was possible for him to travel between *all* the realms. Where Sierra had grown up knowing the truth, Sandeen hadn't. He'd been raised with the rules of his kind. Demons could travel through the Gloom, the veil between Daemon and Earth, to search for a host. Sylphs could ghost through to Earth and be invisible nuisances. For angels, the Mist was similar to the

Gloom, and her kind could use it as such, minus the host factor. Time and distance were nebulous in the Gloom, based more on individual intention. But since her kind was charged with human safety, angels could also transcend between Numen and Earth. They only needed permission from the senate to remove the wards that bound her kind to Numen.

Would Sandeen need permission? Was his heritage the anomaly that defied the rules of each realm?

A half angel raised in the underworld should be unbelievable. Yet Harlowe had seen how much he cared for Alma. Yes, he'd used her. He'd also taken care of her. Protected her. She should write that off as part of his cunning plan. She'd tried to. He was intelligent enough and had enough self-control to be the most dangerous demon of them all. But she'd seen him cook. Seen him try new food, food that wasn't carrion—or worse. Good food made with quality ingredients. He'd been enamored with it.

Would an evil demon get a kick out of the idea that there was such a thing as cream of mushroom soup?

His innocence had enraptured her. It was . . . endearing.

The senate might not see him as anything more than a demon to put down. They'd want his wings at the very least. Her warrior director, Bryant Vale, had kept the information about Sierra and Sandeen to himself. An omission he was risking his own wings for, but there had been some concerns with their senate. Director Vale wanted to protect Sierra, but he wanted information on Sandeen too. Her director had never said, but that information could determine if the demon was to be executed or simply imprisoned.

There would be no "simply" imprisoned for Sandeen.

The demon heaved himself to the top of a craggy rise. Harlowe did the same, sweat prickling along her hairline.

Before them, the land stretched out from a sheer drop. Trees spread out below them, sweeping into a deep valley she'd had no idea was there.

"Nice escape plan, demon."

Sandeen aimed those unnerving blue eyes at her and snapped his wings out. "Isn't it though."

"You can't—"

"*You* can't. Your realm's laws aren't my problem."

"My realm's laws will be a major problem if you fly in broad daylight."

He lifted a big shoulder. His dark feathers fluttered. "The sun's going down. Anyone close enough to see will think I'm an eagle or something."

An eagle with legs and a beard. "Sandeen, you can't—"

He grinned. "See you around, angel."

She couldn't let him get away.

He jumped, his wings spread wide. Jealousy knifed her. She knew exactly what he felt. Ultimate freedom. The wind sweeping below his wings, the air caressing the rest of his body. He hadn't hit his ascent yet. The damn demon was reveling in the fall.

She jumped. Her wings stayed securely in their morph, but she careened after him. Just as his body arched to lift into the sky, she slammed into him.

A whoosh of air left him and they fell, somersaulting in midair, but the male was strong. His wings strained wider, seeking more air current. They were skimming the treetops when he shifted her onto his back between his wings, her arms clinging around his shoulders.

"Aren't you toeing a thin line, angel? Flying in broad daylight?"

"The sun's going down," she echoed. "I'm apprehending you."

"Yes. You've done that." His body shook with laughter.

Her envy hadn't dissipated. Flying in Numen was fun, especially after periods when she'd been on Earth for long stretches. But overall, it was a tame event. The skies were always clear. Her realm had no cliffs. No mountains. No storms. What would it be like to fly like this all the time?

"Wrap your legs around me, angel." The rumble of his demand sent heat to all the wrong places.

"I'd rather strangle you."

"We'd be more balanced, but that's fine. I don't mind having your entire body glued to mine."

She didn't mind as much as she should. "Keep us in the air." She twined her legs around his waist. The beat of his wings around her buffeted the air and his wing joints flexed under her belly. Strength and power, yet graceful.

"How do other demons fly?" she asked.

"They don't. Their wings are weapons."

"And you didn't think hey, I'm kind of different?"

His body tensed under hers and he didn't answer. Such a sensitive subject. She shouldn't exploit it.

"After learning about Sierra, how did you not connect the dots?"

"If you had ever been to the underworld and met my sire, you'd understand." He veered to the right.

She tightened her embrace. "You did that on purpose."

"I would never."

She'd glare at him if she could face him. As it was, her face was buried in the nape of his neck, her nose in his surprisingly pleasant-smelling hair. He'd used the soap from the bathroom. She should pay attention to where he was headed, but she was focused on him and how he felt.

She didn't push him. The rest of the trip, while the light faded and he flew between mountaintops that had no roads, no houses, no signs of civilization, she strategized. He had her weapons, but she couldn't lift them off his body in midair. Had he left her phone behind? Her kind weren't clairvoyant, and communication used to be an issue when working on Earth, but not since humans had invented phones. She was younger than many immortal Numen. She didn't remember a time without a phone of some sort.

Sandeen changed course and aimed for a clearing miles away. Blue glittered from within it. A thin break in the trees must be a road leading there. The lake wasn't far from Green Valley but the road wrapped around it from the opposite end.

He'd already scoped this place out. It shouldn't surprise her that he had a plan B. Was there another cabin hidden by the shore? It would only be a matter of time before the sylphs found him. The underworld wanted Sandeen and his secrets. If the underworld hadn't known he was wandering around in his own form, they did now. The search party would be expansive and brutal.

He soared above the treetops. It was tempting to close her eyes and enjoy the energy, the freedom, of open flight. Exhilarating, yet forbidden. So damn forbidden in this realm her back ached to think about the consequences.

As if the demon sensed her thoughts, he barrel-rolled. Her yelp disappeared into the air and she squeezed him. His laughter reverberated through her.

"Afraid of a few scratches, angel?"

"No." She wouldn't die if she fell, unless she was shattered so badly she couldn't care for herself. But she didn't trust him to pick her up and carry her to wherever he was going. He was tolerating her presence. He could dump her whenever he wanted, he just didn't want the trouble. "Where are you going?"

"Alma's car."

"Alma's car got stolen before she moved to— Damn."

More laughter. The rumble between her thighs almost

made her jerk away from him, but they were still above the treetops.

"You stole an old woman's car?" she asked as he circled the lake for a landing.

"You wanted Alma driving in Las Vegas?"

"She could've sold it for money."

"You're taking care of her."

A stolen car wasn't the hardened crime she needed to pin on the demon. He hadn't done it for Alma's safety, but that didn't change that he was right. Alma didn't need to be driving in Las Vegas.

He swooped along the shore, slowing as they reached a clearing that looked like a rudimentary beach. Large rocks that would claim an ankle morphed into larger boulders that disappeared into the water.

Gravity dragged on her as he landed on his feet. He kept his wings stretched and smirked over his shoulder. "Don't worry. I don't mind if you hang around a while."

She abruptly let go and dropped to her feet in a crouch. His broad back and those magnificent wings were all she could see of him. He couldn't see her glare. Which was a good thing, since her gaze was hovering over his feathers like she was going to pet him.

She clenched her hand into a fist. No petting. What was she thinking?

That she'd been touching him practically from head to toe, but thanks to her clothes, she hadn't felt how soft his wings were.

She spun around, searching their surroundings. "Where's the car?"

The grinding of rock made her spin, only he was walking toward the tree line.

She jogged after him. How had she gone from tracking

him, ready to fight to the death, to wanting to snap at him to wait up?

BRONX WANDERED THROUGH THE CASINO. Ah, Vegas. At the end of the neon blinking lights and mass of tourists was his target—a nightclub full of people looking for the same good time as him. "It's my night off. Can't I have a little fun?"

Urban scowled next to him, scaring off most women willing to approach them.

Nights off meant getting laid. Sometimes, working also meant getting laid, depending on what the job entailed.

He caught the eye of a woman dressed like Sailor Moon. She flashed him a sultry smile, but when her gaze skated to Urban, her eyes flared and she veered in the opposite direction.

Bronx let out a disgusted grunt. "Dude. You're killing my vibe here." Was it too much to ask for some harmless flirtation that led to fucking in the back of his car? Maybe he'd find someone who had a room in the hotel attached to the nightclub. Hookups were easier when he could leave when he was done instead of trying to usher out someone who thought they had a future with him.

"There's demons all over," Urban muttered. His friend would blend in with the other humans in jeans and polos if his expression didn't read *I'll murder you in your sleep.*

"There's always demons. We have an eternity of job security." All Bronx wanted was a night off. Was it bad that he was burned out already? He was a fairly young warrior as far as angels went. He'd be approaching his golden years if he were human. He had centuries of demon tracking ahead of him. Being personally assigned to Director Vale's team of bitches was a pleasant change from straight-up demon hunting, but still.

He wanted more.

"I need to restock." Urban had said it three times already. What he really wanted was Bronx to abandon his night of pleasure seeking, transcend to Numen, and pilfer weapons and angel fire from the warrior storerooms.

Urban didn't take silence as a rejection. He'd just keep asking.

"Night off, Urban." The air between them weighed heavier. Bronx sighed. "Why can't you go on your own?"

On Earth, they were supposed to hunt in no less than pairs. Bronx had no plans to hunt more than pussy tonight. Like he had since he'd been old enough to descend to Earth, since he'd learned how to blend and that humans liked indiscriminate sex as much as many of his kind. Only they were more open about it. He'd done this a million times, and he'd do it a million more—on his own or with a buddy. So what was Urban's issue with going back to Numen alone? His friend still hadn't answered.

"Why don't you just go? I'm fine. You're clearly not into it."

"I've been getting looks."

Bronx stopped. A couple dressed in Hawaiian shirts and fresh sunburns drifted around them. "What do you mean?" Urban wasn't self-conscious. He was one of the most dedicated warriors Bronx had met. A few looks?

Urban scanned the casino. Pings resonated around them. Servers with trays wove between slots, taking orders. Laughter and conversation maintained a steady din that swallowed their words should anyone try to listen in.

"We lost Bryant—Director Vale. Then we lost Sierra. But we gained her father. We're still one member short and it's become clear that we're not just an ordinary team. People want to know what's going on."

"What people? Other warriors?" There was bound to be some jealousy. Director Vale had been their team leader before he'd been promoted, and he'd been chummy with the former director. Other warriors assumed the team had become Director Vale's errand angels. Most didn't mind. They wanted to be left alone to do their job and to do exactly what Bronx was hoping to do tonight. They'd heard about the mess with Jameson and Andy and wanted to distance themselves.

They wanted what Bronx wanted. To enjoy some parts of their long life, and that was harder to do when they were always on guard, sometimes literally. Guarding Odessa. Guarding Felicia. Guarding the old lady and Sierra.

"Senators."

Bronx cocked his head. Not the answer he'd been expecting. "Senators are trying to get intel from you instead of Director Vale?"

Urban stepped closer and lowered his voice. "They know the boss is hiding something."

Yeah. A big something. More than one. That Sierra was half demon. That was a biggie. That there was a demon wandering Earth in his own form—and was also half angel. That fallen blood allowed him to do that and might work the same for other demons.

Director Vale had secrets that could lock down the realm. But he was doing his due diligence and gathering all the facts. He was also abusing his position to keep all hell from breaking loose in the realm.

"Can't Felicia run interference?" Not only was she the director's sister-in-law, she was mated to one of their teammates.

"Not many trust Felicia. The younger senators, maybe." Urban glanced around the casino again. He wasn't the best at covert ops. His expression was shady and made them both look guilty as hell. Which, to Urban's credit, maybe meant they blended in Vegas after all. "But the older ones? The ones who have found ways to supplement their lifestyle and feed off their power? They don't trust Felicia and they know Bryant's hiding something."

"Have you told Dionna?" The rest of the team looked to her as Director Vale's replacement, but she hadn't fully accepted the mantle yet.

"No, she's taking some time off."

Dionna never took time off. Never.

"That's why I want you to come with me," Urban continued. "Tell me if I'm being crazy."

Bronx had done that plenty of times over the years. Urban wasn't an idiot. He had concerns and they were likely justified. "Fine. But can I get laid first?"

CHAPTER 5

*B*y the time Sandeen reached the car, his body had redirected a small portion of his blood back to his brain. Flying with an erection wasn't an activity he'd ever planned on doing. Not even the heels of her boots jammed into his junk had diminished the effect of her body locked against his.

Her sunshine-after-a-thunderstorm scent still clung to him.

He wasn't a cranky demon. He thrived by keeping a calm mind and planning ahead. Reading the room and learning others' weaknesses.

Maybe he wasn't a cranky demon because he was half goddamn angel.

It made so much sense it hurt. Pressure built in his brain and tension coiled so tightly in him he was ready to combust. Was he the underworld's best-kept secret? Obviously, his sire knew. Zadren. Or as Sandeen had started calling him, Big Z. The father he wished he didn't have.

Your mother would be ashamed of you.

Pick yourself up, whelp. Your mother is keening from her shallow grave.

It's a good thing your mother's not alive to see this.

Those were probably the only times Zadren hadn't lied. An angel for a mother. An angel birthing an abomination. A creature her kind sought to destroy.

Yeah, she would've been ashamed.

Sandeen stomped to the car. He'd kept Alma's keys on him at all times in case he had to leave quickly.

Harlowe was still with him. She wasn't trying to tackle him or fight him for her weapons. He didn't know what she wanted with him, but he doubted it was anything in his favor. He was no one's prisoner. Just because Numen smelled better didn't mean he'd be any less of a captive, at the mercy of whomever wanted to grow their power.

He didn't trust anyone in Numen. He didn't trust the leaders of that realm. He didn't trust angels, period.

The car waited for him in the rugged parking lot. There was little more than a dirt path leading to this space. Alma's car was a tank and sailing over the rough terrain had been as fun as flying.

Harlowe didn't know it yet, but the angel was going for another ride tonight.

He unlocked the door and got in. He didn't unlock the other side—no reason to make it easy for her—and fired up the engine. It sputtered but steadied into a purr.

Harlowe marched to the driver's window and shouted through the glass. "You know I'm going to cling to the top of the hood, so you might as well let me in."

He rolled the window down. "Why?"

"I'd draw more attention."

"No, Lowe. Why do you insist on following me? Why shouldn't I leave you here? It's not like you're going to fly to follow me."

Her mouth set in a line. What a rule follower. "We can't let you roam free."

"Your kind does." He leaned his elbow on the window's edge. "Your kind can stay on Earth and eat, drink, and fuck as much as they'd like. Why can't I? You saw I wasn't hurting anyone."

Her pupils had flared at "fuck." Did she know how readable she was? "We're not free to do whatever we want." Her gaze swept the trees towering over them to the narrow path he'd drive through any minute, and by the time she returned those gems to him, resolve filled her expression. "Not all Numen are approved to go to Earth. When we're there, we're supposed to be aiding the human population."

"But all work and no play makes wild Numen dull angels?" At her consternation, he couldn't stop his sly smile. "What about you? Do you use some of your time to eat, drink, and fuck?"

Her glare was amethyst ice. "I don't drink."

His fangs pricked his bottom lip as he laughed. "I got you away from the sylphs before they swarmed the cabin. We're even."

"Even for what?"

His answer was to throw the car in gear.

"Demon!"

"Exactly." He pulled away.

She dove through his window.

"What the—" Her shoulder knocked his mouth, then her hip. He caught his bearings in time to nip at her. His fangs plunged through the heavy material of her pants and she squealed.

"Sandeen!"

That got her to say his name.

Her taste filled his mouth. He hadn't done more than nick her but it was enough. Sultry heat wicked along his tongue and made his mouth water. He was a lot of things, but a vampire wasn't one of them. Didn't stop him from craving more.

She rolled into the passenger seat, nearly taking out his nose with her boots. "Did you bite me?"

He steadied a knowing stare on her. "If an ass is in my face, I bite it."

Her ferocious blush returned. Metal glinted off a knife she brandished at his throat.

He slapped his hand over his right pocket. "Smooth, angel. Smooth."

"Keep your fangs to yourself."

"Usually females beg for them."

Her eyes narrowed but she slid the knife into the empty holster above her boot. "I will carve them out of your mouth and wear them as earrings."

Her threats rang empty. She was too good for that, but he enjoyed how the words rolled off her red tongue. "Buckle up, buttercup. This is going to be a ride."

She didn't question him and buckled herself in. He did the same. His horns had taken a beating from the top of the cab, driving on the rough road.

He pressed the gas. The car bounced and shook over the trail. He'd weave left and right as much as the trees would allow to miss the worst of the divots.

He'd found this lake on one of his nightly scouting trips. With dark hair and dark wings, he'd blended in with the night. No one had seen. And he'd found this lake. He'd sat by the shore for a while, soaking in the peace. The first time he'd ever truly relaxed. Then he'd seen the old road some campers had carved out through the years and a plan had formed.

Harlowe pressed a hand to the ceiling to keep from

getting thrown around as far as her seat belt would let her. "Where are you going?"

"Somewhere else."

Her gaze bored into the side of his face, but he had to concentrate on the path. The headlights cut through the shadows. He hoped to reach the road before full darkness descended.

"Unless it's another secluded cabin, you need to morph your wings. And get a hat or something."

"I have a coat in the trunk."

"A trench coat won't fully conceal your wings. Morph them."

His hands tightened on the wheel. Another bump bounced him until his belt stopped his upward progression.

She was watching him again. His skin tingled wherever her gaze stroked him. "You can morph . . . right?"

He concentrated on the road. The narrow highway it hooked up with was ahead, but there was a drop from the pavement. He had to hit the right spot or he'd bottom out the car and pop a tire or two.

Jerking to the left, then the right, the car heaved onto the pavement and settled into a purr. A few decades ago, he had possessed a teenaged thrill seeker. The kid had lived like he laughed death in the face on a daily basis when the reality had been that he was so afraid of life he could barely breathe. Driving had been his drug of choice, and Sandeen had been bored and intrigued by the kid's conflicting emotions and actions. The boy had felt too much, and when Sandeen had possessed him and dulled everything, they'd each found a few moments of peace. They'd made a good pair until . . .

Until his sire had set another test.

Sandeen visited the kid's grave at least once a decade.

"You can't morph," Harlowe said, her voice filled with disbelief.

The road was smooth, no other car in sight. But he didn't look at her. "When would I need to?"

"Can you though?"

"Demons can't morph their wings."

"But you're . . ."

Half angel. Right. "I'd still have the horns."

"A hat versus a trench coat that looked like you stuffed five wild turkeys into it? You need to morph."

"Are you going to teach me?" This time he met her flat stare.

"Stop the car."

He glanced back at the road. "Why?"

He didn't have to look at her to know her gaze brushed his wings. "Just do it."

EIGHTH TIME'S THE CHARM. Harlowe waved her hands like she was conjuring fairies. "Just like . . . imagine them folding into your skin."

"You said that already. It's not working." With a growl, Sandeen ripped his shirt off.

Her jaw dropped, but she caught it and snapped her lips shut. Rippled abs. Firm, defined pecs. And biceps that looked like he was flexing when his arms were relaxed at his sides. Veins protruded in lines down his arms, crowded over his forearms, and—

For heaven's sake, they were just veins.

A little blood vial hung around his neck. "Is that the fallen blood?"

He touched it with a fingertip. "Yes." He spread his hand

over his chest. "I tried to tattoo it into me, but I healed too quickly."

Something about the blood of a fallen angel circumvented the rules of traveling between their realms. The closest theory they'd gathered was that since the fallen weren't allowed back into Numen, they could be brought to the Mist and vanquished if the need arose. When the Mist sensed demon blood—or fallen angel blood—it expelled the creature as fast as possible. Warriors had learned to dispatch demons quickly and efficiently.

Usually a demon was sent back to their realm. But something about fallen blood on a demon fucked up the process, and it wasn't like this demon would be the one to help them figure it out, being half demon—and half angel.

Her gaze landed on the vial again. "What if you don't even need the vial?"

He gave her a flat look. "The drawback of failing is being stuck in Daemon."

That he was so done with his realm only supported the idea that he meant no harm on a grander scale. Didn't mean he couldn't be harmful. "Haven't you tried to leave the Gloom without possessing a host?"

"Of course, angel."

The road to a better realm was paved with good intentions. She didn't get the impression that Sandeen had no bad intentions, but he certainly wasn't evil. She held her hand out. "Give me the vial." He drew back and she waved her hand. "Come on. You're not here to hurt us or humans. I have a feeling you don't need anything. You're half angel."

"Sierra can't cross into the Gloom."

"She's never tried, and she'd never want to." Harlowe knew her friend better than that. Perhaps it was the sisterly connection that was getting harder to deny the more that

Harlowe thought of Sierra. "Come on. If you think you need to rely on a little vial of blood—which I know isn't Sierra's, so I know you must have procured a stash somehow—then it's a weakness we need to know about."

"It's Jameson's blood. We had a deal going. Back in the day."

She fluttered her fingers. Best-case scenario—he was forced back to the underworld.

Why did that feel like the worst-case scenario? She *should* be gleeful about the Gloom sucking him out of the realm, yet she didn't want to see him go.

With a scowl, he drew the chain over his head, then paused with the vial dangling over her hand. He dropped it into her palm. She didn't wait to see if he wavered or disappeared. She dropped it on the ground and stomped on it.

He remained in front of her, his body tense as if he hadn't taken a breath since removing the necklace. A moment later, he blew out a gusty exhale and flattened his hand on his chest. "I can't fucking believe it."

"Well, that's answered. Do you have any more blood?"

His shoulders relaxed. "Ah, ah, angel. A demon's gotta have a few secrets."

She couldn't push him more. They had to get to the morph. "Fine. Now imagine folding your wings into your back."

His eyes were closed. His nose scrunched and his lips disappeared into his beard as he concentrated.

Had the first time morphing her wings been this tough? All angels learned the trick. It was a special ability her kind possessed in order to help humans while protecting the secret of their kind. The wings sort of just folded in on themselves and disappeared. But she could feel them. She knew they were there. They weren't invisible, they were just morphed into her body.

She'd done it so many times, it was like breathing. She could morph her wings fully clothed.

Was it an ability limited to angels or a learned skill?

His wings were lifted high behind him, twitching as he tried to cram his shoulder blades together. As if that would do it.

"Sandeen."

His eyelids lifted. His blue eyes were subdued in the dark. The moon was half full and a cloud floated across it every few minutes, but she'd rather it were pitch black out, given Sandeen was in all his nonhuman glory in the middle of a road.

"Maybe don't concentrate so hard?"

He rolled his eyes.

A demon rolled his eyes at her.

The more she was around him, the easier it was to see why Alma had such a soft spot for the burly male. Sandeen reminded Harlowe of the guys on her team, Bronx and Urban, and to some extent Jagger. They were deadly, but also pains in her ass, like Bronx pouting when she demanded he clean his cracker crumbs off the couch in the safe house they were working out of. Or Urban humming to himself while he cleaned his equipment in the barracks in her realm. The guy couldn't hit one single note, but that didn't stop him.

They were real, with personality quirks, and they were all important males to her.

Sandeen was real. She was learning his quirks and not just the irritating ones. He was trying really hard to morph. If he couldn't do it, he was still a threat to her kind. Humans could see him—wings, horns, and fangs. She couldn't risk him getting recorded. Becoming a meme. Getting shares.

Many humans would brush it off. Cosplay or something. But others would hunt for the truth and find demons that weren't like Sandeen. Demons that would tear them apart from the inside out, then discard them as soon as their usefulness had passed.

Sandeen let out a frustrated breath. "It's not working."

She crossed her arms and walked around him. She glued her gaze to the seam of his jeans. It was better than his hot flesh. She stopped behind him and studied his back. His head was turned, his profile stark against the backdrop of the forest.

"When I morph . . ." She stepped closer. She had no idea if this would help, but they had to try something different. Spreading her fingers wide, she skimmed her hands over his feathers, barely touching them. "I can still feel my wings. Only, it's like when I'm going to sit cross-legged on the floor. That time between fully standing and totally seated. Your knees are bending. Your ankles. You're hinging at the hips."

She followed the arc of his wings and traced down, his feathers only tickling her palms. Heat radiated off him. Power. Strength. She stopped and reversed. Up. Around the arc and down. He remained still, half looking over his shoulder.

"And when the morph is done . . ." She danced her fingers over the joints where his wings were anchored to his back. Strong cords of muscle and tendon and ligaments twined together. "I can feel them. Only it's not like they're hanging down. It's like they're hugged against me."

She closed her eyes, her fingers flattening on his joints. Soft feathers brushed along her skin. Heat soaked into her hands. She tuned into her own back. "I can feel them.

Tucked into me. They're there, but they're not. They're invisible, but they're not. Their energy has changed, adapted, to fit into my back. Like camouflage, but not. Their energy is now in my shoulder blades. My spine. My skin."

She stopped, her eyes closed, her hands on him. Attuned to herself and to him. His frustration roiled under his skin like a living being. Desperation. He didn't want to return to the underworld. Sadness. Heartbreak?

Why was his heart aching? What did a male like him love?

Light pierced through her eyelids.

She flipped them open and had to stand on her tiptoes to see over Sandeen's wings. Had he lifted them to conceal her?

The car was a ways off, but it was traveling at highway speeds.

She yanked her hands off him. "Shit. Get in the car."

Sandeen didn't move. He was looking at her, his expression full of yearning.

"*Move*." She gave him a little shove.

He didn't budge. "It's dark. They won't see."

"And if they stop to check if we're all right?"

The headlights gleamed off the tips of his horns, sticking up from his hair. He sauntered to the driver's door.

"No." Harlowe elbowed him away. "I'll do the talking if they stop. Get that coat on."

By the time Sandeen had pulled a long jacket out of the trunk and gotten around to the other side, the car was slowing down. As it got closer, the light bar on top became visible.

"Damn," she muttered, sliding behind the wheel. "Get your hat."

"For an angel, you swear a lot." He stuffed a black stocking hat on his head.

"We're not *divine* angels."

He chuckled. "You say it like it's a motto drilled into you from birth. Handy excuse, that."

She shot him a glare before concentrating on the car.

The deputy pulled alongside them and she rolled her window down. "Everything okay here?"

"Just stopping to swap out behind the wheel," Harlowe said easily. She'd dealt with enough human law enforcement officers over the years to know the best thing to do was act like it was just another day.

The deputy's scowl deepened the frown lines around her mouth. "It's not a good idea to stop in the middle of the lane."

A nowhere highway in the middle of Montana didn't exactly have wide shoulders. "We weren't sure where a good place would be." Harlowe lifted her chin. "Our map app got us all turned around. What's the nearest town?"

"You keep going, you'll be in Idaho."

That didn't answer her at all. It just told her they were heading west. "Okay, great. Thank you."

The deputy peered past her, her shrewd gaze raking over Sandeen. The jacket bunched around his neck thanks to his wings. The horns kept his hat from sitting neatly on his head. He was big and rumpled and Harlowe got what must be setting off the deputy's alarms. Something just wasn't quite right with him.

Harlowe kept her expression steady and calm. The deputy slid her gaze back and her eyes narrowed. "You two have a good night. Drive safe."

"Thanks!" Harlowe pulled away, not wasting any time. The deputy's taillights faded. Harlowe didn't breathe until they'd rounded a curve and the patrol car had disappeared entirely.

"I don't get how demons get such a reputation about lying when humans do it all the time."

Harlowe shot him a look and he lifted his hands like *what?*

"She did not want us to have a good night. And Idaho is hours away."

"At least it'll give us time to figure out how to hide you from humans."

"You worry too much about humans, angel."

She glanced at him. He sounded weary, like he knew it was a fight he couldn't win. He wasn't an idiot, and it wasn't as if she hadn't been justifying all the reasons why she hadn't transcended to Numen and reported to Director Vale everything she'd learned. The longer she was gone, the farther away Sandeen would get. He could go in any direction he wanted, but he'd have to stay hidden. Forever.

"Our duty as Numen is to protect humankind. Yes, humans are resilient. Yes, they do things that endanger themselves and others. But the fact is, they aren't equipped to fight demons and I am."

He grunted and shifted in his seat. Sitting on wings wasn't comfortable for long and his coat must hinder any movement. They drove in silence for several more miles until he was continuously shifting in his seat.

"We need to find a place to stop," she said.

"I'm fine. Keep driving."

"I'll stop so you can at least get in the back seat."

Lights appeared behind them. They hadn't passed anyone else on this road. Another vehicle might mean they were getting closer to the interstate. The highway had to hook up to something larger soon.

Red and blue started flashing behind her. "Are we getting pulled over?"

The same deputy from earlier? Harlowe maneuvered to the side of the highway. There wasn't much of a shoulder to stop on. "Let me handle this."

"Sure. It worked so well the first time."

"Maybe she's just passing us—" The patrol car slowed and moved to the side of the road as well. Damn.

She rolled the window down. She didn't have a license, and even if she did, it wouldn't match the car's registration. Alma would vouch for her though. Alma would fly up here and bail them out if she learned Sandeen was here.

This would go so much better if Sandeen could morph.

The car door opened and the same deputy who had checked on them earlier swaggered out. Her hand hovered by her hip and she shined a flashlight toward them with her other hand.

"Please get out of the car slowly."

"At least she didn't wait for backup," Harlowe muttered as she put her hand on the door. "Please let me handle this."

Sandeen stayed quiet, but his blue eyes glittered in the lights flashing through the night.

Harlowe got out, her hands raised. "Can I ask what this is about?"

"This car has been reported stolen."

"Oh, right. I'm a friend of Alma's. I came to Montana and found it abandoned—"

The deputy's gaze traveled down her body. Harlowe wasn't wearing casual clothes meant for doing nothing shady in the middle of Montana during the dead of night. She wore the same long-sleeved black shirt and black tactical pants she'd had on when Sandeen had jumped her.

"I don't care, ma'am. Put your hands on the hood." She

pointed the flashlight in the car. "Sir, I'm going to need you to—"

The lights on the car they'd been driving flicked off. The flashlight beam jumped in time with the deputy. "Sir."

Sandeen didn't say anything. The headlights of the patrol car highlighted the car but only added to the shadows in the front of Alma's car.

"*Sir.*" Alarm and determination rang in the deputy's voice.

The passenger door opened, but the dome light didn't turn on.

What the hell was that demon doing?

Harlowe straightened, but the deputy barked, "Keep your hands on the vehicle. Stay right where you are."

The coat was draped over the passenger seat. Didn't he know that patrol cars had cameras? And where was he?

With his dark hair and black wings, he blended into the night.

The telltale slide of a weapon being removed from the holster resonated above the noise of the engines.

"Stay where you're at," the deputy said as she sidestepped toward the front of the car. She swung out far enough to see around the front. There was no sound other than the engines' humming. The deputy's steps were slow enough to be silent.

Harlowe ducked her head. No one was in the vehicle and the door was hanging open. How were they getting out of this mess without the sheriff's department bearing down on them?

The deputy circled around the vehicle, sweeping her flashlight, looking for the huge male who'd just been in the car. Harlowe watched, interested herself. Demons and angels had a lot of special abilities humans didn't have, but they weren't *that* special. They couldn't go invisible.

She couldn't hiss his name. The deputy would hear. Saying "demon" was out of the question. She was as helpless as the deputy to see how this played out.

The woman was in front of the car, taking measured steps as she rounded to the other side. Then a whoosh of air preceded her, careening into the hood, her head bouncing off the metal. A gust of wind fluttered Harlowe's hair as feathered wings knocked against the woman's head. She slid off the hood, passed out.

CHAPTER 6

Sandeen drove while Harlowe seethed next to him.

They rolled into a little town outside of Great Falls. The car they were driving needed gas. The car they were driving was also not Alma's car.

Harlowe's jaw was rigid and her violet eyes hadn't quit promising retribution. If nothing else, his intervention with the deputy had given her more reason to stick to him like a sexy nicotine patch. He was almost glad. He was becoming addicted to having her around.

"We can't stay in this car," she snapped. "It's stolen too. And the deputy's probably awake by now."

The woman was fine. He'd knocked her unconscious using only as much force as needed. Harlowe had been worried for the human, made Sandeen carry the deputy to her car and radio for help. They'd taken back roads to a small ranch. It had looked empty, but there'd been a little two-door sports car. He'd hot-wired it.

You can't cook, but you can hot-wire a car?

Why was she hung up on the cooking thing? A lot of his

hosts could steal a car fifty different ways but hardly make toast. Those were the humans he'd been in.

So the sports car owner now had Alma's sedan. But these wheels were too flashy to drive around in for long and had shit for leg room. His wings ached from being sat on.

He rolled into a gas station and handed a few twenties to Harlowe. She growled as she snatched them out of his hand. She'd have to go in, pay, and grab food and supplies.

"Is the money stolen too?"

He gave her a look that said *don't ask questions you don't want the answers to.*

She huffed and strode away. The kid working the night shift drooled out the window at the leggy blonde heading his way. Sandeen got out, his coat pulled tight around his shoulders and his hat in place, and pumped gas.

She returned after the gas was paid for, bag in hand. "He says there's a little motel on the other side of town."

He got behind the wheel. Driving took his mind off how uncomfortable sitting in a car was for him. When she slid into her seat, he asked, "And when we get there, then what?"

She dug through the bag and pulled out a water and two protein bars. She handed him one. "What do you mean?"

He frowned at the bar. "These taste like shit."

"So? They're nutrition. That's all we need right now."

"If I wanted to waste my taste buds' time, I could return to where I came from and eat sylph. A little chocolate doesn't kill us. A lot of chocolate doesn't kill us."

"It's just a protein bar, demon."

He tossed it back. "It's worthless. I didn't plan my freedom for years to eat organic cardboard." He eyed the water. "Don't tell me . . . That's all you got to drink?"

"Don't tell me," she mimicked, "that you'd rather have soda."

"Something fun. Or why bother? Anyway, you didn't answer the question."

She shook her head as he idled through town. "I'm not hunting down my team tonight. I need some rest first and to think about what else we might be facing before I call them."

He believed her. They were both fatigued. It wasn't just fleeing through the night and jacking a car. It was the days before tonight. Her sleep had probably been shitty, chained to the floor of a cabin with a hunted demon.

His sleep hadn't been bad. But with her so close . . . It'd been its own form of torment. The angel he couldn't have, but couldn't quit wanting. Now that he'd tasted her? He wouldn't be sleeping well tonight either.

He parked two blocks away and they walked to the motel lobby. He loitered in the shadows while she checked in. When she came out and walked to the room at the end of the building, she didn't look at him, just unlocked the door and went inside. He slipped in a minute later.

"Tomorrow we'll need new wheels—" There was only one bed.

"You'll have to take the chair," she said as she sauntered toward the bathroom.

Nope. He'd slept on a stone slab for decades. He flopped on the bed and closed his eyes.

Water ran in the bathroom for several minutes. She wouldn't strip down and shower with him a wall away . . . Would she?

Blood rushed to his groin as the water cut off. The door whipped open and movement ceased.

"Get off the bed." Her voice could sever an artery.

He didn't bother opening his eyes. "No."

She sputtered, then stopped. He cracked an eyelid open. Her glare hardened. Her arms were crossed over her chest. His lips nearly twitched into a smile. This angel had been ready to draw blood just days ago. Now she was just pissy with him.

"There's room for both of us." He lowered his voice. "Or don't you think you can help yourself around me?"

"Shut it." She sat on the corner of the bed. "Don't touch me."

"Hadn't planned on it." He closed his eyes again. It was easier to control his body's reaction if he couldn't see her. It was hard enough, remembering her taste and dealing with her sunshine-after-a-rainstorm smell.

"Move your wings over." Hostility mingled with exasperation.

He shifted to his side, turning to face her and draping his left wing over his side.

"What the fuck, Sandeen?"

He kept his eyes closed but his lips curled up. There was something about his wings with her. "Angel, you need to quit talking dirty to me."

"You— No— Demon! Move over."

"I did. Good night, Lowe."

She huffed and shook the bed as she made herself comfortable. This had to be a first for her. Sleeping next to a demon. Aiding and abetting the assault of an officer and stealing a car. Using stolen money.

She must hate it.

This was pretty tame for his life. It was what he needed to do to hide from the underworld, and the longer she was around him, the more she'd become an active participant.

He didn't like that. He didn't want to be the one to corrupt his angel.

DOWNY HEAT BLANKETED her and she turned into it. Stretched her hand out onto a hard chest. Inhaled the scent of pine, brawny male, and stale hotel room.

Her eyelids fluttered open. The room was dark, covered even more by the large wing draped over her.

The demon. Half demon.

She should jerk away. At the very least, take her hand off his chest. Kick off the wing that had covered her at some point during the night.

But she didn't. His steady breath moved his chest under her hand.

This male was confusing. He should be undeniably evil. Another demon would've killed that deputy, but he'd only knocked her out. A love tap, for a demon. She'd still have a concussion, but Harlowe hadn't thought of a better way out of that situation.

Another demon would have killed the angel in his bed, or worse, but he'd draped a wing over her like he worried she was cold.

She couldn't make out details, just his big body in front of her, wrapped around her. The even rise and fall of his chest. He had his shirt on. What would his skin feel like?

She crept her hand higher. A few more inches and she could touch his beard. Not many warriors wore beards. They preferred a tight haircut, much like human military, and a clean-shaven appearance. What would Sandeen's beard feel like? Soft? Coarse? Hot?

She was burning up under his wing, this close to his body.

She shifted her hands. Little higher. Her gaze traveled up his body with it, roaming until she met his lazily slitted eyes.

"I thought you were sleeping," she whispered. He was supposed to be sleeping. He'd acted like it. She should be ashamed, but in this warm cocoon he'd made for her, she couldn't bring herself to care.

"I didn't want you to stop." His low rumble went straight to her belly. She almost groaned with the pleasure.

This was wrong. So many shades of wrong. "Why?" she asked to delay her desires.

"Because you're touching me like I've never been touched before."

"How's that?"

"Gentle."

This wasn't the first time his words had torn at her heart. She had no reason to believe a thing he said, yet she had a hard time pinpointing a time he'd outright lied. And the way he'd talked about life in the underworld . . .

If the heart beating under her hand was bloodred instead of dark and shriveled, then it was heartbreaking. It made her want to hold him.

She brushed her hand along his beard, the strands whispering against her skin, until she cupped his face. He tilted his chin down and his lips were there. So close. Ready to kiss.

So she did. Pressed her lips to his. Energy vibrated along his body from where they were connected, down his torso that was inches from hers, and through his wings.

She added more pressure until she was rolling into him, her hand digging through his hair. When her fingers glanced off his horns, she should've recoiled, filled with horror. She should've jumped away, found a phone, and called her team. Demanded a replacement.

But she didn't. She let the silky strands of his hair run through her fingers. Arched into the hand on her hip, his fingers digging in but not moving her. Met the parted lips and slipped her tongue in, careful of those sharp fangs that had given her a delicious bite earlier.

Her body had zinged with life when he'd pricked her. His mouth at her hip. How could something so wrong feel so right?

His tongue swiped across hers, a dash of softness from a hard male.

A low moan left her and she deepened the kiss. Somehow, he kept from nicking her again. Tiny flares of disappointment lit in her belly, but she ignored them.

Heat thrummed through her body. She'd never felt this alive with anyone. Her other partners had been fellow warriors. No one from her team, but males she'd trusted to leave their tryst behind in some small bedroom somewhere on Earth.

He was moving his hand at her hip, untucking her shirt. Her grip tightened in his hair. The need driving her wiped out all thought beyond getting more.

His rough fingers touched the skin at her abdomen and another moan escaped as her belly clenched. More. He wanted gentle but she wanted demanding—

A shotgun blast ripped through the night.

She was on her feet, the dagger she'd pilfered from him in her hand. Sandeen was on the other side of the bed, his wings flared out like he was protecting her. All he was doing was blocking her view. She edged to the side.

Dust filtered through the air, through blades of light that shone through where the door had been.

Another bang and the door to the room flew open.

The deputy from earlier strode in, shotgun barrel entering the room first. A sneer curled the woman's lips. Her brimmed hat was gone and her blond hair was wild, half in and half out of her bun. An image of an obsidian demon overwrote the human's features. Beady eyes, sharp horns, and a perpetually pissed-off expression.

Harlowe had faced this demon before. Zanda.

The host's eyes widened as her gaze landed on Sandeen. She stepped back as if admiring him. "Well, well, well." The tone didn't sound right in the deputy's otherwise no-nonsense voice. "I almost don't want to kill you for tricking me." Her gaze shifted behind him and narrowed on Harlowe. "Are you fucking an angel?"

"She's technically my prisoner."

Zanda gave an appreciative hum. "Fucking prisoners is the most fun. Kill her and let's go."

Harlowe tensed but Sandeen said, "I'm not going back to the underworld."

The other female aimed her barrel at Harlowe. "I'm willing to deal. I can see the appeal of shedding the human skinbag and feasting on them with my own fangs, but we have to leave. Gerzon is working on finding a host. He'll be here soon. So will the hick cops." She swung the barrel of the shotgun toward Harlowe. "I'm going to fill you with so many holes—"

This bitch had obviously forgotten who she was dealing with. Harlowe leaped over the bed, shoving Sandeen out of the way as she spoke the incantation that would yank the demoness out of the human and into the Mist.

Zanda jerked backward, hit the wall, and pulled the trigger. Harlowe didn't stop, her fingers curling into the deputy's coarse shirt, knocking into the rigid bulletproof vest underneath. Cool droplets closed around her as she entered the Mist.

Her hands were empty.

Damn it! The demon got away.

Harlowe stepped out of the Mist, back into the dark hotel room. Voices rose from outside the room. The deputy had passed out as soon as Zanda had left her body and was slumped on the floor against the wall.

The human had had a shitty night.

"We have to go."

Sandeen grunted, his expression strained as he palpated his chest. She couldn't make out details in the low light, but wetness gleamed beneath his hand.

"You were hit?" The barrel had been aimed at her, but had he blocked it?

They didn't have time for her to ponder how she felt about that. She yanked the comforter off the bed and draped it over his head and wings. Circling her arms around him, she rushed him out of the room. He stumbled, but once they hit the pavement, heads bowed together in case anyone was filming, he steadied and ran with her.

"Fucking stings," he mumbled. It wouldn't kill him, but it'd hurt like hell.

"Your girlfriend got away."

"She's quick like that."

He didn't deny the girlfriend part. Petty jealousy seared her, made worse because it was a piss-poor time to feel it and because she shouldn't be jealous anyway. "Everything's going to blow up now. We need to find a phone."

It was time to call her team.

CHAPTER 7

Harlowe missed the days of pay phones.

They were on the road again. Different vehicle.

Sandeen had ignored the blood dripping down his torso and hot-wired another vehicle. A pickup this time. Older. Beat-up with rusted fenders. She'd feared they'd wake the whole town, but the house it'd been parked in front of had remained dark.

They were heading west once again, only hours after they'd stopped for the night. He'd insisted on driving, said it took his mind off sitting on his wings, and since he was full of lead because of her, she'd let him.

"We need to find a phone," she reiterated. They hadn't spoken about the kiss and she would be fine if they never did. Ever. They also hadn't spoken about Zanda, or what her finding them meant.

"There should be a gas station coming up." His mouth was drawn back in a chronic grimace, but he didn't mention the shotgun wound either.

"I can't go inside. The clerk that checked me in will be

able to describe me to the cops, and you . . ." She waved her hand at him.

"All right." He turned at the next road, a wide dirt road that disappeared into the trees.

"What are you doing?"

"Finding a phone."

As they crested a hill, the trees thinned. Lights were scattered in the distance. "We can't just break into a house to use the phone."

He blew out a gusty breath. "*You* can't. I can do whatever the hell I want. But I won't be able to if Zanda finds me again. And if what I'm doing gets beyond her to Gerzon, he's going to make plans for me. And if the news gets beyond Gerzon, to my sire?" He shook his head. "Your people are looking like the better option. For now."

Fine. They were breaking into a house and stealing a phone. She didn't like to break human laws. Sometimes it had to be done, but like a human with their taxes, she made damn sure she could prove the expense was necessary.

It was necessary in the days of cell phones. Any other phone would be in a public spot. They were in a sparsely populated area, which was an advantage, but it also meant more scrutiny if they passed a patrol car. It meant sticking out more when they drove through a small town.

They neared a farmhouse. The trees cleared as they entered a wide, swooping valley. A small ranch. Maybe a hobby farm.

Sandeen parked and killed the lights. "Good luck."

So he'd come to the same conclusion. It was safer for her to break and enter. "You're coming with me. I need a lookout." What if he left her?

"So I can spook the cattle and wake the household?" Moos echoed around them. She didn't know what cows normally sounded like in the hours before dawn.

"You're not going to ditch me?" She'd have no way of finding him.

"I'm backed into a corner, angel. No money, no weapons, and a set of wings that'll only bring me trouble. Gerzon wants this power. Your lot failed to get him, but he fears my sire. And if he can't catch me, he's going right to Big Z and tattling on me just so I can't keep the toy he can't have." He sighed and sank into the seat. "And they're going to hunt your fallen. Thanks to Andy, they know how I'm doing this."

Sierra. Sierra's baby. Protectiveness swelled inside of her until she was ready to palm her dagger and carve her way into the underworld. Gerzon was not getting to Sierra or that baby. She had to notify her team. "Promise me you're not going anywhere."

He grunted and arched his back. Was he finally healing? Did he heal as readily on Earth in his own form as he would in the underworld? "I don't make promises, angel. I make deals. You find a phone and get me somewhere I can sleep this off and I won't tell anyone you kissed me."

She sucked in a breath. "You wouldn't dare."

His grin showed a flash of fang. "Care to test me?"

"Fine." She flung the door open, then slammed it behind her and stalked into the trees. *I don't make promises, angel. I make deals.* Somehow, that made her trust him more.

BRONX WANDERED through the weapons room. Warriors were supposed to be meticulous about keeping track of their weapons. If they lost one, there was a chain of command to report to. Paperwork to go to the analysts. Tracking procedures to determine if their lost weapon had been obtained by demons and used against humans or angels.

The window of accusation it created caused more problems than it prevented. Warriors were afraid to intercept a demon and risk losing a weapon, opening themselves up to a zealous senator. Some of the more obnoxious ones liked to start by calling for their wings, then move down to removing the warrior from the field and making them a trainer, or worse, kicking them out of the profession entirely.

Numen had callings. Bronx had wanted nothing but to be a warrior, and though he was a little tired of the fight now, he couldn't imagine doing anything else. The angels in the senate were usually born into the role, and there were far more of them than the actual population of Numen needed if you asked him. But no one had asked him.

If anyone had, he'd tell them they needed more warriors. But then his kind would have to admit that they could die. Easily. Demons had nothing to lose when they fought. It made them dangerous, ruthless, and deadly.

"Need more angel fire?" Urban pocketed a crystal vial. Crystal was the only substance that could contain the deadly plasma. Most of the time, they didn't have to open the vial and pour it on their opponent. Bronx had good aim. He could nail a demon on the horns, shattering the vial and dissolving the bastard from the head down.

Wicked way to go.

"Nah. I'm fine." He'd been an errand boy more than a warrior lately. He hadn't been in many fights. Was that why he was antsy?

"I'm done."

They walked out and locked up the weapons room. The male on duty gave them a cursory glance and went back to his game. Weapons-room duty used to be the most hated assignment until human electronics infiltrated the realm. Now, angels would gladly use their energy to power the devices rather than train.

Bronx walked out with Urban. Only other warriors were around. Bronx's phone buzzed. He glanced at the message. "The director wants to talk to us."

They changed direction between two marble buildings. One slate-gray rectangle was the barracks he used to stay in with his team. But since Bryant had mated with Odessa and moved out, the rest of the team had filtered out too. Sierra couldn't even return to the realm. Jagger split his time between Earth and his mansion in Numen. Dionna kept her personal life private. Harlowe had been hunting the demon for months and rarely came back to Numen. She was a workaholic. That left him and Urban. They used whatever safe house they were working out of as a temporary residence or got a hotel room. Ransom was new to the team, but he had his bachelor pad. They all avoided the barracks. And the inevitable questions about what they'd been up to.

Without a word, they marched up the steps to the front door of the administrative building that housed the director's office. Director Vale and Odessa had converted a part of the building next door into their new place after Odessa's mansion had been consumed by angel fire.

The front door opened as if someone had been waiting for them. A petite angel strode out, her pouty red lips turned down. Her flinty gaze landed on them and her eyes narrowed.

Tosca Smith. She was an enforcer. She'd been one of Odessa's guards when the director's mate had been threatened.

Enforcers and warriors didn't get along. Enforcers

were the police force of their kind and warriors liked to ask them what the fuck they did all day. That didn't go over well.

Bronx didn't ask. He'd met enough corrupt enforcers not to trust them as a whole. Tosca was different. She might also be in the pocket of a senator.

She blocked the entrance to the door. Enforcers dressed like warriors, but Tosca looked like a princess playing soldier. Her hips flared wider than her tactical belt. Bronx didn't know what she carried as weapons—he had a hard time taking his eyes off the hips and round thighs that could really lock around a guy.

"What are you two doing back in the realm?"

He dragged his gaze up, brushing over her chest. Damn. Tosca was a poster child for the hourglass figure.

Her eyes were narrowed on him. Busted. He gave her his best panty-melting grin. One time, he'd literally melted the edible underwear off a woman. Licking her clean was one of his favorite memories. The taste lingered in his brain even if the woman's name and looks didn't.

Tosca's lips curled into a snarl as if she could read his thoughts.

Urban cut through the tension by answering. "Replenishing."

Tosca's garnet gaze slid to his teammate. "Oh, yeah? You lost some weapons and discharged your angel fire? I can check the records about how it happened?"

Disappointment ricocheted around his chest. So she *was* in the pocket of some senator. Why else would an enforcer be up in their business? "If that's what gets you off."

The force of her gaze was like getting bitch-slapped with a sock full of rocks. "While others might admire the crassness of warriors, I find your language as charming as the bottom of your shoe." She rolled her gaze back to Urban. "Warriors have been in their own world for too long."

Bronx closed the distance between them and she backed up until she hit the closed door. "And it's up to you to do something about that? Is that how it works?"

"We were just leaving." Urban ran headlong into a fight with a demon, but tiptoed around conflict in Numen.

She pushed away and wedged between them, her wings flaring out until he had to step back or get a mouthful of feathers. It'd serve her right if he nipped her.

Blood rushed between his ears and down to his groin. Hell. She was sexy, but she was a corrupt pain in the ass. Still. No more thinking about biting the ripe enforcer.

He couldn't let her get the last word when he was the one leaving. "Maybe you should watch over your own profession, enforcer."

She stopped at the bottom of the stairs, her downy, storm-gray wings held off the ground. "I'm good at my job, as are my counterparts."

"Likewise." He trusted his team. Her expression was full of doubt as he turned his back to her and pushed into the hallway. This enforcer could take her haughty attitude and cannonball into a tornado.

"Damn," he said.

"Bronx. Urban." The bark came from Director Vale. He stormed down the hallway, his wings flared behind him. The director glanced between them. "Harlowe needs an extraction. Which one of you is going?"

CHAPTER 8

The sun was high, heating the car too much to be comfortable. Sandeen and Harlowe reclined against a tree, shaded by overhanging branches.

His chest and shoulder had quit burning. The skin had mended, but lingering zings of pain shot from where the wounds had been. He could go for a good steak, one cooked by someone else.

Would the warriors let him cook?

He'd have time to work on his morphing.

He wasn't as worried about being imprisoned by the angels as he'd let on. Nothing they dealt out could be as bad as what he'd been through in his own realm. They also wouldn't let him near Numen. Earth was their only option. He'd have a roof over his head, the bills would be paid, and he could work on morphing his wings.

Then he could escape. Because one thing he knew for damn sure was that the underworld was going to find him if he didn't learn how to blend. Big Z would sit back and let Gerzon do all the heavy lifting with his bull-in-a-window-factory routine, and then he'd swoop in.

Sandeen didn't worry about his sire's influence on Earth. Not since the incident with the kid. No. His sire was too vulnerable to warriors on Earth and he was shit at containing himself in a host. Only that one time. When it had hurt Sandeen the most.

His sire had claimed Sandeen's entire life that humans and angels were too weak. Yet Sandeen was here. Half angel. Had Big Z been testing the other beings all this time? Learning where their weaknesses lay? He was one of the oldest demons in the realm. He'd been the one to reveal to Sandeen the connection between the metal used in all their non-earthly metals and angel fire. He'd been the one to tell Sandeen about the deal between the realms and exactly why it had fallen apart. And Sandeen doubted many angels knew the story. Big Z could've been lying, but Sandeen doubted it. There were certain facts his sire fixated on, and getting screwed by angels was one of them.

"Did they stop to piss every ten miles?" He was hangry. Shotgun blasts and having the best kiss of his long life getting interrupted did that to him.

"You're lucky any of us has been within two hundred miles of this place."

"Can't you just go through the Mist instead of only going to places you've been before?" He didn't think Daemon had many advantages over their counterparts, but if they could find a host to inhabit anywhere in the world, then they could *go* anywhere in the world. The sylphs made sure they kept a lot of humans in all walks of life feeling burdened and disenchanted. Made possession a lot easier.

"We can, but it's too risky. If a human saw, it'd look like we just appeared out of thin air. This isn't life threatening."

"I'm going to threaten someone's life if he doesn't get here soon," he growled.

"I'm going to threaten your life if you don't quit complaining."

"Now, angel. We've been through so much together."

"Shut it, demon." He wasn't the only one hangry.

"So, who's our rescuer? The player, the stoic one, the rich asshole, the serious one, or the new grandpa?" He knew their names, but this was more fun.

Her mouth tightened, but more like she was fighting a smile instead of annoyance. "It could be Bronx or Urban. Jagger's probably busy with Felicia and the senate. You're lucky it's not Dionna. She's not as patient as me. And Ransom is new to all this." She waved her hand to encompass the trees and him.

"The player or the stoic one, then."

"Bronx isn't a player."

He grinned. "Ah, but you knew who I was talking about."

She glared at him. "Shut it."

Numen liked to fuck around, and warriors were the worst. Faced with mating for eternity, most Numen probably fornicated to get it out of their system. But a warrior's mating meant extra healing capabilities. Since warriors were faced with more opportunities to lose life or limb, they mated earlier and at higher rates than other Numen. And they fucked like their eternal life depended on it. Or so he'd heard.

Some stupid voice in his head whispered that he was part Numen as well. Did that mean a mate? He brushed it off. If he couldn't do a basic wing morph, then higher achievements were likely locked. He was a demon.

But he wasn't ready to drop the subject, not when it came to Harlowe. "Are you like that?"

"Getting personal, demon."

"Seriously though. I have sex when it's to my advantage.

Otherwise underworld sex isn't exactly pleasant. I'll spare you the details."

"Getting with the female that peppered you was to your advantage?"

Zanda had been aiming at Harlowe, but the demoness would probably be delighted to know she'd shot him. "Always. But she was more palatable than the rest."

Harlowe shot him a dirty look.

"What?"

She shook her head.

"She didn't gut me during sex, and that can be hard to find."

"God, stop talking."

"No need to bring Him into my sex life."

She sputtered, then stuck with shaking her head. "You're incorrigible."

"That's the best compliment I've ever gotten." He played it off like a joke, but he was serious. Being called an asshole was the tamest thing that could happen in his former home. At least she'd put some thought into "incorrigible."

An engine hummed in the distance. He hoped it was the warrior. There was only so far back in the trees they could hide the old pickup. They were taking a chance that someone nosy wouldn't notice and stop to investigate.

They were welcome to—after he and Harlowe had left.

The hum got louder. He stayed where he was. His wing covered him and anyone looking would see nothing but shadows underneath the boughs of the pine. He stretched a wing out to conceal Harlowe, but she slapped it down.

"Stop it with the wings, would ya?"

"Why? You seem to like them."

She ignored him and crawled out from under the big branches. He watched her heart-shaped ass the entire time. His fangs throbbed to sink into her flesh.

Would she kiss him again? How badly was she regretting what she'd done? She seemed to fear losing her wings. Would she be in danger of it from making out with a demon? That had to be against the rules.

A black four-door sedan approached.

"It's Bronx."

Sandeen didn't rise. He waited for her to flag the other warrior down. Bronx rolled out of the car like he was driving a Bentley and wearing a five-thousand-dollar suit instead of jeans and a black T-shirt. His clothes blended in with the locals' better than Harlowe's ripped tactical clothing. But the male wouldn't blend. He was almost as tall as Sandeen with jet-black hair, an athletic build, and attitude like he'd just walked off the set of *Crazy Rich Asians*. Every human between puberty and death would gawk at his beauty.

Angels looked like the world they were welcome to inhabit. Demons were a hodgepodge of open sores and defensive adaptations. What was the balance there? That angels didn't have horns to gut their opponents?

Didn't seem like a fair trade.

Bronx eyed him. Sandeen eyed him back.

The male folded his hands under his armpits. "I wouldn't have believed it, but damn. How are you staying like that? Do you have to keep, like, dipping into the fallen's blood?"

"He used to have a vial of blood around his neck and he regularly tattooed it into himself. But he doesn't need it."

Bronx's dark brows popped. "Nothing? You're just here?"

Sandeen held his arms out. "Apparently."

"It might have something to do with his heritage," Harlowe added.

Bronx's jaw worked. "Right."

Right.

He wasn't alone. There was a whole realm of angels unhappy to hear about the circumstances of his birth.

Harlowe started for the car. "We'd better get going. Where's the safe house?"

"Vegas." Bronx went to the trunk and popped it open. He stood next to it, gazing expectantly at Sandeen.

"One," Sandeen said, "I'm not going to Vegas. That's the stupidest place on Earth I could go. And two, I'm not riding in a trunk."

Bronx gestured behind his back as if his own wings were unmorphed. "This is kinda a deal breaker, big guy."

He hadn't expected the male to be so flippant. It was annoying and reassuring at the same time. If his life had gone another way, Sandeen would've been like Sierra. He would've been raised in a loving home, would've grown up with friends and worked with guys like Bronx.

Your mother would be ashamed of you.

Big Z hadn't been lying.

He gave himself a mental shake. He'd never bemoaned his lot in life. He wasn't going to start now just because he'd learned a fact that changed nothing about him.

Sandeen stood his ground. "I didn't leave the underworld so I could fold up into a pretzel and suffocate in a hot trunk."

"He likes his creature comforts." Harlowe got in the car. "Just let him ride in the back seat. He's stubborn."

Bronx cocked a brow and mouthed *stubborn?* like he couldn't figure it out.

"You've gotta quit throwing the compliments my way, Lowe. It's going to get embarrassing." Sandeen crawled into the AC-cooled car. Better than a tree branch. He peered into the front seat. "Got something to eat?"

Neither angel answered.

"Vegas isn't a good spot," said Harlowe. She didn't expressly say Sandeen had been right, but it was close enough. He smiled enough so that if she looked back at him, she'd know exactly why. But she didn't. Eh, it had been worth a shot. "There's still too much demon activity."

"They're going to look all over Montana," Bronx countered. "They're going to comb Montana and the surrounding states, searching through mountain ranges and fields, molesting cattle, and defiling run-down motels. Vegas is too obvious, and that's exactly why we're going there. Hey, big guy. Lie down or something. Your wings are blocking my rearview."

Sandeen didn't feel like arguing. He had two Numen responsible for him on a long drive. He might as well get some rest. Who knew what would happen in Vegas?

HARLOWE RESISTED the urge to turn around every twenty minutes and check on the demon. His breathing was even, but she'd been fooled before.

She was also envious. He'd been snoozing for hours while she and Bronx had been making plans. She'd been messaging up a storm to Director Vale with the new phone Bronx had brought her. There wasn't much she had to keep secret from Sandeen, but she hated how little she worried about speaking around him. As if the half-angel fact was a game changer when he didn't seem to accept it.

Did Sierra accept her demon half?

"How's Sierra doing?" She hadn't meant to ask. She was tired and the sexy beast with wings she wanted to wrap around her naked body had frazzled her.

"Good. Arik's doing well. Ransom is the proudest granddad ever."

"Except he's not."

Bronx slid his amber gaze toward her. "He's her dad."

"Yeah, I know."

It'd been an asshole thing to say. Ransom was Sierra's proud, loving, engaged papa on a normal day. Being a grandfather would be like supercharging his fatherliness. Envy as hot as angel fire burned through her body.

Harlowe had lost her mother. Not because of Sierra. Harlowe wouldn't blame anyone but demons for what had happened to their mother. But Sierra had been adopted and raised by an attentive father.

Harlowe's father checked out of the land of the living a little more each year. Whenever she went home, her father was quieter. Lost in memories. It was why she didn't often go home.

"I just don't know what to think about all that." And she wasn't just talking about their fathers. After dedicating her life to fighting the underworld, Harlowe wasn't knowingly allowing a demon in her life—even if that half demon was also her half sister. But after spending time with Sandeen, things had gotten complicated. And she missed Sierra.

"I don't know what to think about a half demon in the back seat who asked me for a snack." He blew out a breath. "Shit's changed in the last couple of years. Things we were taught were impossible are very real, and very close to us."

"My sister. Maybe I'd feel different if I'd been outright lied to. More righteous about the deceit. But we all just assumed she was an angel, like us, because why wouldn't she be? And she couldn't say otherwise." To protect Harlowe. To protect the entire realm.

She glanced at the big body taking up the back seat. He'd covered himself with the wing he wasn't lying on, managing to keep his feathers from poking between the seats. "How many more do you think there are?"

"Not many."

"What do you mean?"

He lifted a shoulder but kept his arm draped across the wheel. "If it was more common, we'd have heard rumors or something. That must mean it's not easy. I mean, his father?" Bronx tipped his head toward the back to indicate the demon. "Have you read the fact sheet on that male?"

Harlowe shook her head.

"Nasty stuff. He would be the one that made it happen. And we keep discounting Gerzon cuz he seemed to need his hand held by Andy. But someone helped Andy stockpile all those weapons."

Andy had claimed it was to keep any demon from getting their hands on both Numen weapons and fallen blood. But the guy had been a psychopath. "The female working under Gerzon is savvy. She'll turn on Gerzon in a heartbeat and use her relationship with"—Harlowe tilted her head toward the back like Bronx had done—"to do it."

"Is she his mate?" Bronx asked as quietly as possible.

She shook her head. She didn't think so, but she whispered, "Do demons mate?"

"No," Sandeen answered from the back.

"Dammit!" she shrieked. "Will you quit pretending to sleep?"

She snapped her mouth shut before she could spill any more details. Bronx liked to play casual and relaxed but he was one of the best warriors she'd ever fought with and it wasn't because he didn't pay attention.

"Your fellow warrior is correct." Sandeen ignored her outburst. She wished she could. It was unlike her. "Big Z is nasty, and he's smart for a demon. He didn't sire me just because he could. Well, he did, but ultimately it was a test."

"Of what?"

"I don't know. My whole life, he's tested what I could

withstand. He's probably sitting on his throne of bones and getting reports on what I'm doing. Gerzon wants a piece of the pie. Big Z controls the pie and the whole damn oven. This?" His wing fluttered. "Is probably just another test. What can I do on Earth? Can I morph? Can I get to another realm? Will I be accepted and where will my loyalty fall? Once he knows for sure, he'll determine if it's worth trying again."

"Where does your loyalty fall?" Bronx asked.

"Myself."

"That's not a surprise," Bronx muttered.

Harlowe clenched her jaw. She didn't know why her irritation rose so high when the demon said stuff like that. He wasn't loyal to the underworld. And he wouldn't fall for that demoness's promises when he was looking out for number one. But that also meant no one else factored into his priorities.

CHAPTER 9

The safe house looked much like the last one Sandeen had stayed in when he'd possessed Alma. Off-white stucco with brick-red shingles and accents. The inside was open concept. Ceramic tile floor. A square patch of carpet in the sitting area. A staircase along the wall that went upstairs. There was a sliding door that led to a rectangle of grass that didn't have much more square footage than the carpet. A wide-finned ceiling fan spun lazily overhead. The only difference was that this house was in North Las Vegas instead of Henderson.

Last night Bronx had parked inside the attached garage and come inside first to make sure all the blinds were drawn. As if some dude with horns and wings would get that much attention in Vegas. The bigger threat about anyone seeing him was who they blabbed to. Or that they were haunted by sylphs. Those little bastards wouldn't ignore him.

Sandeen let his wings fall across the couch on either side of him and he kicked his feet out. The place had a TV and internet. He was streaming his fourth cooking show of the morning.

Harlowe paced behind him. She hated safe-house duty. She hadn't said anything, but the disgruntled set to her shoulders spoke volumes. His only experience with her in safe houses was when she was guarding him. So she might only hate safe-house duty when he was involved.

"Get this—people use zucchini instead of crust for pizza." He snorted. "What a waste of effort."

She stopped at the edge of the couch. "Stand up. You need to practice."

"But the Southern lady is on. I don't want to miss her show."

"They're all Southern."

"Not the celebrity."

"They're all celebrities."

"So jaded, angel. Sit and enjoy the show."

"And then eat a can of soup for lunch? No, thanks."

The groceries were an issue. He'd eaten better for weeks on what Boone had left behind in the cabin. Then he'd ordered in food and eaten like a real human, albeit one who couldn't cook.

He watched the opening segment of the show. An older woman was surrounded by her kids and grandkids in front of a giant barn that looked like it held dances instead of animals. Every person wore a smile a mile wide. Was it genuine? Or a show for the camera?

What kind of life would that be like? To be surrounded by beings that loved you and shared in your passion?

What would it be like to have a passion that included more than survival and freedom?

He wouldn't have to worry about it. Figuring out a way to ditch the angels and blend in well enough with society to evade demons and angels alike was his passion for the foreseeable future.

"Practice what?" he asked since Harlowe continued to glower at him.

"Morphing."

Morphing was now part of his passion.

He stood. Bronx had stocked his bedroom with a few simple T-shirts, ones with slits in the back that fit him properly. But Sandeen took his shirt off anyway.

The way Harlowe's pupils dilated and her throat worked as she swallowed was worth it. He closed his eyes and summoned the memories of his time with Harlowe on the side of the road when she'd first tried to teach him. Her hands stroking his back. The way her voice dropped the closer she was to him. How she described the sensations of a morph.

He stayed in that place and waited.

Nothing. Not one feather fluttered.

Damn.

He opened his eyes. It had to be possible. He had to figure this out so he could disappear.

Harlowe walked backward, keeping the couch between him and her. "Umm . . . Maybe if we—"

The sliding door opened. He didn't have any weapons on him, but he made fists and tilted his head down. His horns made good battering rams. They'd been here less than a day. How many people knew about this place?

Bronx strode through first, wearing his T-shirt and jeans combo, but his expression wasn't casual. Another male entered. A big angel, half his face scarred. Angel fire burns. Must've hurt like a bitch. He wore clothing more like Harlowe's. Black and tactical. His hard whiskey-colored stare landed on Sandeen, lifted to his horns, and roamed over his wings. The corner of his mouth on the uninjured side of his face turned down farther. This must be Director Vale.

A male with loose blond curls, dressed like the others, came in and slid the door shut. He didn't recognize this one, but the avid curiosity in the male's gaze told Sandeen it was likely Ransom. The warrior had knowingly raised a half-demon daughter. He must've thought she was the only one in all the realms. They all must've taken turns transcending from Numen to the privacy screen surrounding the little pad of cement outside the door.

Sandeen flopped on the couch, spreading his wings out again. After the long car ride, he wasn't sitting on his wings anytime soon. "Is this it? Judgment day?"

The director tilted his head toward the door. On cue, the other three warriors filed out, leaving Sandeen alone with their boss.

Director Vale grabbed the high-back chair next to the couch and spun it. The chair wasn't some light piece of crap furniture, but he flipped it like a cheap plastic lawn chair. Sandeen would be impressed if he cared.

The male perched on the edge, his long legs making it look more like a squat. "I'm not going to beat around the bush." His voice was gravelly, like someone had taken sandpaper and had a go at his vocal cords. How had he sounded before the angel fire incident? "You're a demon and you're walking around Earth with your wings flappin' and your horns all shiny. That's a problem."

The hint of an accent broke through the male's words. British? He must've spent a considerable amount of time out of Numen to pick up an accent. "I admit, it's a bit of a problem for me too."

The director's expression didn't change. "We can't prove you're half angel, but . . . bloody hell. Look at you."

"Do you know who my mother was?" He hadn't meant

to ask that. He hadn't meant to show such vulnerability to someone like this, a male who thought he held Sandeen's future in his hands. A male who thought he had a say in how Sandeen lived his life.

The male was wrong.

But Sandeen would play along for now.

"No. Tell me your age and we'll go through our records." Director Vale's gaze narrowed on nothing. "She'd be listed as missing, I'm guessing. We keep thorough records on death, but if she perished in the Gloom, we'd never know."

Most of those missing angels probably had perished in the Gloom. Demons might bring an angel to the gloomy realm separating the underworld from Earth—but they'd never let them leave. It was like bringing the enemy to your doorstep. They might see things they weren't meant to and demons were a secretive kind.

Angels dragged them to the Mist out of necessity. They couldn't kill a demon on Earth, they couldn't have human witnesses, and demons weren't going to bring the fight to the Gloom. The Mist had safeguards woven through it that expelled demons after a length of time, not that many wanted to linger.

"Do you know anything about her?" the director asked.

"Only that she suffered." *And that she'd be ashamed of me.*

"Does that bother you?"

He didn't reply. It wasn't the director's business. It also wasn't anything he'd thought about, or that he wanted to spend time pondering.

"My team tells me you want to roam free. That you claim you wouldn't bother anyone."

He'd never claimed that. "The goals of Daemon and Numen are not mine. Seeing as I don't exactly belong anywhere, I'd rather just . . . be."

"You know why that can't happen."

"You toss the fallen out and turn your head. They're free to do whatever the hell they want."

"They're being monitored."

"Do they know that?"

"Since you let everyone know that you can strut around with your wings out thanks to their blood, yeah, they know. They're being hunted."

Was he supposed to feel guilty? "I capitalized on some information."

The director studied him. "I'm the only thing standing between you and an entire senate that would call for your eradication if they learned about you."

"If I were you, I'd be concerned about whether anyone already knows about me in your precious senate."

Director Vale pressed his lips in a line. Yeah, the male would like the same information. He wasn't stupid. Even worse, he was realistic. Sandeen was caught between wanting to trust him, and wanting to put as much distance between them as possible.

Angels and demons had worked together far longer than this male likely realized, but several older angels in the director's senate would remember. They'd also remember the balance the realms had attained for a short while, and who had tipped the scales.

The director put the tips of his fingers together. "Half angel or not, you prefer to work with bargains. Am I correct?"

Sandeen lifted a shoulder. Director Vale wasn't wrong. But bargains were like a game of chicken. Who would betray the other side first? Most angels didn't understand, just like they didn't understand that the trait wasn't unique to demons.

The director's eyes narrowed. "You stay here. Watch

TV, cook, whatever. Don't cause trouble for my people." Short of defining trouble, the deal didn't sound terrible so far. "And my mate will search for information on your mother. We'll go from there."

Hope pierced Sandeen's chest, but terror shoved it out. *No.*

No, no, no. He didn't need to know his sire's victim. He didn't need to know her name, or the loved ones Zadren had stolen her from. He didn't need to know that she'd had an idyllic life that would make what had happened to her look as atrocious as it was.

But he said, "Deal." The bargain bought him a few more days to figure out what to do. A few more days to work on morphing his wings. Once he had that down, he'd deal with his horns, and then he'd disappear forever.

THE HOT VEGAS sun scorched Harlowe's bare legs. She'd shed her tactical pants—too odd for the neighbors to see when she was in the backyard. Her shorts were black. Sandeen had asked if it was her favorite color and she'd told him she wasn't here to party. For the last week, she'd cared for the lawn and made a show of being outside. Bronx took the car in and out of the garage at least every other day. Just normal people in this house here.

She sipped from her lemonade. The demon had hand-squeezed the stuff. Added mint leaves and enough sugar to challenge her angelic ability to prevent diabetes.

Mint leaves.

Forget using up what was in the pantry. Once Bronx had learned that Sandeen wanted to cook, and that when he did, he wasn't half bad, he'd been incorrigible. Those trips Bronx made every other day were to the grocery store, and he returned with fresh produce, baking staples, and custom cuts of meat.

Custom cuts of meat.

Sandeen had even talked Bronx into grilling.

A week of recipes, cooking shows, and delicious meals.

Harlowe was going out of her mind. She should be patrolling the streets. Shanking demons in the Mist. Not sampling the best chicken cordon bleu she'd ever had.

This safe-house assignment was going to be the end of her.

Bronx stepped out of the sliding door. Harlowe squatted and pulled a weed out from between the rocks. Bronx stuffed his hands in the pockets of his basketball shorts and roamed toward her. "Everything's still pretty quiet."

They did their updates outside. Sandeen wasn't allowed out with his massive wings, and he was an expert-level eavesdropper.

"He's up to something," she said.

Bronx drew his brows together. "How do you figure? He has everything he wants here. We're even buying him groceries."

"He's lulling you into a false sense of security. I'm telling you." She didn't know how she knew, she just did. Sandeen was soaking up AC, free food, and their protection. But he wasn't free. He was their captive.

She hadn't lost sight of the fact that her kind couldn't just let him be. He was a problem they had yet to deal with. If she hadn't forgotten, then neither had he. Bronx liked to assume all sentient beings were as logical and accepting as him. When he wasn't dealing with demons, he was an amiable guy. Sandeen acted a lot like him. But it was an act.

Bronx edged closer, his voice low. Neighbors were

nosy; it didn't matter how big the city was. "Say he were to escape—where would he go?"

She rose and took another sip of her lemonade. It'd been a struggle not to gulp it down. "That's what we need to be discussing."

Bronx crooked his lips as he thought. "He has nowhere to go. Vegas is still a demon hotbed thanks to Jameson and Andy. Sandeen has no money. No friends. He can't transcend. The only place he could go is back to Daemon, and he's not afraid to admit that he's not going back. Do you think he's lying?"

No money. No friends. "He's stuck. But he's not a guy who likes to be stuck. He doesn't want to be dependent on anyone about his future. He's using us." The demon had to have somewhere else he could go. A place he didn't want to go to, and that didn't make a lick of sense.

Frustrating male.

Displeasure rippled through Bronx's features. He was starting to like the demon. That was part of Sandeen's ultimate deception. He made himself likable. He used his charm and his looks and got overtired angels to kiss him. "All right. I see your point. We've already mapped out the nearest bus stops. Sierra set up alerts on this address if any car rides or taxis are ordered."

"She should do the entire neighborhood."

"Why don't you let her know?" Bronx's brown gaze was steady, his voice quiet.

Harlowe kicked at the turf with the toe of her athletic shoe. She couldn't do sandals. Not when demons might be after them. Her Las Vegas Aces shirt and the shorts were baggy enough to hide her daggers and vial of angel fire. "Fine. I can message her."

"Or call. She is your sister."

"Then you get how complicated it is."

He didn't have time to answer. A shuffling of feet by the door snapped Bronx's attention around. Harlowe forced herself to remain relaxed. One of their team was here. The latticework wood panels around the sliding door were angled to block an outside view. The second layer of lattice paneling tucked inside the first wasn't visible other than to make it impossible to tell that someone was appearing or disappearing from behind the privacy wall.

Ransom Cormorant popped his curly blond head out. Sierra's father. The male who'd raised her, and had kept the secret of Harlowe's mom for decades. So completely dedicated to his daughter.

A mix of emotions welled inside of her. Despair. Anger. Regret. They swirled, a tempest centered around envy, but she kept it all from showing on her face.

His pale blue eyes flicked to hers, then away. He was new to their team, since he'd been the first to keep the whopper of a secret that was Sierra. It made him the perfect addition. Dammit.

Relief crossed the male's face when his gaze landed on Bronx. Harlowe's feelings might not be as secret as she meant them to be. "The director sent me. You and I can stay and watch the captive." Ransom's resistance to talking to Harlowe was revealed in the heavy slide of his blue gaze to her. "The director would like to talk to you."

"Where?" The word was a whip snap.

"His office."

She strode to the privacy screen. He edged out, plastered against the wood. He was dressed in khaki shorts and a slate-gray polo shirt, a good-looking guy in his midthirties—if he were human. He was probably a few hundred years old, and more experienced in the field than her, but his strained expression said he'd rather take on a horde of demons than face her.

Harlowe felt the same. Being around him made her want to ask questions. How bad had it been for her mother when she'd died? How much had she suffered? Did he feel guilty that Harlowe had grown up believing a lie?

Being around him also made her want to claw his eyes out. So it was better she leave immediately. Because then she might start wondering if the demon had the same questions.

CHAPTER 10

*H*arlowe eyed Odessa as the female dug several scrolls out of her robe. Had the female sewn pockets inside her robe so she could smuggle documents to Director Vale's office?

Harlowe had changed into her standard pants and long-sleeved shirt before coming here. No one but her team knew of her assignment. Returning to the realm looking like she'd been on vacation might inspire unwanted questions.

"There are several missing persons, more than I ever expected." Odessa arranged the scrolls. Her vivid gaze bounced between Harlowe and Director Vale. "And that's not all that's odd."

Harlowe counted twenty-two scrolls. All missing? That should be bigger news, but they were a long-lived species. Twenty-two on record over centuries wasn't a fact that would set alarm bells off. Perhaps if the realm thought something nefarious had happened, ripples of worry would course through their society.

Odessa tapped a scroll. Particles of dust puffed off and

mingled in the air above it. "They're all scrolls. We'll never keep up with the advancement of humanity if we don't advance ourselves, so we've worked to automate as much of our records as possible. Watchers' notes on human activities are dictated. An analyst transcribes them. Same with warrior records. We have staff who are working on backlogs and converting these scrolls to an electronic format."

Odessa's point was easy to see. "But the missing angels' information is left in a dusty corner."

The female nodded, her long, mahogany hair sliding over her shoulder as she peered at the lineup. "Just like the fallen scrolls had been shoved in some cart that would be easy to pass by."

The director ran a hand over his shaved scalp. "As if someone would rather we not look into the details. Which is the most recent?"

Odessa tapped the yellowed scroll on her right. "This female went missing a few years after Sierra was born. Ransom had reported that Sierra's mother—uh"—her gaze jumped to Harlowe—"*your* mother was killed, so there's no scroll on her."

Harlowe's chest burned. Sierra's mother. Her mother. They were one and the same. She nodded as if Odessa hadn't ripped a bandage off a wound a mile wide and willed the female to continue.

"Less than a decade before your mother was attacked, another female went missing." Odessa double-tapped that scroll. "Within a thirty-year period before your mother died, three females and one male went missing. The others before that are spread out over several centuries."

Director Vale scowled. "A male? Were they mated?"

"Only one female was, but the missing male wasn't her mate. There are no notes that he'd been dating or had a relationship with any of the females, but he had to. I mean, he had to. Who wouldn't at least check?"

"He could've gone legitimately missing." The director crossed his arms and glowered at the scrolls. "Which means he meant to go missing, or he didn't mean to and something bad happened. Or he could've gone searching for one of these females. Or . . . he could've been responsible for it. Maybe the male went on the run and the demons got to him and took care of the problem for us."

It would be convenient if that was the case, but that wasn't how Harlowe wanted to work with demons. "Which one was mated?"

Odessa pointed to the scroll of the female who'd disappeared before her mother was killed.

Harlowe unrolled the crispy parchment. The information hadn't even been annotated on their good material. It was like someone wanted these to disintegrate into nothing. "Sandissa Colbert. A chaperone who never returned from assignment." So the angel had been allowed on Earth. That made it more complicated. Not all Numen were granted access to Earth, but those who were could live there. They could go to Earth and never return.

Sandissa. Sandeen. What were the odds? "Think there are any pictures?"

Sandeen had hair a shade darker than Odessa's rich mahogany locks. His eyes were a stunning blue that couldn't come from a demon. Demon eyes were mostly all pupil, a trait she'd assumed was from living in the underworld. Looks alone wouldn't confirm this Sandissa was his mother, but it wasn't like they could get a DNA sample. They had no ability to do tests like that in Numen.

Harlowe carefully rerolled the scroll. "We need to talk to her mate."

"He lives on the edge of the realm," Director Vale answered.

Harlowe's brows popped. The realm had a fountain of angel fire in the center and the buildings spread out from there. Commerce. Residential housing. Barracks on one side, the enforcers' headquarters on the other, then more residential. With each layer winging out, the homes grew grander and more ornate.

"Senator?" Supposedly any angel could become a senator, but being born into a political family helped. Those families tended to be the best connected and the most affluent.

"No." Suspicion rang in the director's gravelly voice. "But his mother is."

"That could complicate things." Had the mate been involved? Had the mother? It'd be easy to bury the missing case with a senator behind it.

"I'd tell you to be discreet, but let's see what happens when you tell Sandeen."

Odessa blinked, her shocked expression a mirror of how Harlowe felt.

"Director . . ." What would Sandeen do? How would she tell him? He might be as cool as when he'd learned of his heritage, but he couldn't be unaffected. He just couldn't.

"It's part of our deal with him anyway. Tell him we may have a lead. Hell, tell him her name. He may know more than he's letting on."

She didn't think so, but she had no proof. "Okay. I can talk to him."

He appraised her. "Do you have an issue with that?"

Normally, she wouldn't. But this time? Yes. People thought she was a dedicated hard-ass, and she was. Her work was her life. But telling the demon this information as part of some bargain left her with a sense of wrongness.

She hadn't made that deal with him, the director had. Bargaining with information about his mother.

She needed more than just teasers. She didn't know why she felt like she owed him more. Maybe because she'd learned in the middle of a dangerous situation what had happened to her mother. There'd been no sitting and talking it out. Parts of the story had been gleefully shared with her to be pieced together later after the mission. By herself. With no one to talk to.

She couldn't do that to Sandeen. "No, sir. But if you don't mind, can I talk to Sandissa's mate first? Maybe see if he has any pictures?"

"Good idea. I'll send you the information on where to find him. If he's a senator's son, he probably splits his time between the realm and fucking around on Earth."

Harlowe nodded and left. The delay while Odessa searched for information on Francois Colbert wasn't unwelcome. Normally, she'd be antsy, maybe charge ahead and find him herself. But this time, she needed a moment.

She was searching for background on a female who might be Sandeen's mother. Memories of growing up without her mother struggled to break free. Asking her father why she didn't have a mommy like other children her age. His calm explanation. Then his silence.

Father had always been supportive of her work. When she had first told him she wanted to be a warrior, she'd thought he'd beg her to be a watcher. Better yet, an analyst who rarely left the realm. Someone safe behind the scenes, not charging ahead and engaging the enemy in battle. But his eyes had brightened and he'd told her that was great.

She could really use some of that zest at the moment. Some encouragement to continue on a case that was bringing her closer to a demon and making her rethink her stance on her half-demon half sister. The ex–best friend she missed and would otherwise talk to about the feelings tangling inside of her.

HARLOWE STARED at the big house in front of her. She hadn't grown up in a mansion like a senator's family, but it wasn't like there was a slum in Numen. White shutters. Stone accents on the exterior. Green grass that was as unchanging as AstroTurf, no water or mowing needed.

She hadn't noticed what a stasis Numen was in until she'd spent a considerable amount of time on Earth. Overgrown lawns. The rise and abandonment of neighborhoods. Many of the humans she'd helped earlier in her career had passed on by now, brought to the light by chaperones of her kind.

Maybe that was what bothered her about coming back home. It wasn't that she was an adult and being in her childhood home was an odd juxtaposition. It was the unchanging nature of this place. Not the rest of Numen. Parts of her realm upgraded itself, adopted technology, and progressed, however slowly.

Her home did not.

Harlowe edged into her house. No warm smells greeted her, same as always. A coolness, much like the rock on the exterior of the house, surrounded her. If there was any scent, it was stone. The place was quiet, but it was never not quiet. Daylight fought against the heavy blinds on the windows and lost. No lights were on. There shouldn't need to be any, but with the blinds drawn, any sunshine was muted.

Father might be napping. Just in case, she said his name loud enough to carry, but quiet enough that it wouldn't rouse him out of a decent sleep. He wouldn't mind if she woke him up, would he? She didn't come home too often, other than to stow her things now that she wasn't living in the barracks. She didn't visit as much as she should.

No answer.

Should she shout? He had to be home. Some days she worried he'd quit leaving the house and succumb to starvation. Their kind could heal from a lot, but severe injuries and starvation could tax their healing abilities enough that they never recovered. Most life-weary angels walked into the fire when they decided they were done with eternity.

Familiar tension traced across her shoulders. Was this the time she'd find Father gone for good?

Letting out a tired exhale, she took the circular staircase. She shouldn't have come. What had she hoped for, that her father would greet her at the door and suddenly be like the guy she remembered from before her mother died? She should've polished her weapons while waiting for the information on Sandissa's mate. But she was here. She could grab an extra set of tactical clothing or something.

In her room, which was as unchanged as the rest of the house, she dug through her drawers. Everything she needed was at the safe house. She'd learned to live on the go. To not have a home base.

She and the demon had a lot in common.

There was a light knock on the door. "Harlowe. Is that you?"

A spark of joy flamed to life in her chest. She'd become disappointed in her father over the years, but after the short comments Sandeen had made about his, she should be grateful. Father loved her. He didn't show it. Maybe he didn't know how, but he cared for her.

She opened the door. Gray streaked through Father's

brown hair, crowding out the darker color. Bags hung under his eyes like he didn't get enough sleep, or got way too much. "Yes, Father. Sorry to bother you. I had to come back to Numen for work and thought I'd stop by."

"It's no problem." His smile was kind, though it only touched his eyes. "I'll let you get back to what you were doing."

He shuffled off and she was left staring at the plain white wall across the hall. She stepped back and shut her bedroom door.

She'd been so young when her mother had passed. He'd gone through the motions of raising her. He loved her, in his own way. Yet when she'd left to become a warrior, he hadn't gone to Earth for humanitarian work. He still didn't go out with friends. He didn't really leave the house. He merely existed.

He was in stasis, and she realized he always had been.

She rolled her neck and held back another sigh. It wasn't as if she could talk to him about what had been happening in her life. But still. It'd be nice to talk.

Sinking onto her childhood bed, she scanned the drawers. She didn't need anything from here.

Demons had stolen her mother, and her father too. She needed to be out there, avenging her parents. So why wasn't she storming out of the house and scouring the realm for Francois Colbert?

Her phone buzzed. Without looking, she knew it was the location of Sandissa's mate. She rose and swept through the place without seeing her father or saying goodbye. Nothing had changed. She had her job, and she had a mission to do.

Sandeen swung the mallet again and again, beating the piece of meat until it was a half an inch thick.

"Could you keep it down?" Bronx had his feet propped up on the end table. Sandeen had tossed him a cloth to polish off his dusty smudges. Bronx had yet to clean them, and if he didn't soon, Sandeen would use this mallet on him instead of a chicken breast.

"Do you want to eat tonight or bitch about the noise?"

Bronx craned his head over his shoulder. The TV flickered with *The Bachelor* reruns. "What are you making again?"

"It's a surprise." It wasn't. Sandeen didn't feel like talking. He'd been cooped up in this house for a week. Two full days beyond what he'd told himself he'd handle. Yet here he was. Cooking.

The sliding door opened. Harlowe stepped in. Her grim expression and the pinched corners of her eyes gave him pause. Something was wrong.

He tossed the breasts in the hot pan on the stove. He

usually enjoyed the sizzle, but his concentration was on Harlowe. She murmured to Bronx. The male nodded and popped off the couch. He went out the sliding door.

It was just him and Harlowe.

"He's going to be disappointed. This is going to be some epic chicken."

Her gaze softened when it landed on the mess on the counter.

Prickles traveled down his spine. Harlowe wasn't an empathetic angel. She snarled at the groceries that Bronx bought for him to cook. She'd stayed as far across the house from him as possible since the forbidden kiss in the middle of the night. If Harlowe couldn't be across the room from him, she was working on the yard. No weed had a chance to thrive under the punishing sun, thanks to her.

"What's going on?" He had to make the sauce for the chicken, but he wasn't concentrating on the recipe.

"It can wait until after we eat."

"Even demons don't like bad news. Spill it, warrior."

She tilted her head and considered him. He flipped the chicken over but held her gaze.

"All right." She took a seat at the little table in the kitchen. If he hadn't been busy cooking and cleaning up the kitchen, he'd have bugged the warriors for a puzzle. Alma had gotten him hooked on the zen that came with searching for the right piece. "How old are you?"

He put his tongs down. "Hard to say. Somewhere north of sixty. Close to a hundred maybe?"

She frowned. "You don't know how old you are?"

"We don't throw birthday parties."

"But . . ."

"There is no rising sun in the underworld to calculate time. We sleep when we think we won't get murdered or violated. The length that we sleep is determined by whether we're murdered or violated or if we think we're going to be. We don't have the ability to possess a host until we're older." He lifted a shoulder. "I've been coming to Earth for fiftyish years. I could be around sixty-five. I dunno."

She blinked. Then scrubbed her face.

He took the pan off the stove and tossed it into the preheated oven. The angel was stringing him tight. At this rate, they were having plain chicken. Fuck the herb cheese sauce.

"We've found some angels who went missing around when you could've been born."

Muscles cramped around his shoulders. He didn't want to hear this.

"Four females and a male."

"Well, we can rule out one."

"Right. But his disappearance might be related."

Again. Didn't care.

"There's one missing angel that I checked on. Her name was just . . ."

Sandeen rolled his neck. Acid ate its way up his esophagus. Cheese sauce. Herbs. He should start on that—

"Her name was Sandissa."

He stilled. A name so close to his own. Hearing it made her real. Not some imaginary female who hadn't given a shit about him. Not some imaginary angel who'd been forced to bear him. Sandissa. Someone who'd suffered. Because of him. Someone who probably hadn't wanted to have him, much less share her name with him.

"I talked to her mate, asked about her looks, and while this isn't definitive by any means, she had blue eyes."

His patience snapped. He couldn't hear any more about Sandissa with the blue eyes. He took a step and cool, haunting droplets surrounded him. The Gloom. He hadn't been sure he could get into the Gloom with the fallen blood tattooed into him, but he no longer had that obstacle, nor did he wear the vial anymore.

"Sandeen!" Harlowe's shout wavered. She couldn't get into the Gloom without him bringing her in.

He stumbled farther away from the kitchen. He needed to get away. And he needed to get the fuck out of the Gloom before he was spotted by one of his kind.

Concentrating, he wandered. Space didn't work the same here. He homed in on a soul that had called to him before. She still called to him. She was safe from others like him, but because he'd inhabited her before, he'd always be able to find her.

He had nowhere else to go. No one else to go to. He walked toward the beacon and charged right into the human realm, into a kitchen not much different than the one he'd left. No wonder it'd been so easy to find her. She wasn't far away.

He squeezed his fists together. This hadn't been planned out. He was charging into a new place, as himself, without checking to see if anyone else was here.

Spinning around, keeping his wings off the floor, wishing for the thousandth time that he could morph them, his gaze landed on the incomplete puzzle on the table. A landscape picture. Mountains and flowers. Like Montana.

He lifted his gaze to the woman seated at the table. Her hand was poised over the puzzle, a small piece between her gentle fingers.

Alma's wrinkled face split into a grin. "My demon. I'm so happy to see you."

HE WAS GONE. Just gone.

Shit, shit, shit.

Harlowe hopped up. Had she been that terrible at telling him their suspicions? She'd thought he might walk away, not *disappear*. Why hadn't that occurred to her?

She pressed her fingertips to her forehead. What the hell? Where would he go?

Could demons enter the Gloom from indoors? That had to be how they got close enough to their targets to possess them.

Her gaze landed on the oven. He'd never leave mid-meal. News of his mother bothered him. The way his gaze had blanked out, and his rote actions when he'd tossed the pan into the oven and hip-checked the door shut, played through her mind.

She turned the oven off. She was shit at feelings. Maybe Bronx should've told him. Would her teammate have been any more compassionate? Why had the director told her to do it? Sure, she'd been with Sandeen the longest.

She was a warrior, not a counselor. She'd become a warrior to avenge her mother.

A mother who'd suffered like his had. She'd relayed the information better than how she'd learned the truth about her own mother, but that was all she'd done. Rattled it off to check it off her to-do list.

And he'd left. He'd severed his part of the bargain. But she still had a job to do.

She rubbed her chest and strode to the sliding door. Once outside, she ascended to her realm, outside of the building that housed Director Vale's office, and walked right in.

Bronx's head whipped around. Director Vale lifted his unscarred eyebrow.

"I messed up," she announced after the door closed behind her. She told them how Sandeen had disappeared.

The director stayed hunched over his desk. "Where could he have gone?"

"Anywhere if he went into the Gloom," Bronx said.

"Yes, but no." Harlowe flung her braid off her shoulder. "He was adamant about not returning to Daemon. I think I know some places to check. I don't think he went far. He might even be back."

"He can be back, but he can bloody well leave whenever he wants. From wherever he wants." Director Vale's tone was serious. They hadn't considered how little of a prisoner Sandeen was. "Can we promise him something? Give him something that'll make him want to stick around until we sort this mess out?"

"He wants to be left alone." But did he want to *be* alone? "To live freely in the human realm."

"That can't happen. Ever."

"I know." Sandeen wouldn't accept that. He'd been determined to be free before, but after learning that beings in Daemon, and possibly in Numen, had hurt his mother? Never. "Give me some time to find him?"

The director's eyes narrowed. She couldn't tell him why it was so important. She didn't know herself. Other than a sense of obligation. She'd hunted him. She'd been the first to find him. She knew him better than anyone.

But she'd also driven him away. And she knew how much it hurt to learn the truth after you could do nothing about it.

"Use the mother angle to get him to stick around. He clearly cares." Director Vale dipped his head. "Keep us posted, yeah?"

"Holler if you need anything," Bronx said, chill as ever. Like she hadn't lost the captive he'd been helping guard for a week. Like she hadn't announced that their captive could leave at any time.

She stepped out of the office. One of her skills was tracking through the Mist, and it did fuck all for her right now. She thought about where she'd go if she were Sandeen. They knew so little about him, about his time on Earth. So she considered what she did know. The nightclub where she'd first run into him. The place had burned down. The cabin. Maybe. Green Valley, Montana?

There was one clear answer. And the idea that he might go there when he was emotionally unbalanced seeped into her heart.

She appeared back at the safe house and went straight for the car. However, once she was on the road, she looped and wove through residential areas, running a couple of red lights for good measure. She had to find Sandeen, but she couldn't risk anyone following her.

She pulled up in front of a home she'd been to several times and rang the doorbell.

Would anyone answer?

The lock clicked thanks to the remote entry Sierra had asked Urban to install. Easier on Alma's joints when she didn't have to run to the door. She could see who was on any part of her property from at least five different cameras and unlock her door from her phone.

Harlowe charged inside and stopped. The small entry opened next to the dining room. All Alma used the table for was her puzzles. The woman clicked in a piece and grinned at her.

"Oh, Harlowe. So nice to see you again."

The big male sat next to Alma, scowl firmly in place, his wings wrapped around the back of the chair. He glanced at Alma and then to her phone. He hadn't known about Harlowe's arrival. "You're a wily one," he said to Alma.

Alma patted his arm and pushed her chair back. "It's time for my siesta. You two need to talk. Lock up if you leave."

Once she was standing, she wasn't much taller than Sandeen when he was sitting. She leaned down and pressed a kiss into his hair, right next to a horn. His eyes drifted shut and longing flickered over his face.

Harlowe's heart clenched. The demon had a startling depth of emotion, and he trusted Alma with it. Alma championed the demon like he was her own. Harlowe had kept him alive and hadn't hurt him, but that hadn't been enough.

Sandeen kept his attention on the puzzle.

Harlowe took Alma's vacated seat. "I'm sorry." She never thought she'd be apologizing to a demon. Half demon. "I should've told you about your mother better." She suppressed a wince. She sucked at this.

Sandeen leaned back in his chair. His loose black T-shirt didn't hide the rippled abs, nor did the jeans hide the strength of his thighs. "I don't want my mother to be an angel."

"You'd rather be full demon?"

"I'd rather have a goat for a mother than an innocent angel who suffered as one of my sire's test subjects." He clicked a piece of a vibrant red petal into place. "I'd rather have a mother who didn't know that she'd birthed her worst nightmare."

Not even a warrior hell-bent on doing her job could remain hardened against the most staggeringly unselfish admission she'd ever witnessed. "You're not exactly a worst nightmare."

His bright gaze landed on her. "I'm a demon."

"Yeah, well . . . I can't say how she'd feel. All I can think about is my mother. And Sierra. Is Sierra a nightmare?"

"She was raised in Numen."

"Exactly. By someone who knew what she was. I don't know what my mother would've thought either. We can assume the worst, we can assume the best, or we can just accept that they're gone and we'll never know. We'll never, ever know." She blew out a hard breath.

"Zadren taunted me with her disappointment. That was hard enough when I was younger, but he lies as well as he breathes. Now that I know she was an angel . . . He wasn't lying."

"You're not evil."

"I've done things."

"Have you? Like, how bad?"

His brows drew together. "I've killed plenty of angels."

She winced. "Right. I mean, you were raised to do that." He clicked another piece of the petal into place. Alma had her puzzle pieces sorted by color. *A little work ahead of time pays off in the end.* "Why did you come here?"

"What do you mean?"

"What I was telling you bothered you, and you went right to Alma. Why?"

"She's . . ."

"A maternal figure?"

His jaw flexed and he drew his hands back like he was afraid he'd crush a piece of the puzzle. "She's a mellow woman. Calm."

"Did you tell her? About Sandissa?"

His eyes darkened as soon as she said the name. "No. She just invited me to the table."

"So you used to possess Alma." A demon couldn't get much closer to someone. Sandeen had learned everything about Alma. Part of the corruption of the possession was what the demons made the host do. The other part was housing pure evil. Alma put together puzzles and ordered pizza whenever Harlowe came to visit. She wasn't corrupted. "Yet she trusts you. She likes you. She cares for you. Alma knows all about demons and angels. If she feels that way toward you, why are you so convinced your mother would be ashamed of you?"

His body went rigid. He'd done the same when she'd arrived at the safe house and started talking about Sandissa and the missing angels. "I didn't capture and torture and rape Alma."

"You didn't do that to Sandissa either."

His steady blue gaze pinned her in place. "What did her mate say?"

"What?" The spin in topics left her reeling.

"Sandissa's." He worked his jaw like he was tasting the word. Like he was seeing if it fit, if she could be the one who gave birth to him.

Harlowe should fib, just a little. Keep him in the dark, but she couldn't. Director Vale had been with her when they talked to Francois, Sandissa's mate, who lived in a large mansion in Numen, had a bigger place on Earth, and smiled as if he knew your deepest secret. "Francois didn't say much. He described her. Said she went to work one day —she was a chaperone—and she didn't return. He pines for her, thinks about her all the time, planted a huge garden around his big-ass house in honor of her."

Sandeen's gaze narrowed. "And you think this Francois disingenuous?"

She paused. His sudden interest was suspicious. She also knew what she would do with any information about someone who might've betrayed her mother. And . . . the director wanted to keep Sandeen around. This could be the way to do it. "He was shifty as hell."

"Then I have a new bargain for you."

Success shouldn't make her feel dirty. "I would have to gain approval." Director Vale would approve.

"Then pass it up to the scarred one. You want me to stay in that safe house so you and your team can wander around and think you're doing good in the world? I want that mate. I can make the angel who sent my mother to hell suffer. I can make him pay."

"We don't even know—"

"Then find out."

"It's not that simple."

"It can be," he said simply and stepped away from her.

No. She knew that look. "Don't you dare leave—"

He lifted a brow and time slowed. He lifted one booted foot. If that shoe touched the ground, it'd be in the Gloom.

She launched from her chair and closed her hand around his wrist, but the rest of her barreled into his chest. His brows drew together, but he couldn't stop the momentum. The crash of her weight into him pushed him the rest of the way.

Foul water droplets encircled her and she pressed closer to Sandeen as if his hard body could block each drop from touching her.

Pinching tingles danced along her exposed skin. She glanced up and met Sandeen's alarmed gaze. She was in the Gloom.

CHAPTER 12

"What the hell did you do?" he growled under his breath, as pissed at her as he was at himself.

A symaster with wide yellow eyes skittered out of the Gloom. Shit.

Harlowe blinked away from his gaze and stood straighter. She didn't remove her hand from around his wrist. "Can't we just step right back out?"

"Yes. Just like the witness that saw not just me, but you. The witness who had time to leave since I was busy propping you up and couldn't gut him as soon as I saw him." He should've let her fall on her ass.

"Shit."

"Exactly. Now they know that I'm with your team. They might even suspect I'm working with you. Come on." He used her grip on him to haul her away from where he'd been.

"Where are we— Damn, the mist burns."

"It's not the Mist."

"I thought the Gloom would be gloomy. Not acidic."

"Your skin is too soft." He'd never spoken truer words. His wrist tingled under her touch. Strong, but soft in all the best ways. What would it be like to feel her entire body against him without a stitch of clothing to hinder—

"Sandeen. You brought us a gift."

He held in his sigh. That was fast. The symaster must have known exactly where to find Zanda, and had gone to her immediately.

He spun, yanking Harlowe to his chest as he slipped the vial of angel fire from around her neck. Zanda was flanked by a stooped archmaster that was as vicious as he was ugly. His mottled-cream, leathery skin hung from sharp bones. The worst part about him was the calculating gaze in his eyes. He wasn't as old as Sandeen's sire, not as intelligent, but he was ancient and experienced. On her other side was one of Gerzon's daughters, a squat demon with angry red skin and a fairly square head. She was like a female Hellboy, before the horns were filed down.

He couldn't negotiate with Zanda around witnesses.

"Zanda, this bitch is mine to use, not yours." Harlowe elbowed him in the gut, but he fisted the vial in front of her face. He dropped his voice to as menacing of a tone as he could muster and popped the cap of the vial. "You're going to look like your boss if you keep doing that."

She sucked in a breath but stilled. She was either playing along or believed he'd do it.

Good. But his gut churned like he'd eaten roadkill sylph.

Zanda narrowed her onyx eyes. "Why is she still alive?"

"Like father, like son."

Respect shone in Zanda's eyes. Did she know the truth? Or did she like the idea that he was doing what his sire would? "He would be proud."

"No, he wouldn't. He'd try to steal her."

"Bastard," Harlowe snarled.

"Don't let us stop you." Zanda swept her hand out. "Proceed."

"Unlike the rest of the realm, I don't like witnesses." His tone was pure velvet when he said, "You know that better than most."

Harlowe's chest rose and fell under his arm. He kept the vial poised and tried to ignore the weight of her breasts on his forearm and how it whipped up a storm in his veins. His blood raced and rushed, not knowing whether to give him a hard-on or prepare him to fight or both.

Zanda took a step forward. "I do," she purred, but her dark eyes were as frigid as mud in the Arctic in the middle of January. "But you two looked pretty cozy the other night. I think you're working with the angel bitch."

He measured Zanda's resolve. She wasn't bluffing. She'd been stalking the Gloom, waiting for him to fuck up. Not only had he fucked up, but he'd drawn Harlowe into the trouble.

"The angel bitch is getting me what I want. Can you do that?"

The two demons behind Zanda shifted, restless. They were working for her, or more likely for Gerzon, and feared both him and Zanda. That obligation was the only thing keeping them from attacking.

"What do you want?" Zanda inched closer. Sandeen wiggled the vial in his hand. Harlowe stiffened and Zanda stopped. "We can deal."

No, they couldn't. Not with two witnesses.

The moment of pause was enough of a distraction. Harlowe elbowed him. His breath whooshed out as her sharp joint dug into his ribs. She snatched the angel fire out of his hand and whipped it at Gerzon's daughter.

The demoness couldn't pivot fast enough. Angel fire

splattered her and she shrieked, twisting and writhing, swatting at the searing substance to get it off of her but only spreading it more. Before she could recover, Harlowe had launched a dagger from her belt. Steel buried itself between its eyes.

"Shit," Sandeen muttered as he intercepted Zanda's attack.

Claws stabbed the skin of his arms and she tried to rip him open, but he heaved her off before she could.

Harlowe had spun away and was embroiled in a fight with the nasty old demon. She was out of angel fire. She probably had two more daggers, but this hadn't been a planned attack. She'd been caught by surprise and they'd started outnumbered.

Zanda snarled, trying to use her fangs to tear at his flesh. He batted her away but took a blow to the head from one of her wings. He flared his own out and deflected her claws. It was a familiar dance, and they were old partners. This fight wasn't much different than sex. Zanda wasn't trying to kill him though.

Why? To hand him over to Gerzon?

He ducked a kick and narrowly missed getting impaled by the small talons on her feet.

Harlowe's roar jerked his attention away. The angel had buried a knife in the male's chest and she was attached to his back with another knife, sawing at his horny neck. The demon bellowed and whipped around trying to dislodge her, but between the two of them, Harlowe was obviously more experienced at decapitating demons.

Zanda's right hook slammed into Sandeen's jaw. He staggered back, barely righting himself before the female renewed her attack. Claws ripped at his shirt. At this rate, it'd be death by a thousand cuts.

Then Zanda ripped herself off him and spun away, disappearing from the Gloom.

The demon that Harlowe rode like a bucking bronc was on his knees, his jaw hanging open as his life spilled out. Harlowe's lips peeled back as she hugged the male's head and wrenched it the rest of the way off.

Whoa. He'd seen warriors in action, but he'd never seen them dispensing Daemon.

A strangled yell came from the female demon as she bolted upright, ripping the dagger out from between her eyes as she went. Her skin was still dissolving under the burn of the angel fire. "I'm going to enjoy killing you," she gargled.

Harlowe dropped the demon's head and lasered her gaze on the demoness. She didn't have a pithy reply. She just stalked forward.

Gerzon's daughter swung her head toward him. "You always were worthless." She charged him. He braced himself and let her attack. All those fights in the rings, his sire's chants still ringing in his ears.

Kill them slowly. Savor it.

If you can kill, my son, you'll be greatly rewarded.

Make your mother proud. Be brutal. Big Z's knowing grin after he'd said that made sense now.

Rage filled Sandeen and burst out of him in the form of energy, of pure intent. He yanked the dagger from the demoness's grip, spun her, sliced across her throat, and ripped her head off in a move that made Harlowe's look like it had been in slow motion.

He let out a roar as he threw the head.

Everything was getting fucked up. This was supposed to be simple. Get access to the fallen blood. Leave the realm. Be left the fuck alone.

But the angel had tracked him down. The angel that

wasn't leaving him alone. The angel that was the only other thing he'd ever wanted for himself in life.

"Goddammit, Lowe!"

Her stunned gaze was still on the felled demoness. His efficiency had been unexpected. The fact that he was pissed about getting into a fight must surprise her. But it's not like she knew the real him. The him that had been raised to fight for no other reason than to kill. The him that hated where he was from.

He grabbed her arm and dragged her through the stinging droplets of the Gloom.

"Sandeen, where are we—"

He dragged her to the safest place he knew: the abandoned farmstead that proved he'd never be anything more than a demon at his best.

~

"Why did you follow me?" Sandeen roared.

Harlowe had barely righted herself. Sandeen had pushed her out at an abandoned farmstead. She shouldn't be able to see it as well as she did. Thick clouds crowded out the moon, but after the murkiness of the Gloom, it was like the world had gotten a good scrubbing with Windex. The house didn't look particularly old, but it stood stark against the overgrown landscape. Tall grass brushed against the peeling white walls. For as run-down and empty as the place seemed, the glass wasn't broken. Someone was taking care of this place and keeping local kids from messing with it.

"Where are we?" The fresh smell of impending rain hung in the air. A flash of lightning lit the farmstead, revealing the emerald green of the grass and the deep red of the old barn. A roll of thunder traveled over and around them.

"Somewhere they can't find you." Sandeen shoved his hands through his hair. "Fuck, Harlowe. I could've worked with Zanda, but she'll never deal with me now."

"Why would you deal with her?" A few large drops of rain smacked her in the face. She didn't blink or break eye contact.

He spun on her, his blue eyes blazing as rain spattered off his horns. Drops hit his forehead and tracked down his face, giving him a sinister effect. She took a step back from the intensity. He advanced. "Why would I deal with you?"

"You can trust us." She lifted a foot to take another step away from the wall of angry, hot male in front of her. This was not the time to find him magnetic. They were bleeding from small scrapes. She was covered in demon blood and there were guts stuck on her daggers. She'd barely had time to holster them before Sandeen had stormed out of the Gloom. Now those had to be cleaned out too.

She put her heel down. This wasn't a sexual situation and the male was infuriating.

His wings flared out. If he were closer, he'd block out the night sky. "If you don't know why I can't trust you, then you know nothing about your kind."

She threw her hands to the sides. "They're your people too!"

The sky opened up and rain hammered down on them. Cool, clean water washed the worst of the grime away. His feathers gleamed as they reflected the water hitting them. He crowded closer. "Just because you went all AncestryDNA on me doesn't mean it changes who I am."

"And who are you, Sandeen?"

She expected a caustic response, but his gaze dropped to her lips. Rivulets streamed down her face. She blinked away the moisture. She had to be seeing things. He wasn't looking at her like he wanted to devour her in the middle of a storm in a strange place that she hoped was as abandoned as it looked.

He couldn't be looking at her like that, because it made her want him too.

Adrenaline burned through her veins, looking for an outlet after the fight. After the way he'd held her to him, the way he'd made her heart pound. After the way she'd been confident that he wouldn't hurt her, but how, for a little while, she hadn't cared. He thought it was simple, that he was a demon and that was the end of it.

He was a layered male. Intriguing and cunning and frustrating and so damn sexy.

The blue of his eyes was as liquid as the rain hitting his face. He crushed his mouth to hers, and instead of shoving him away like she was supposed to do, she wrapped her arms around his neck like she was terrified he'd stop.

This kiss wasn't like the motel room. They were still in the dark, but they were outside, where anyone who braved the storm could see them. And this wasn't a tentative exploration.

Sandeen wanted and he took. She let him.

His tongue invaded her mouth. Cool rain wicked in with it, tempering his heat. His hands were everywhere on her body. He yanked her shirt up and off, breaking the kiss only momentarily to do it. She did the same with his, pulling it free of his wings. The material got tossed to the grass and she didn't give a shit how soggy it got.

His hands were at her waist next. Her tactical belt hit the ground. The backs of his knuckles scraped the skin of her abdomen. Her muscles tightened from her abs to the quivering muscles between her legs.

He yanked apart the clasp of her pants. Seams ripped, the sound lost in another peal of thunder. Cool air hit her skin as he rolled down the wet material. Her legs trembled and it had nothing to do with the soaking rain. She watched as he crouched and tugged each boot off, her hands gripping his bare shoulders. The chill of the rain hadn't penetrated his sweltering skin. His heat burned into her palms like a brand.

His wings flared out. Lightning cut through the clouds, lining his inky wings with shadows. She was naked in front of him, but mesmerized by his wings. He curled them around her, encompassing her with their heat and protection. Strong arms swept under her, lifting her feet from the wet ground and laying her back.

She expected a back full of sopping grass, but his soft feathers protected her from the worst of the onslaught.

All those days of admiring his wings and now they surrounded her. As soft as his kiss that dark night. As warm as the rest of his body. They were more than she thought they'd be.

"Sandeen." The need in her voice surprised her. The yearning.

His only answer was to nudge her legs wider to accommodate his size.

She hadn't had time to deal with his pants. Wet denim was between her thighs as he kneeled, bracing his weight with his wings as he yanked open his fly.

She wanted to see all of him, to admire the rest of him like she had with his wings and his horns.

His horns.

When had her restraint disappeared? Probably when she'd succumbed to how nice it felt not to be alone.

She brushed her hands along their warm, smooth surface.

Sandeen went rigid, his gaze pinning hers. "Do you like them, angel?"

They were fascinating, like the rest of him. "Yes," she whispered.

A line formed between his brows and was gone just as quickly. "I need to taste you again."

The light show in the sky above them made the white of his fangs glow. "Please?" Practically a whimper as she recalled the way he'd pierced her skin with them before.

He dipped his head and licked along the base of her neck. The cool of his damp beard contrasted with his hot lips. A quick sting preceded the hot brush of his tongue.

A ragged groan left her as pleasure as powerful as the electricity in the sky streaked through her body.

He lowered his hips. He hadn't touched her otherwise, but she was ready for him. Needy.

She pressed her heels into the top of his ass as he pressed closer. The blunt head of his cock hit her opening. She hadn't seen him, but he was big. He pushed in, a steady and welcome invasion.

As he entered, her body welcomed him. Her hands gripped his horns and his tongue swirled at the base of her throat. Could he tell how hard her pulse pounded as he pushed farther and farther inside, filling her in a way she'd never been?

"Demon," she breathed. Full. Stretched. Her walls clutched around him, demanding more, ordering him to move in the same way he was at her throat.

Her body asked and he answered.

His restraint had gone the same place as hers. He withdrew and thrust, increasing the pace. She didn't mean to score her fingernails down his back, but her body coiled tighter as he hit every pleasurable spot she hadn't known she had.

He surged over her, inside of her. His mouth claimed hers once again. She tasted a faint, metallic saltiness that was intimate and familiar in a way she hadn't expected. She stroked a hand down his strong jaw as their tongues twined together.

She arched as he pulsed inside of her. Energy built, more powerful than she'd ever experienced. "Sandeen, this is—" *More than I can take.*

He angled his hips up and thrust hard, his pace punishing, and she loved every second.

Ecstasy washed over her, drenching her as thoroughly as the rain. She hovered on a precipice, and if she went over, she'd never be the same. But the fact was, she would never be the same anyway. Not after being fucked by a demon in the rain and wanting to do nothing but this for the rest of her life.

His name ripped out of her once more as she exploded. Lightning coursed inside of her, getting lost in the light show above them.

He roared, going taut over her as he thrust and pulsed. Heat spread inside of her, again like a brand, but from within.

As her climax faded, leaving her pulsing and tender in foreign places, she clung to him. Her hand cupped his face. They were no longer kissing. Their mouths were a breath apart. She lifted her gaze to his.

Wet hair was plastered to his face. His horns glinted under the lightning. The rain had slowed to a steady patter. But it was the look in his eyes. Stark vulnerability.

Was that how she looked too? Shaken? Changed in a way she should've never been?

She'd been weak. Swept up in emotions she wasn't used to dealing with. This male threatened everything she worked for. She'd been determined to do right by her parents, yet she'd had sex with a being of the underworld. A demon. Yes, he was half angel too, but did that matter when he had no plans to claim that side of himself?

She could blame the way she softened toward Sandeen on their similarities. Losing their mothers. Having less than ideal fathers, though hers was nothing like his. All that had ceased being an excuse when she'd let him strip her down and make her come. She'd been pretty clear on what she'd wanted then.

An "Oh no" left her before she could think better of it. Hurt flashed across his face and he withdrew from her. The loss of him inside of her twisted a knot in her gut she wanted to ignore. She pressed her fingertips against his chest to cover the conflict raging inside of her. She wanted to hug him closer, to do this all night until the storm cleared and the sun rose in the morning, but she needed space. She needed to get away. She needed to figure out what the hell had happened and why she'd ditched a lifetime of duty for a male who was less than angelic.

He shifted backward, his wings slipping out from under her. There were no take backs. She couldn't undo what she'd just done. All she could do was stop blurring the lines from here on out. She'd lost focus on her mission. It wouldn't happen again.

"Damn. Damn. Damn." She couldn't stop chanting as the cold of the night soaked into her body now that the large, hard furnace had been removed. She lifted her pants. Water dripped from them. No way was she putting those back on.

She found her shirt and struggled into it. The cold material stuck to her skin like plastic wrap, but she didn't straighten it out. She found her boots and belt. With her arms full of her sodden items, she turned and faced him.

He looked like an avenging angel. Dark outline. Stormy

background. She didn't dwell on the slump in his wings that normally wasn't there. Or the way he tipped his chin so his hair hung over his face, so she wouldn't see the devastation in his eyes.

He wasn't supposed to be devastated by her behavior. He was supposed to be heartless. He was supposed to be laughing at her. He was supposed to not care about her, or about his mother. She couldn't fool herself anymore. She was falling hard for a male she shouldn't want. A male who could cost her everything when she didn't have much more to lose.

"I can't . . ." She pressed her lips together. She couldn't stay. She had to go. She wanted to run. To get the hell away from this male who made her crystal-clear life cloudy.

So she did something she'd never done before. She ascended without knowing one hundred percent that there were no witnesses. Just another rule she willingly broke around the demon.

SHE WAS GONE.

He'd seen the panic darkening her violet eyes. The self-recrimination. And she'd fled.

What had he expected?

She was who she was. And he was . . . who he'd always been.

Where had she gone? To tell her boss where he was? To offer her wings as punishment for what they'd done?

"Fuck!" he yelled, the sound swallowed by the thunder.

Fitting that it was fucking storming. The night his teenaged host had died, it had been storming too. And the day the sale had closed on this house.

This place had been his first human purchase. What

would Harlowe think of the story? He'd used deceit and stolen money to buy the place. Angels would definitely frown on the methods he'd used.

"Fuck," he said, quieter this time.

Pleasure sang through his body. It'd been that powerful between them. All his life, sex hadn't been about feeling good. It had been just another power game. Until now. Every moment of being with Harlowe had been nothing but pure rapture. Ironic for a demon to put it like that, but there it was.

What had it been like for her? The way her body had clamped around him when she'd come had made him sure he wasn't alone in his experience. But then she'd left, so . . .

He'd drive himself crazy remembering the sex. Blood was already redirecting to his cock. It wanted more. So did he.

But he couldn't make an angel want him. This occurrence had been a surprise. Harlowe would never have been with him if she hadn't been distracted from the fight in the Gloom. Harlowe didn't *want* to want him. That much he knew.

Yet he'd fucked her anyway. Just like the bastard he was.

His sire was right. His mother would be ashamed of him.

CHAPTER 13

*H*arlowe stared at the cabin up the drive. Night had settled on the land, but the moon's soft glow created the perfect amount of shadow for her to hide in. She'd been here once. Out of duty, in case she had to come help for whatever reason, and she'd made sure to never return. A half-demon half sister hadn't fit into her plans. She'd told herself that risking her wings wasn't worth it.

Then she'd spent months and months alone while hunting another half demon. All those months, she'd been able to keep a tight lock on her thoughts about Sierra. Until Harlowe had found Sandeen. Two separate parts of her life had collided and had forced her to open her eyes.

She hadn't liked what she'd seen. But she'd liked being around Sandeen.

She'd more than liked what had just happened, and she could no longer make a straight line out of her ideals, or the way she'd been living her life.

Then she'd panicked. And she had no-fucking-body to talk to.

She gazed at the cabin. She'd ascended to Numen, stared at her father's place while holding her sopping wet clothing, and descended right down here.

The place was buried deep in the trees outside of Helena. The smell of pine and wildflowers surrounded her. She stayed for a moment, letting the peace sink into her bones. She wasn't exactly creeping. Sierra and Boone had cameras stashed all over the forest and around the house. They tracked every living being that crossed their land. They had known she was here the second her feet touched the ground. Yet Harlowe had come despite that.

It was time. Sierra needed an apology. Harlowe could start there while she figured out what the fuck she was going to do moving forward.

Yet it was night. And she couldn't march up to the cabin wearing nothing but a shirt and knock. She needed to clean up and be alone with the cascade of her thoughts.

What had she done? Why was she so drawn to the demon? Why couldn't she stop wanting to go back and do something about the hurt look she'd put on his face?

She risked Sandeen taking off again, but she couldn't go back to the stormy little farmstead. Neither could she tell Director Vale that she'd ditched him. Then he'd obviously ask why. Bronx might be at the safe house, wondering where the hell they'd gone, but he was probably just hunkered down and waiting to see if she'd return with the demon.

Either way, she'd need to answer to someone eventually.

First, she had to answer to herself. She'd avoided Sierra after learning that they were sisters. And then she'd seen how Sandeen reacted to learning of his mother. Seeing what it had done to the demon, and how he refused to acknowledge it, made her realize that she'd been jealous of Sierra for something imaginary. As if Harlowe had to share the mother she had lost, as if Sierra had gotten a part of their mother Harlowe could never have.

In fact, it was Harlowe who was fortunate to remember her mother. Her kind smile. The way she'd winked when she was joking. How she'd sung a lullaby every night.

"Are you going to stand here all day or come on up?" Sierra's voice came from behind her.

Harlowe's pulse kicked up, but she didn't turn around. She should've known Sierra wouldn't let her be. Perhaps she'd gambled on it. "I thought if I stood here long enough, I'd chicken out and leave."

"I can pretend I never saw you."

"Nah. It sucked pretty bad when I had to pretend that you didn't exist." This was just like them. Light tone. Serious subject.

"How about when you kept telling yourself that we weren't really sisters?"

Tears pricked the backs of Harlowe's eyes. "Yeah. That really sucked. I don't know why admitting the truth was so much harder."

"Because your mother was stolen from you. And you felt like I did it."

"Dammit, Sierra. You never did pull your punches."

"I've pulled plenty. Gets exhausting."

"Yeah." Harlowe let out a long breath. "But you got an awesome father and I think I was more upset about that. But I'm glad. I'm really, really glad you"—*didn't suffer the neglect I did, or the same horrors Sandeen did*—"had a good upbringing."

Why couldn't he just . . . be different? Why couldn't Sandeen embrace his angelic side more? Be more willing to help stop the destruction demons wreaked on both humans and angels? Why couldn't she just find him mildly amusing and highly frustrating instead of sexy, heartfelt, and irresistible?

Sierra would understand better than anyone her epic fuckup. "I made a mistake."

"Want to come in and tell me about it?"

"Honestly? I'd rather stand out here and tell the trees. Seems easier that way."

"Trees don't judge."

"I slept with Sandeen."

A soft whistle came from behind her. "Was not expecting that. Well, maybe a little."

Harlowe whirled, her feet twisting in the weeds. Sierra leaned against a tree that was bare for several feet above her head before the branches started. She was dressed in loose camo pants and an off-green tank top that should have looked unkempt and baggy but only made her look tough and cute.

"What do you mean 'maybe a little'?"

"The chemistry between you two was off the charts, and when I figured out that he was half angel . . ." She lifted a bare shoulder.

"He doesn't want anything to do with his other half."

"I don't see why he would. We've been hunting him his entire life."

Not him, specifically, but Harlowe got the point. "He's still half demon. And an assignment."

"Is it the 'half demon' part or the assignment that really bugs you?"

"Sierra, I could lose my wings." Sierra didn't flinch but Harlowe did. "Sorry." Her head sagged back. "I'm sorry for so much, but I just wish he . . . could be more like you."

Sierra stuffed her hands in her pockets and pushed off the tree. "Seemed so much simpler back then. Even though I had a helluva secret, it was still just us versus them. Now I'm fallen and we can't ignore fallen anymore. The fallen that have persevered and made a life for themselves have been uprooted by Numen once again. This time they're told it's for their own good instead of Numen's own good. Like somehow that's better."

"You don't agree?"

"No, I do. But . . . it's not so clear cut anymore. We know there's corruption in the senate. Just because Senator Kenton's gone doesn't mean it's not still happening. There's Arik, a child of two fallen, being raised by one fallen and a human. That human is now helping Numen, and if they knew about him, they'd demand all our wings *and* that we still work for them after."

Harlowe's back twitched. Her morph stamina was strong after working in the human world for so many years, but she longed to let them hang free. To walk around like Sandeen.

"And here you are," Sierra continued. "You care about two half demons, but you'd rather not."

"I don't—" That was the trouble with a best friend. They called you on your shit. "I wish I could care about you without the fear. I thought I lost you once. Twice. Three times, actually."

Sierra's head tilted as she calculated. Harlowe had lost her best friend as soon as she'd learned about Sierra's betrayal. Then again when she'd fallen. And again when she'd learned the truth of who Sierra was.

"And the demon . . ." There was so much about him.

"Is he still acting like a demon?"

"Not really. He walks in shades of gray. He lives by

negotiations he has no intention of fulfilling. He has no honor."

Sierra did the head-tilt thing again and Harlowe braced herself. "What do you think Alma would say if you told her he has no honor?"

Harlowe scoffed. "Alma has a serious soft spot for him." She fell quiet. "He's complicated. Like you said."

"I think maybe you're no longer as black and white as you want to be."

"So he's not a monster. I can't trust him, Sierra. He might not intentionally want anyone to get hurt, but he's not doing it to keep others from getting hurt. He just wants to be left alone to walk the realm with those long, magnificent wings hanging out."

Sierra smirked. "He does have nice wings."

"Shit. Sorry."

"I've had plenty of time to get used to no wings. It's getting easier. I have Boone and Arik. And Pa. More than I thought I'd have when my wings were taken. I'm grateful, Harlowe. I'm in a really good place. That's all Sandeen wants. That's all any of us want. But the way we get there is what complicates things."

"Yeah. I should probably get back to guarding him." The job she'd been so scared of losing. She pressed her fingers to her temples. "God, I just left after we . . . you know."

Sierra laughed, an easy, joyful sound. "Well, I'm no longer wondering why you're in nothing but a shirt. Sandeen is either in whatever bed you left him in or long gone. You need to talk and you have a nephew you haven't met yet. Want to stay for a bit?"

Harlowe had left Sandeen on the grass in the middle of a storm. Was that better or worse than ditching him in bed?

Sierra's words sank in. Harlowe had a nephew she

hadn't met yet. Just one more thing she hadn't faced in the last several months. If she didn't resolve issues here, she'd never figure out how she felt about Sandeen, or what she should do. "Yes. I'd like to meet Arik. The mess I made can wait."

Zanda crossed her arms under her bare breasts. "You know I don't trust you."

Sandeen gave her his best *you don't say?* look. "I don't trust you either. But you want to get something over on Gerzon and I want vengeance."

"After the mess you made in the Gloom, I can't get caught working with you. I should sever your head right now."

One of them would likely die if she tried, and she must not be confident she'd be the survivor or she'd have already tried. No doubt her desire to climb higher up the Daemon food chain than Gerzon was what kept her here and her claws sheathed. She was hunting him, knowing full well that his head on a pike would earn her respect in her own right, rather than riding Gerzon's coattails. Sandeen didn't know what his sire would do, and he didn't care. But Zanda probably cared. Big Z was a powerful demon. He controlled the mines. And because he controlled the mines, whoever messed with him had to be ready to take on the power, and in the event of his defeat, to keep the power.

Zanda had aspirations, a rare demon with ambition. It was why Sandeen had had no trouble locating her in the Gloom. She was hunting him for a reason and it wasn't to kill him. Another rare trait. Patience. She was plotting, or waiting for an opportunity to strike.

Either way, Sandeen could deal with her, but first he had to learn what she knew. "You knew that Gerzon fathered the fallen Sierra."

Zanda's lips drew back like she was going to heave. "That he fornicated with an angel? Yes." Her gaze turned wary. "How do you know?"

"My sire did the same."

Her eyes flared. She tried to cover her surprise. A poker face was a necessity in the underworld, but he'd seen enough to read her. No one else knew what he was. She was Gerzon's right-hand demon. It made sense that she'd known about Sierra. But him? Why wouldn't his sire tell anyone?

"I want to know who supplied them with angels."

Her lips twisted. "You don't think they wooed them? And don't think I didn't notice that you didn't answer my question. How do you know about Gerzon's relation to the fallen?"

"I pay attention."

"There's another half demon roaming Numen, who'd have thought?"

"Not Numen."

Her eyes went impossibly wide. She must've seen the grim acceptance in his expression.

He did jazz hands, his fingers disrupting small droplets in the air. "Surprise."

Shock, disgust, and fear rolled through her dark irises. "You? No. *No.*" She took a step back. "How— What—" She worked her jaw. "But we . . ." She retched, backing up and doubling over, but she didn't turn away. Her instincts were too acute for that. "Gross."

Perfect. He'd been rejected by an angel who hated the idea of sleeping with a half demon. Now he was watching a demon heave because she'd learned she'd fucked a half angel.

"I want the person who delivered the angels to my sire and Gerzon." His tone was hard enough to make her stand upright. She was moving her tongue like she had to spit out a mouthful of shit. "My mother and Sierra's couldn't have been the only ones."

"Are there more of you?" Zanda made it sound as if that was worse than getting her eyes plucked out by bored sylphs.

"I don't know."

She crossed her arms, the tips of her claws tapping on her skin. He could see her working through the situation. She could find the information. It wouldn't be easy, but since she was one of the few who knew about Sierra, she'd have a better chance than anyone else. But she didn't want to get on Big Z's bad side. "You think it's an angel?"

She was smart enough to know it would have to be. Most demons weren't interested in capturing angels and even fewer were skilled enough. Add in the fact that no angels had launched massive search parties, and all signs pointed to both sides keeping things quiet.

"Maybe I can get some information. Then what?"

"I can get you a warrior."

"The female?"

He nearly bared his fangs. No. Not Harlowe. "The director. He deals with me."

"The director? The scarred one?" Interest lit the yellow specks in her eyes.

He couldn't offer much as far as bargaining chips, but it

didn't matter. He only needed enough to get her to take the deal, and killing the director would raise her profile over Gerzon. She'd be more fearsome and could command her own underlings. Gerzon's power would diminish as hers rose.

Zanda crossed her arms. He'd snagged her interest. "Information in exchange for the director?"

Good try. "No. The trafficker for the director."

"The scarred one doesn't come to the human realm."

"Doesn't he?" Sandeen's tone was amused.

"Fine." Her gaze raked his body. "Normally, I'd seal the deal like we used to. But . . ." She shuddered. "No, thanks."

That was for the best. He didn't think he would be able to get his dick up.

She gave him one last calculating look. He forced his expression to remain bland. This was a deal like any other they'd done. With a final narrowing of her eyes, she walked away and disappeared into Daemon.

He wandered for several minutes until he was certain he wasn't being watched or followed. Then he stepped out of the Gloom and onto damp grass. The sun peeked over the horizon, lighting the sky with various blues.

Fatigue haunted him, growing heavier the longer he was here. He had a plan, he'd put it into motion. It was time for rest.

Awareness prickled along his skin. Someone was here.

He backed toward the house and crept to the corner. Long grass brushed along his pants, leaving streaks of moisture behind, but he ignored it. Who would be here? He'd worked hard to dissuade any humans from stepping foot on this abandoned property, and he'd only been here a few times in thirty years. Not even a sylph would care about this place.

When he stuck his head around the corner, he almost ducked back and hid.

Harlowe. She stood at the foot of the porch like she was deciding whether the steps would hold her weight or splinter under her. The steps would hold. The house only looked decrepit. It was strong.

He steeled himself and rounded the corner.

Harlowe sheathed the dagger in her hand when her wary gaze landed on him. "I thought you'd left."

"I have nowhere else to go." Not a total lie.

"We need to get back to the safe house."

"You need to, angel. Or did you come back because you like hating yourself?"

She ignored the question. Was that confirmation that she hated herself for what they'd done? She scanned their surroundings. This would be the first time she'd seen them in the daylight. He stared at her rather than follow the direction of her gaze. There was the failing picket fence that surrounded the yard. Kelly had helped his mother put it up when his father had died. The barn that was nothing more than a mouse shelter. Maybe a few raccoons made their home in there. And the long grass. The trees that Kelly's dad had planted when they'd first moved into this house. It'd been Kelly's parents' dream home. A place to raise their kids and entertain their grandkids.

Until Sandeen had destroyed it all.

"What is this place?" Harlowe still wouldn't look at him.

"Just a farm I procured years ago."

She finally rolled her violet eyes toward him. "You never do anything just because."

"Aw, angel. I'm touched you know me so well." He'd aimed for mirthful sarcasm and landed on bitter.

"What happened here?"

He'd felt the love a son had for a father. His dedication

toward his mother. The crushing inadequacy resulting from simple human interactions. Sandeen had tapped into empathy, the worst thing that could've happened to a youngling in the underworld. Then he had learned what an atrocious monster his sire was long before he'd learned about his mother.

But he answered with, "Nothing. Just knew it was on the market."

Her solemn gaze settled on him. Would she call him on his lie? "We need to get back. Bronx has probably reported us missing by now."

"That sounds like a warrior problem." He spun and went up the stairs. They creaked underneath his boots, and before he hit the top, he knew she'd left.

THAT DAMN MALE. Harlowe opened the sliding door of the safe house. She had to update her team, but thanks to Sierra, she'd been able to clean up and could at least appear normal even if she was a mess inside. A little more of an organized mess, but thanks to a long talk with her sister, she'd realized the heart of the matter—and it went beyond her work obligations.

Regardless, she was still a warrior. Duty didn't wait. She had to brief Bronx. She wouldn't go into specifics, but she had to let someone know that Sandeen was somewhere else and she still had tabs on him.

She'd also have to tell her team that he refused to leave the farmhouse. That she suspected there was a story behind the place but he wasn't talking. Would he eventually, or had she shattered any trust between them?

Bronx was on the phone in the living room. When he saw her, he said, "Wait. Harlowe's back." Speaking to her but keeping the phone to his ear, he asked, "Everything square?"

"Sandeen is secure, but he won't cooperate."

The person on the phone must've heard her. Bronx nodded and signed off. "I can give the director an update after you fill me in."

"Is Dionna still on leave?" Their de facto leader since Bryant had been promoted was oddly absent from this mission.

"She's with her family, yes."

"Dionna has a family?" She hadn't meant to sound so oblivious, but Dionna had never been open about her private life. She was a dedicated warrior, to the point Harlowe had assumed the female didn't have a private life.

Bronx shrugged. "A mate in Nigeria, I guess. Grown kids too. I think they're all schoolteachers."

Grown kids? For whatever reason, Dionna hadn't talked about them. The news eased the tension between Harlowe's shoulders. Dionna didn't talk about her mate and kids. Harlowe wasn't the only one with secrets.

Totally the same.

"Sandeen refuses to return." She braced for Bronx's reaction. But true to Bronx, he was chill.

"Okay," Bronx said. "I get it. His world is turning inside out. So where's he at?"

"An abandoned farm."

"Where?"

Harlowe chewed the inside of her cheek. She'd gotten no details. At all. To be fair, she hadn't spent a lot of time there. Much of the last twelve hours had been spent with Sierra, and her sister wouldn't tell anyone. Boone wouldn't either. If they said anything, it'd be that Harlowe had been there to make amends and see her cherubic nephew. No one would question it. But that didn't explain her inattention toward important details.

"You didn't find out the location?" Bronx's incredulous tone made her feel worse.

"It was storming and I was worried he'd flee again," she mumbled. The superficial answer tasted sour on her tongue. "But he's not leaving. It's isolated and he claims it's safe."

"All right. Well, send me the details once you get them. I'll update the director when I make my other report. He sent me a message about the male that went missing during the same time frame. Odessa found records that his family eventually reported that he walked into the fire. They were in mourning and slow to notify the analysts."

Tragic, but not uncommon. "No doubt whoever dealt with the scrolls didn't want to disturb them, and thought it'd throw anyone off the trail if they went looking too hard. Did the background investigation on Sandissa's mate check out?"

"It did, actually." Bronx scowled. "But it doesn't feel right. There's something going on with him."

"Gut feeling?"

He nodded tightly. Seasoned warriors didn't ignore their gut. But when the kid of a senator was involved, it was difficult to dig deeper without ruffling some robes.

Harlowe rubbed the middle of her forehead. "I could talk to my father." Would she get more than a vacant look in his eye, or would her questions make him check out completely?

"He knows Francois Colbert's parents?"

"I doubt it. But he could give us details about what my mother was doing before she went missing. Other than that male, most of the other missing angels over the centuries were single females with no children. But my mother had me. And Sandissa had a mate. Both she and my mother disappeared closer together than any of the other females. If the usual targets were single females, why them? It seems like a long shot, but maybe their disappearances are related."

"Good idea. But find out where that farm is first. I don't need the director growling at me."

"Will do," she said as professionally as possible when the thought of seeing Sandeen again left her stomach swirling with both dread and anticipation.

Sandeen finished in the shower. The water worked, but judging by the sizable puddle on the floor, there was a leak somewhere. He toweled off with his T-shirt, hung it on the towel rack next to his pants, and went to the basement to shut off the main valve.

The bottom level of the house reminded him of home. Dark. Dank. Shadows that could be deadly or not. But the basement had more bugs than sylphs and the dankness was less oppressive. The darkness wouldn't change. He had money squirreled away for electricity, but he wasn't sure he wanted to spend that much time here. He'd bought the place as more of a memorial. A standing lesson about attachments.

He pushed his damp hair back through his horns when he reached the top of the stairs.

A creak alerted him. He tilted his chin down, ready to use his horns as a battering ram.

"Oh, shit. Oh, sorry." Harlowe spun, her fingers pressed to her temples. "Oh, damn, you're naked."

"Back so soon, angel?" He tore his gaze off her, and especially off her heart-shaped ass.

To keep his dick soft, he concentrated on the puddle and the plumbing issues as he strode toward the bedroom. His privates didn't get the message. Semisoft would do. He didn't plan to get dressed until his clothes were dry.

In the bedroom, he yanked off the sheet that had been draped over all the furniture left behind. Dust particles scattered in the light streaming through the faded floral curtains. The fairly clean mattress beckoned him. It'd been a long damn day.

"Where is this place?" Harlowe asked from behind him.

He suppressed his groan. The angel was in the same room with him and a bed. It'd been tolerable before. But now he knew how hard her body milked him when she came. "Earth."

"Dammit, demon. Can you give me a straightforward answer for once?"

"Depends." He leveled his gaze on her as he sat on the edge of the mattress. His cock had surpassed semisoft. Between Harlowe's velvet heat and the way she cried his name as she came, it was going to be impossible to stay soft around her. "Are you going to admit that you came back because you want a repeat of what we did out there on the grass?"

She sputtered and shifted her weight on her feet. "I'm not— That wasn't—"

"Are you going to admit that was the best sex of your life?" He regretted the words as soon as they were out. It'd been the best sex of his life, but his comparisons were closer to torture. Harlowe might've made sweet love a thousand times in her life, with harps and shit.

Her mouth dropped open and a spear of alarm hit her

gaze. He sat straighter. Was he right? It wasn't just true for him?

"You're being ridiculous," she scoffed, but her gaze jerked to the wall and her cheeks flushed pink.

"Am I?" He gestured to his growing erection, wanting to burrow deeper under her skin.

He'd taken down the sheet over the large mirror on the vanity before he'd showered. He'd wanted to try out his morph skills, but his wings hadn't budged. He was sitting across from it now, wings spread behind him, cock straining toward the ceiling. All this picture was missing was her.

"It was the best I've ever had. Fucking amazing." He blamed the fatigue for that admission.

Her resolute expression flickered. "I need to know where we're at. Otherwise, I'll have to walk down the road until I find a sign or something."

He hung his head back, enjoying the softness of the mattress but wishing he was on top of her instead. "What will you give me if I tell you?"

"I don't barter with sex." Her tone was hard.

"Consider yourself fortunate. But I wasn't talking about sex."

She cursed under her breath. "I can let you stay here instead of the safe house."

He didn't want to stay here. This was the last place he cared to spend any time. If his mother knew what had happened here because of him, she'd be more than ashamed. She'd be mortified. "We're in Michigan. Isabella County."

"Town?"

Her hard voice washed over him. He wanted more. Just hearing her talk was enough, but he wanted her needy whispers in his ear again.

His cock throbbed. She was in the same room. The perfect distraction for the way this place made him feel. He wrapped his hand around his erection. A low moan emanated from him. "Now, angel. You're asking for a lot of details."

Her feet scraped the wood floor as she turned away. "Demon. What town?"

The corner of his mouth kicked up. She was a stubborn one.

Oh, well. It wasn't as if he'd invited her into the bedroom. And she wasn't leaving.

He pumped his hand. Once. Twice. He rarely masturbated. The last thing he wanted in the underworld was to get taken down while stroking one off. He'd had to be ready to defend himself at all times—or to barter with his body when the moment arose.

"What town?" she gritted out, but he only smiled and sank into the pleasure.

"Do you ever take time off, angel?" He cracked his eyes open. Her back was to him, but when he spoke, she tipped her head like she was trying not to peek.

"There's work to do. People depend on me."

He groaned, imagining her lowering herself onto his cock. He hadn't been able to see much when they'd fucked. His wings had added to the shadows. But there were two spots on his ass that still ached from the way her heels had driven into him. "What do those people do for you?"

"They don't need to do anything. They're the innocent, and I protect them."

"Such a good angel."

"You need to quit touching yourself while we're talking." Was that a note of panic in her tone? She was the one in his bedroom.

"I'm way past touching myself. Know what I'm picturing?"

"I don't care."

The breathless quality to her voice said she very much cared. "I'm picturing how you looked when you came. You screamed my name, Lowe. Did you realize that? In full passion, you didn't call me 'demon.' "

"Don't like it when I call you demon?"

Her question wasn't what he'd expected. "I don't care. It's what I am. But I like my name on your lips. I wanted a lot more of me on your lips."

He stroked faster and pinned his gaze on her.

Not only hadn't she left, she'd pivoted toward him, her gaze on his hand. She swallowed hard. "We're not supposed to—"

"I don't care what I'm supposed to do, angel. Expectations come from others." He recalled her slick heat. The way her body gripped him until he'd thought he'd melt into her. It hadn't been the push-pull of sex he'd experienced before. The clawing, the biting, the fight for power.

She'd taken all of him. She'd wanted him.

He wished she'd admit it. Wished she'd accept him, but it wasn't meant to be. They were realms apart. "You know what I want?"

"World peace?" Her voice was so thick, he was surprised she could get the words out.

"You coming over me again. I want you, on top of me, with your wings out. They're beautiful, aren't they?"

She didn't answer, and she didn't look away. Her bright gaze jumped to his eyes, then dropped back to where he was stroking himself.

He slowed as he watched her reaction. He'd never be more truthful than he was in this moment. "I want to see all of you. I want your wings dipped back from the strength of that passion you hide. I want your light hair free of its restriction and flowing down your back, over those round breasts. I want to hear you whisper my name, I want to hear you scream it. I want to feel your release spilling over me with that sensual heat you keep bottled up."

Pressure coiled at the base of his spine. He was ready to blow, but she was captivated. By him. He wasn't wasting her attention.

"Angel, you're the sexiest damn thing I've ever seen, and I want more than a taste. I want to devour. I want to spread you wide and sink my fangs into your sweet flesh."

Her lips parted. Her eyes were no longer bright. Pink tinged her cheeks and her pupils had blown. The tight knit of her shirt did nothing to hold back the force of her peaked nipples.

"Do you want to know how you tasted, angel?"

Her gaze lifted to his. Need raged in her eyes, held back by only a sliver of restraint.

"You tasted like the only slice of heaven I'll ever know." With that, he came, pumping his pulsing flesh as hot jets shot out, landed on his skin as he envisioned it streaking across hers instead.

A choked gasp left her.

He was breathing hard as his hand came to a stop. He didn't have the strength to remove it, his flesh too sensitive to disturb.

Shock played across her expression until it was chased away by dogged resolution. "You're right, Sandeen. I do want you." He sat up at her admission. "But I can't have you. Not because you're a half demon. Not because of what you've done in your life. But because you refuse to do anything but live life for yourself. I need more out of a partner. I need more from a male who could endanger me and my entire team. A male who could endanger not just one realm, but all three. I want a male who can get beyond his past and his pain and be there for me. And until you quit being selfish, I can't be with you."

She spun on her heel and left the room, leaving him alone with his mess.

BRONX SNAPPED HIS FINGERS. "Earth to Harlowe."

Despite his action, her attention was sluggish in returning to the scrolls in front of her. She and Bronx had set up at the safe house with the scrolls and more information Odessa had been able to get them about the missing angels. "I'm paying attention."

"What did I just say?"

If it wasn't about how she'd watched Sandeen jack off while telling her exactly what he wanted to do to her, then she didn't know. Last night was all she was able to think about. She shouldn't be here. Jagger could've come and worked with Bronx. Urban. Even Ransom, who was fairly new to their team and all the information they were withholding from the senate. But she'd needed to get away and practically begged Director Vale to be in on the investigation. She'd assured her boss that Sandeen wasn't going anywhere.

She wished she could assure herself.

"I know you weren't listening. Where's your head at?" His gaze was too keen. She wasn't as close to him as Sierra, but they'd worked together long enough. Would he figure out her secret? That she had to be in a different realm in order to keep her distance from Sandeen?

"You were talking about the annoying enforcer you want to fuck."

He gave her a look that said he knew damn well she was trying to divert his attention. "She's more than annoying. She's a threat, but more on that later. Did you see that Sandissa's mate, Francois, likes to frequent a nightclub right here in Las Vegas?"

"What's his excuse for being on Earth?" There weren't many humanitarian missions in nightclubs.

"Exactly. I should go there and see what the place is like, how many angels frequent there. We can't have another Fall From Grace."

"Right. I can get changed and go with you."

His mouth formed a tight line. "Harlowe."

"What? Urban can go to the farmstead." She'd gotten the exact location, but no one else had been there and she'd liked that too much.

"I have a feeling the only thing keeping the demon around is you. If you start finding other places to be, then he will too."

She sighed. "I need a break from him."

"Something happen?"

The image of his body poised over hers as he drove into her shot through her brain. So many things had happened. "He's just . . . I know why we have to watch him, but he doesn't want our help."

"He can't exactly hide those big wings of his, so we need to at least make sure he doesn't rampage through some small town in Michigan, flashing his fangs and horns."

She'd told Sandeen she was leaving to get food and supplies and update her team. She'd hollered it as she'd walked out the door. It'd been the truth, but she'd needed the escape.

Bronx was on the phone, probably messaging Urban.

The two lived for missions that took them to human locations full of women down to fuck. They didn't need dating apps. Their looks alone got them enough action. The nightclub was right up their alley. Harlowe could blend when she needed to, but her concentration would ordinarily be on work. For the foreseeable future? Her concentration would be on a male who twisted up her mind and body until she didn't know which way to face. Bronx and Urban would be better options.

If other angels were there, they'd know the males wanted to get laid and it'd be easier to evade suspicion. Harlowe had done the nightclub scene before, both for work and for pleasure. She could go, dance, hit up some guys. But while her body still throbbed from what she'd done with Sandeen, it wasn't like she would go home with anyone. She didn't think she could stomach making out with someone in public to preserve her cover.

Damn that demon.

She pointed her mind toward work and willed it to stay there. "Any hint that Sandissa used to visit Vegas? What do Odessa's notes say?"

Sandissa had been a chaperone. She'd guided souls to the light. Her work had kept her busy and away from Numen. Her parents had been centuries old when they'd walked into angel fire together. The angel fire fountain in the middle of Numen was her kind's way of leaving the world when they were ready. Sandissa's mate's parents had been friends with her parents. Had Sandissa's mating been an arrangement, or had they been destined? Not all angels liked to wait for their fated sync mate to appear.

Had Francois been ready to mingle and itching to be single instead of attached to a mate who was a damper on his good time with her work in the human realm?

Chaperones were well respected in Numen. But they

were also avoided. A heaviness weighed on their wings. Continually witnessing the end of a life and the circumstances that brought it to fruition was mentally taxing. Chaperones were solemn individuals. Harlowe couldn't see Sandissa partying it up at some nightclub.

Bronx's finger tapped on the keys. Odessa had sent all the information she could find that wasn't etched into scrolls. Harlowe and Bronx were combing through that data instead of sneezing through dusty scrolls.

"Most of her work *did* center in Vegas." Bronx's dark brows lifted. "Vegas sixty-five years ago. It wouldn't have been hard for her to go missing and for the realm to write off her disappearance. Daemon have been busy in Sin City for decades."

"And Francois?" Harlowe leaned over the chair to watch the documents flip by as Bronx scanned them. He stopped on one and it took her a minute to register the information. "Francois's father used to do a lot of humanitarian work in Nevada?"

Bronx poked a finger at the screen. "In Reno. But he seemed to spend a lot of time in Vegas."

She tried to put the information together. "So, Sandissa worked in the Vegas area. Her mate likes to have a good time but he doesn't have a history of coming to Earth for more than a good time, which he resumed soon after Sandissa disappeared."

"His father used to spend a lot of time in the area too. And his mother is a senator." Bronx paged through several more documents. "Doesn't look like Francois's father has been to Earth since the shit with Odessa started hitting the fan."

"Lying low?" She reached over Bronx and paged up to the documents on Francois. "But Francois has kept on partying."

"So either he's oblivious to the possibility that his mate was sold to the highest demon bidder, or he's just a spoiled male who thought he hit a stroke of luck when his mate never returned."

"His father, Jean Luc, is certainly suspect. We should tell Felicia to check out his mother too."

Bronx nodded. "At least get her take on the female. She might be oblivious and Jean Luc's using his mate to fly under our radar and the enforcers' radar—assuming the enforcers ever turn their radar toward the senate and their mates." His glower made the statement seem personal. That enforcer had gotten to him.

"I don't know Tosca, but I didn't get the impression she was corrupt."

"They don't need to be corrupt to be influenced to do corrupt things."

True. Just look at Sierra and the reason her wings had been taken. "Perhaps. But Tosca's far down on the list of individuals we need to check out."

"I'll meet with Jagger and Urban to investigate Francois and the nightclub. See if Ransom is available to check on the father, and if Felicia has an intuition about Francois's mother."

They had a plan of action, and that left Harlowe with nothing to do but face her demon. She couldn't go back and feel like she was two steps behind Sandeen. "Before I go, I need to use the computer to look up a couple of things."

"You talk to your father yet?"

"No. I'll figure out a good time. I'm going to look in the watcher records for anything on the farmhouse."

Bronx gave her another look, like he knew she was stalling and wouldn't tell him why.

A kid shouldn't dread talking to their parent. But he'd

never been much of one, and the older she'd gotten, the more he'd withdrawn. The sad irony was that she was taking after him more than she cared to. She was avoiding both him and Sandeen. If she'd learned anything from her relationship with her father, it was that she needed to deal with her problems. It was time to face her demon.

CHAPTER 16

Sandeen hadn't left while Harlowe was gone. His stomach rumbled, but he'd waited. She'd said she'd bring back food. He wanted to know what information Zanda had found, but it was too soon. The more he left this house and entered the realm, the easier it'd be for his kind to track him right back here. He'd give Zanda time and use it to figure out where to go from here.

He doubted anyone had found his stash of money at Boone's old cabin. The cache of fallen blood should be safe too. He clearly didn't need it. It would be easy enough to return and locate his funds and destroy the blood. But he needed another place to go after that. A spot that was his own.

Boots hit the steps outside. Harlowe's determined cadence. Had it been hard for her to return?

And until you quit being selfish, I can't be with you.

She had said that? In this house, the pinnacle of selfish acts from his past? He wanted to leave this place. To do exactly what she had accused him of, think of himself and never look back.

But he hadn't. He'd learned enough to plan.

Harlowe came through the door, several tote bags in one hand. She stopped and grabbed a few that she had set down to open the door.

He crossed to her and took five bags from one hand. "You could make more than one trip. You know that, right?"

"Or I could do it all in one and be done."

He unloaded the bags. Simple, no-prep foods that could be kept at room temp. Jerky. Fruit cups. Ramen. They could heat water over a fire.

He scanned the pile. "I've possessed college kids with better eating habits."

She pushed a strand of hair that had broken free from her braid out of her face. "Pay for electricity, then, or move into a dorm."

The bags she unloaded had nothing but bottled water.

He grabbed a bag of jerky, ripped it open, and offered it to her first.

She gave him an odd look. "I grabbed two." She dug through the pile he'd made and found her own package. "Do you realize you have manners, or are you trying to mess with people when you do nice things?"

"What are you talking about?"

She lifted the packet she held. "You offered me the food first. You got the bags at the door. And when you cooked at the cabin and at the safe house, you made my plate first. It seems to come naturally."

"I've watched people. It's what they do."

"Mm."

He scowled at her as he bit into his dried meat. Her *Mm* was loaded. "It's part of blending."

She chewed on her food for a moment before she spoke. "You know how we can tell someone is possessed?"

"You can see us," he said like *duh*. Warriors knew how to look at humans and see the hologram effect of the demon inside.

"We can't walk around on Earth staring into the distance. We need to focus, so we look for signs. Heads don't spin around like they do in the movies."

He'd seen a few human heads spin around, but the humans hadn't bounced back from that. "Okay?" Tension crept between his shoulder blades. What was she getting at?

"Rudeness is always a warning sign," she continued, oblivious to the heartburn she was inspiring by wherever she was going with this. "It's not simple rudeness. All humans have varying levels. It's obvious rudeness. People automatically hold the door open for others behind them. They stand in line with automatic compliance. They say 'thank you' absentmindedly even if they don't mean it. That behavior's been ingrained in them. So, when doors are getting slammed in people's faces or someone's charging through a crowd without the urge to say a quick 'excuse me,' we take a closer look."

Because basic manners weren't bred into demons. They weren't raised hearing "excuse me" uttered a thousand times. They barged through doors and didn't care who was coming or going at the same time.

"Like I said, I watched and learned." He might've learned faster than others like him. He shoved another piece of jerky in his mouth.

"What happened at this house?"

The jerky turned to sawdust. His tongue quit trying to work it around his mouth. He grabbed a napkin and spit it out. Harlowe would probably see that as another difference from other demons. He didn't spit or shit on the floor. He was civilized.

"You can tell me, or I can tell you what I think," she said softly.

His blood ran cold and his lips curled back. She didn't flinch from his fangs, but then, she never had.

"You possessed someone who used to live here. And since the events drove you to buy and preserve the house, I'd say that something you did may have led to the kid's death." She inspected him, gauged his reaction. What would she see? He was stony faced, his blood concrete in his veins. "In Numen, analysts keep records. Humans do the same. And I did some reading. The kid was barely eighteen. Wild. But he loved his dad. There are a lot of write-ups of the two of them. Before."

Before. It was what had come after Sandeen had possessed the kid that haunted every corner of this place.

"The kid—Kelly, right? He felt so guilty about his dad's death. That was how you got in, wasn't it?"

Sandeen ground his teeth together. Kelly had wanted to go fishing so badly one weekend. His dad hadn't been feeling well. And if they'd been closer to civilization, maybe Kelly's dad could've gotten help for his heart attack. Instead, he'd died on the boat, with Kelly as a witness, leaving Kelly behind to get to shore and get help that would be too late for his dad.

"He was angry. He was lost. But the kid felt more than that. He loved deeply. You experienced it all. You went along for the ride, maybe even enjoyed the drama."

"I wasn't with Kelly when he died." He should've been. Kelly had been acting more irrational. Yelling at his mother. Drinking his dad's leftover booze.

"No. Another demon took the wheel, didn't he? Literally and figuratively. Kelly was acting out, but not like that."

"No. Not like that." Kelly had gotten drunk on the rest

of the cheap vodka, taken his mother's car, and crashed into another carload of teens heading to the county fair for some good, clean, rural-kid fun. When the cops had come to the house to notify Kelly's mom, they'd found her stabbed to death.

"Zadren. Your sire."

Sandeen's scornful chuckle echoed in the silence of the room. "He's destroyed everything I cared for. I had a puppy once. I managed to get it across the realms. I was going to raise the first hellhound, create a pack of creatures that would protect on command. Train it to protect my place so I could actually get some sleep without worrying about my safety. He crushed it and ate it." Harlowe blanched, but he kept going. "Then Kelly."

"Why was Kelly different?"

The past hung on his shoulders as he recalled latching on to Kelly that first time. "His memories."

"He loved his father, and you saw what it was supposed to be like between a parent and a kid. You saw how much Kelly's mom cared for him and what she would've done for him. And you realized you were different."

Hearing Harlowe utter his feelings made them harder to ignore. "I knew I was different long before Kelly."

She set her bag down and crossed to him. His ass stayed planted on the counter. He couldn't move when she feathered her fingers over his face. "Why'd you buy this place?"

Someone would've moved in. They would've kept farming, they would've kept going, just like Kelly and his mom had never lived here.

"Sandeen," she whispered when he didn't answer and cupped his face.

"Don't read into it, angel. I'm not the good angel you're looking for. I'm the selfish demon you rightly assumed I am. I keep this place to remind me that my sire is an evil bastard who enjoys teaching me morbid lessons. I keep this place to remember that no matter how different I feel, I'm still a demon who's ruined the lives of humans."

~

HARLOWE ENTERED her father's house, not worrying if she was making too much noise. If he was napping, he needed to be awake for this talk. She wouldn't let him drift away from her this time.

"Father?" She crossed into the main area. Neat and tidy. Ready for visitors.

Had they ever had company when she was growing up? Her mind spun, but she couldn't recall a visitor. No other family. It'd been her and Father.

On the sofa, her father sat. His back was to her, his gun-metal gray wings limp, and he stared at the far wall. This wasn't the first time she'd caught him spacing off into nothingness. When she was little, she used to hang drawings on the bare wall. Father had left them until they'd fallen of their own free will.

Harlowe approached, circling around him. His hair was a little grayer than she remembered. He was a few centuries old, but he'd never looked the part until now. "Hey."

The pull from wherever his mind had gone was slow. Life seeped into his pale amber eyes and he lifted his chin. A faint smile formed across his thin lips. "Oh, Harlowe. Hello again."

He folded his hands on his lap as she sat across from him. She took the moment to let her wings unfurl. Relief spread through her muscles as they stretched to accommodate the weight of her wings. She was home. She wished she felt like it. Living in the barracks had provided more comfort than this.

"How's work?"

It was the first question he usually asked, and she had always given him a quick review. "It's good. Pretty quiet right now."

It was the first time she hadn't been honest. She had told him all about the corruption in the senate. She'd held back tears as she revealed that Sierra would lose her wings. She'd described what had happened to the warriors' previous director and how Director Vale had gotten the position. She'd done all the talking and Father had politely listened with the same faint smile on his face.

"Good," he said, aloof expression in place. "Quiet is good."

Why couldn't she be important enough for him to return to the land of the living? But she was here for work, not a visit.

She didn't mean to rip the bloody bandage off, but the question popped out. "Father, what happened to Mother?"

He blanched, swaying in his seat until she worried he'd topple to the floor. "Harlowe." He rarely expressed that much emotion in his voice. The older she'd gotten, the cooler he'd grown. "Wha— Why would you ask?"

She opened her mouth. Closed it again. She'd asked in a business capacity. She'd known she'd have to eventually. Her team had to know if her mother had been a victim of convenience, or if she'd been targeted.

But there was another reason. "We've never talked about it."

"We don't need to," he huffed. Color was returning to his cheeks, deepening to a flush. "She's gone. That's all I know." His jaw hardened and moisture misted his eyes. His voice dropped to a ragged whisper. "That's all I need to know. She's gone."

"I need to know how. Why Mother?"

"Demons don't discriminate." His tone grew heated. "They gladly took the most vibrant female and destroyed her. Took her away from us and rejoiced, no doubt. Celebrated her demise."

This was the father that had supported her decision to become a warrior. He'd wanted to make the demons pay.

Harlowe's stomach sank. He'd supported her because he couldn't do it himself. The loss of his mate had left him broken. So he'd sent his daughter into danger in his stead.

She swallowed past the sour lump in her throat. "What was she doing to put her in harm's way? Do you remember anything she talked about before she disappeared? Any specific issue she was looking into?"

"She's gone, Harlowe. It doesn't matter anymore."

"Father, please."

Sadness draped over his face. The dark circles under his eyes deepened, and his shoulders hung. His wings were already drooped. But his gaze grew faraway. He was thinking. She remained quiet, willing him to remember more than his grief.

"She didn't tell me about specifics. I'd worry too much. But there was one time she mentioned wanting to update the director on something about an old friend who had gone missing, but she worried the director would pass her worries on to the senate."

Which of the females had her mother been friends with? "Why would that be an issue?"

Her father lifted a shoulder, but he frowned. "Well, that friend's mate had a mother who was a senator. I suppose that's why. The senator might have gotten upset if she'd thought her efforts to find a missing angel were being criticized."

"Oh?" Harlowe kept her voice light, but her heart slammed against her ribs. "Who was her friend?"

"I don't recall. Your mother went missing not long after and I couldn't . . . I had you to raise. But I remember thinking, 'Poor family.' At least they found your mother's body." He choked on the last word. His expression shuttered and he turned away.

Harlowe wasn't done. Her body vibrated with anticipation. She was close to an answer that would make all this clear. She pushed her father, insisting once again that he rouse from his misery.

"Father, the friend's name. Please, try to remember."

His brows drew together and annoyance crossed his face. But her tone must've gotten through to him. He sighed and looked to the ceiling, as if that would help him remember. "Let's see. The senator is, um . . . Colbert. I believe the friend's name was San-something. Sandy? Sandrina?"

It couldn't be. But all the pieces fit. "Sandissa?"

He nodded. "Sandissa. Yes. That's it."

CHAPTER 17

*D*rifting through the house, Sandeen made sure that Harlowe was indeed gone and that no other warrior had taken her place. The coast was clear.

He didn't know why they'd quit cycling through with constant guards, but he wouldn't question it. Perhaps they knew they truly had no way to hold him, and that finding a secluded spot to hide from both Numen and Daemon alike wasn't easy. He was left spinning his wheels here.

Or so they thought.

He hated stepping into the Gloom from this house. The risk of being seen at the one place only his sire and Harlowe knew about was too great, but he had no other choice. He couldn't procure a car without drawing unwanted attention, much less drive across Michigan in full half-demon, half-angel regalia just so he could enter the Gloom from another location.

He stepped in and looked around. Nothing.

Hurrying through the stinging mist, it didn't take long to get to a section far away from Michigan. He stopped and waited. Several moments went by before a sylph loped

172

across his path, crossing from the human realm to return to Daemon.

It pretended Sandeen didn't exist. *If I pretend I don't see him, then he won't see me.* Most days, Sandeen let them think that was how it worked. But today, he needed the little fucker's help.

"Hey. Bring Zanda to me."

The creature stopped. It was no taller than Sandeen's knees and this one looked like it'd been ridden hard and put away wet. He didn't think of their work on Earth as being work, but they were creatures that tired from the daily grind just like any other.

The sylph squinted its red, beady little eyes and looked around as if to say *Who the fuck are you to make me?* If the little demon wasn't getting eaten, it wasn't going to be helpful either.

Sandeen didn't have much to bargain with. He wasn't giving away the location of any of Harlowe's team. Doing so would be certain death for the sylph and any other demons the little beast recruited to go with. Money didn't do sylphs any good. Sandeen was on the dirty side of a shit sandwich with most demons in his realm. He couldn't promise his sire's good favor, and if the sylph had two functioning brain cells, he wouldn't want it anyway.

Sylphs were a food source. They wanted to hide.

Sandeen kept his grin from forming. Turned out, he could offer something he'd never planned to use again.

"Get Zanda and you can have my place."

If the sylph had had brows, they'd have risen. It shook its head.

Sandeen shrugged. "Would you go back if you were me?"

The sylph's expression turned greedy, its fangs

protruding as it peeled its lips back and rubbed its small, clawed hands together.

"But if you don't get Zanda here in five minutes, I'm going in and burning my place to the ground." He wouldn't, but the fact that he was never returning to Daemon was beside the point.

The creature slipped away.

It was several minutes before Zanda appeared, the droplets parting around her. "How'd you get a beasty to do your bidding?"

"Trade secret." A foreign emotion stabbed his chest when he noticed blood dripping at Zanda's bare feet. The claws of her hands were fresh with red blood, and the scraps of flesh left behind matched the rotten-cream skin of the sylph.

He almost asked if she'd killed the creature who had done her no harm, but the question wouldn't help him. She'd latch on to the fact that he didn't like killing even sylphs and she'd find a way to use and abuse it.

As if she sensed his displeasure, she lifted her hand to her mouth and licked off a fingertip. Her tongue flicked out, her gleaming eyes gauging his reaction.

He kept his tone bored, restraining the urge to wrap his hands around her throat. "What do you have for me?"

"Turns out some of the demons under your sire are chatterboxes." She licked another finger. To be fair, the sylph might've been his lunch. But still. He didn't like that he'd sent it to its death.

Maybe he had more angel in him than he thought. Or maybe he was just pissy he couldn't hold his home over another sylph when word got out that he expected favors that got them eaten.

She sucked another finger and eyed him like she wanted to sink her fangs into his jugular. His neck ached at the memory. He hated her fangs in his body. His reaction was nothing like Harlowe's when his fangs grazed her skin.

Thinking of Harlowe wouldn't do him any good in this situation. The angel was a weakness around Zanda.

"So," she said and smacked her lips. "There's this angel who likes to party. Just so happens, he's mated—father's orders. The father likes to party too, but the son was risking their time on Earth. Thought it'd center him or some shit. Don't know why he didn't just kill the brat."

A conundrum. Sandeen remained expression-free. If he anticipated the information, Zanda would withhold it.

"So this brat angel—" She snorted. "And they say we're evil. This guy has already sold a couple of innocent angels out to your sire. The females didn't survive. There was supposed to be a long break between females going missing, but low and behold, this brat angel ends up with a mate he doesn't want, so . . ." She lifts her hands, amusement dancing across her leathery expression.

"So he sells her too." Because Big Z wouldn't be able to resist.

Zanda shimmied her shoulders and sang off-key, "Party time."

"Did you get a name?" Sandeen knew it, but he wanted it confirmed.

"Frank something."

Close enough to Francois to seal the mate's fate.

"So . . . You need to hold up your end." Her fangs flashed.

"The deal was the male who sold my mother for the director. You only gave me gossip." She'd confirmed a lot, but he didn't thank her. She had to hold up her end.

Her eyes narrowed and she sniffed, as if she were trying to smell a lie. "He still likes to party, but his father got suspicious. He doesn't deal anymore."

But he had, and his fate was sealed. "I want him."

Her eyes lit. Not because she had a sense of justice. She liked the violence. And that Sandeen wanted to kill an angel. "The director?"

"You'll have him in the scarred flesh. You bag him and Gerzon won't hold the power he thinks he does. He had to have Andy help him. You could get the director."

She poked a claw into his shoulder. It bit through the fabric and into his skin. He didn't move, but damn. It burned like a brand. "When I tell you where to meet with Frank, you bring the director. Or I'll let Frank know exactly what kind of danger he's in and who exactly you are. I'm guessing you don't want that to get out."

Sandeen's fangs throbbed. Francois needed to die. So did Zanda. But only one of them was useful. "Deal."

"SANDEEN?" Harlowe stood inside the front door. She'd just returned from talking with her father and while she wouldn't mind having the house to herself for a while, that meant the demon was off doing something that probably didn't include fixing the plumbing.

To be fair, if it included fixing the plumbing, that wouldn't be good either. He'd have to go somewhere and the wing thing was still an issue.

The house remained quiet.

"Demon!" She didn't take off her shoes, but roamed through the living room. She'd read up on Sandeen's sire after she'd left her father's house. The male was gruesome. That kid hadn't had a chance. He'd been a puppet.

Zadren had been targeted by several warrior groups for centuries before that. He was a brutal demon, and when he possessed a body, he destroyed it from the inside out and trashed everything around it. His behavior was next level when it came to possession. Most demons had some level of survival instinct. They wanted the host to last. They wanted to use it again. Zadren chewed through them like gum.

Sandeen wouldn't admit to an extra dose of guilt because he'd been the one to lure his sire back into the human realm. That'd be too undemonlike for his comfort. He couldn't have foreseen the level of devastation his sire would cause.

No answer. Where the hell was he?

She drifted through the first floor of the house. The couch was like she'd left it, the pillow and blankets she'd brought over piled on one end. The first-floor bathroom was empty.

A creak from the bedroom caught her attention. She put her back to the wall and edged toward the bedroom with the half-open door.

No one knew about this place, but warriors didn't stay alive by making assumptions. Sandeen hadn't answered her for a reason and she doubted it was because she'd made him talk about his feelings.

She curled her fingers around the hilt of a dagger and slipped it from its sheath. Heel to toe, she stalked toward the bedroom. Pushing the door open, she crouched, dagger in her palm and ready to maim.

Sandeen was in the middle of the room with his shirt off and bunched in his hands. The material was pressed to his shoulder. Thankfully, he wasn't staring into the mirror like the last time she'd walked in on him.

"Sneaking up on me, angel?"

"I called for you."

"I was napping." He turned his back to her and tossed the shirt into the corner, where he had a small pile of dirty clothes started. His wings were lifted off the floor as he went to the dresser where he stored his meager supply of shirts she'd carted over on one of her trips.

As he shrugged into a new top, she scanned the bed. He never napped. But there was also nothing else to do here. "I'm going to town to get some supplies so we can fix the leak and use the water."

"It might be a game of catch-up."

"Then I'll keep fixing leaks."

He faced her. "Since when do warriors learn plumbing?"

"Since we got the internet." She spun on her heel. "Besides, I'm not doing it—I'm just getting the stuff. It's your house."

He trailed her. "Get some meat. I'll start a fire."

"Or . . . you could turn on the electricity."

"I'd need a phone to do that."

She rolled her eyes. Frustrating demon could've asked her the first morning they had peanut butter and jelly sandwiches. "I'll call, but you already offered to grill, so . . ."

"Angel. Did I find your weak spot?"

He was still behind her and couldn't see her smile. All of his cooking was becoming a weak spot. Somehow, the demon made the best PB&Js she'd ever had. How did one of those taste different than another? It shouldn't be possible. But then, Sandeen shouldn't be possible either.

He followed her all the way outside. "How are you getting to town?"

"I'm not going there."

"Vegas, baby." He propped his hands on his hips. Green trees provided a backdrop. Emerald fields peeked from between the leaves. The grass was yet another shade of brilliant green. Birds chirped around them. Happy songs of nature.

She was struck by the normality of the moment. She was leaving to run some errands and bring back food. They'd grill, eat, and act like . . . a couple. Friends at the very least.

Was that what they were? He was her mission. She wasn't exactly his bodyguard, but she did guard him. They'd had sex. It was hard to remember a time when she wanted to hurt him, when she'd been ready to kill him.

"What?" he asked.

"Nothing."

He cocked his head and the sun limned his horns until they looked like polished mahogany. If a demon had to have horns, he had nice ones. "It's something. You went quiet and looked at me like I was a new species of bug."

She lifted a brow and the side of her mouth canted up.

His grin revealed the tips of his fangs. "Bad analogy. I am a new species."

"I like this place."

His smile fell. "It's full of—"

"Peace."

He snapped his mouth shut.

She faced the house. "I think . . . I think she knew it wasn't her son. The chaperone would've let her know. She wouldn't have walked into the light without knowing. What happened is done. This place has healed and is ready for life again, and that's because of you."

"Angel, you keep—"

She held her hand up. "Right. You're so evil I'm lucky my eyes aren't bleeding just looking at you."

His lips twitched. "I mean, they might be a little bloodshot."

She laughed. "That's from sleeping on a couch that was made in a different century."

She could leave, but she wanted to linger. She could

help him find wood. Clear a place to make the fire. But his earlier warning rang through her mind. Maybe she should listen.

Was that why she wasn't telling him what she'd learned about their mothers? She wanted to preserve this moment? Or because she didn't want him taking off again? She had a feeling the news that in another life they might have been a normal angelic couple planning their future would bother him more than any other revelation.

"Need anything else while I'm out?" Such a normal question.

"Nope. Get back by dark, or I'm hunting a cow and getting started myself."

She chuckled and transcended to the safe house, making a list in her head. The neighbors had cattle, and Sandeen wasn't really joking.

Two weeks had gone by. No news. No updates.

Every time Harlowe had popped out, Sandeen had risked the Gloom to try and catch Zanda. But she was nowhere to be found and sylphs avoided him.

The last time he'd gone in, three symasters thought they'd gang up on him and survive. They hadn't. Sandeen had returned and used the newly working plumbing to clean up before Harlowe had returned.

The electricity was on. He'd linked all the bills to one of his dummy identities, Sander Lowe. The glare Harlowe had given him when she'd seen the utility bill had been worth it.

Harlowe entered the house, her hands full of tote bags. She brought more stuff after each trip. Life would be easier with a car, but she was probably afraid he'd steal the keys and joyride to town with his wings on display.

Maybe, if it was dark out.

He grabbed the grocery bags from her hands. "Only two this time?" She'd been bringing back supplies after each trip. If she didn't go shopping, Bronx or Urban did it for her and left the stuff at the safe house.

"I have actual work to do."

"I am your job, angel."

She mock scowled at him, but then her expression went taut.

Right. Her work. Their goals were overlapping at the moment and with the radio silence from Zanda, he asked, "Trouble with my mother's investigation?"

Harlowe paused, her expression wary. He hadn't asked about what she'd learned or how it was progressing and she'd been oddly quiet on the subject. She was sharp enough to know he had an agenda. Had Zanda gotten to Francois already? Was she out looking for him to set up the swap?

He hoped he managed to look mildly interested. He didn't want to know more details about his mother's life; he wanted Francois dead. When she didn't say anything, he said, "I've been thinking, that's all."

"Thinking that you want to interfere?"

That was already done. "Thinking I've been ignoring her existence and what she went through and maybe I should figure out how I feel about it."

Harlowe put the milk away. Whole milk. She'd bought skim one time and he'd gagged for three hours. "Well . . . I learned my mother was also investigating the disappearance." She leaned against the counter and crossed her arms. "Our mothers were friends."

Regret coated his guts with lead. He shouldn't have asked. He'd been sullen about his mother's existence, shoving the details away so they couldn't bother him more than they did. But he couldn't ignore this.

His mother hadn't been some angel. She'd been friends with Harlowe's mother. His mother had had a life. She'd had friends. Siblings? Had they cared when she disappeared?

Friends. With Harlowe's mother. He and Harlowe had been linked since before they'd been born.

He worked through the knowledge until he got to the part where he realized that Harlowe had lost her mother because of his. Her mother had suffered. Sierra existed because of his mother. The ripple effect grew until it was a tidal wave knocking him over.

He walked out the screen door and paused. He didn't look over his shoulder when he said, "I'm not leaving. I just need to think."

He kept going, his bare feet flattening the warm grass as he headed down the slight hill behind the house to the little pond that gathered at the base.

Dropping to a seat before he really came to a stop, he folded his arms around his knees.

Harlowe didn't speak but she was behind him. He sensed her several feet away.

"It's not your fault." She'd said something similar before. Repeating it wouldn't make him agree.

"It's someone's fault."

"We're closing in on him."

"Her mate?" They'd better not find him before Zanda did.

"Mmm. He's easy enough to find. Harder to keep under the radar."

"Your director likes to bend the rules more than me." But the director was being discreet on this one. Otherwise, he'd have to tell a hell of a story.

"He's always pushed the boundaries," she agreed.

Sandeen tipped his head back. After an eternity on Earth, he couldn't imagine tiring of the sun on his face.

The rich water smell laced with the summer scents of grass and wet reeds. "I'd think that'd chafe for you."

"It should." She dropped next to him and wrapped her arms around her legs like him. "I guess I crave justice more than following the rules. And some of the politics makes justice hard to serve."

"Humans. Numen. It's all the same. Politics. If Daemon reached that level, they'd be dangerous."

"I guess that's a good thing." She glanced at him. "You think that's why your sire was trying to . . ."

"Breed a new kind of demon that could finish a crossword puzzle instead of just shredding the paper?"

"Basically."

"Maybe. He has a lot of power in the underworld."

"I read up on him."

He could imagine the atrocities recorded about his sire. "But you don't know the real story."

"What do you mean?"

"About why he's so powerful."

"Can he do part of a crossword puzzle?"

He chuckled. The subject of his sire was easier than digesting that their mothers had known each other. He wasn't going to tell Harlowe the rest of his sire's story though. She was still a rule follower at heart. She'd report to Director Vale and then Sandeen would be more powerless than he was now.

He soaked up the moment, sitting by the lake with a female like it was a secluded part of a realm he should've been born into. "Do you think that, as Francois's kid, I would've been a total douche?"

She grimaced. "That's a thought."

"Big Z always said my mother would be ashamed of me, but I think *he* was. Every time I didn't live up to my full evil potential, I made his efforts look like a waste of time."

Every wicked deed had given his sire some smug delight. "Sandissa's mate needs to pay."

Harlowe was full of reassurance. "We'll get him."

Not if I get to him first.

TOSCA WANTED to cross her leg and bounce it as she waited for the director to wrap up whatever bullshit meeting he was in. The leg bounce was her go-to fidget move. But it did her no good when she was so much shorter than the males she confronted, and Director Vale was no exception. It didn't help that his statuesque mate towered over Tosca as well. Odessa Vale was a sweet analyst, but she was on Tosca's list. The list titled "Hiding Something."

Senator Colbert had met with her privately. She'd described some concerning behavior coming from the director, his mate, and her sister, who was also a senator. Tosca had promised to look into it, not expecting to find anything. She'd gotten to know the team when she helped guard Odessa before the female had mated Director Vale, back before he was actually the director.

But Tosca had run into vague answers and a lack of defined missions. Enforcers usually steered clear of warrior drama. The two professions butted heads better than they worked together. But she sensed the director and the rest of his former team were hiding something, with the help of Odessa's sister, Felicia, and it affected the realm. What affected the realm was an enforcer's concern.

Then Senator Colbert had appeared at her house this morning. A senator in Tosca's neighborhood drew attention. Francois Colbert wasn't answering his door and had missed a few appointments. From what Tosca could tell, those appointments were massages and facials, but still. He was MIA.

Tosca took her job seriously. After the betrayal of her old boss, Stede, and a couple of other enforcers, she was determined to restore the trust in her branch of chosen service. The senator trusted her, and Tosca wasn't going to fail her.

Time ticked by. Some angels joked that they had nothing but time. Tosca didn't feel that way. Each minute that went by, her realm was vulnerable to the secrets the walls of this building knew.

The director's door was closed. The antechamber she was in used to have an assistant. Another traitor to the realm, Stede's daughter, if Tosca had heard correctly—and it'd been hard to find out. A direct threat to the realm, and the issue had bypassed the enforcers entirely.

Enough of this. She rose and went to the door. It was locked, but she took out her little kit. Breaking and entering was illegal. Residents liked to think it never happened in Numen, but it did. Enforcers were trained how to open locked doors. Tosca's experience was an added bonus, and one of the few secrets she kept to herself.

The work took seconds and she pushed the plank of wood open. Bronx's astonished expression greeted her. He either hadn't thought she could be so proficient at picking a lock, or he couldn't believe she'd had the audacity to do it to the director's door.

She had a lot of audacity, and she had a feeling Bronx was going to be one of the first to figure that out.

That male pushed her buttons. Hell, he *installed* new buttons each time they crossed paths.

She didn't like him based on principle. He was hot— and he knew it. In a realm of vain creatures, he took it to another level. Jet-black hair brushed to the side. A style some men paid a fortune for but seemed natural on him. An angelic body built for sin—an intoxicating combination. A wide, defined chest that was always on display, as if he wore shirts a size too small. Muscular thighs filled out his pants. And those eyes. Filled with mirth, but also an underlying current of solemn contemplation. She didn't have to follow him to Earth to know that he left a trail of discarded panties and broken hearts wherever he went. Not exactly purposeful work.

And his attitude toward enforcers. Rude. Condescending. Entitled. She tried to keep her learned dislike of warriors in check. Her job came first. But this male could suck it.

A wave of heat swamped her. Bronx could suck absolutely nothing. Maybe that was a better way to phrase it.

She backpedaled her thoughts before the tinge of pink could hit her cheeks. Most people thought she was pissed when she flushed. As much as she disliked Bronx, he'd figure out she flustered easily. The last thing she needed was for him to know that he got to her. That when her guard dropped while she was sleeping, he invaded her dreams.

She plopped on a chair opposite Bronx and across the desk from the director. "I got tired of waiting."

The director didn't cover his annoyance quickly enough. "I was just wrapping up."

She waved her hand. "Don't let me stop you. In fact, I have a feeling that this conversation should include me."

"Why would you think that, enforcer?" Director Vale's tone was low, dangerous.

Tosca ignored it. The male was a lot of things, but he wouldn't hurt her. He'd just interfere with her job in order to do this the way he wanted to. The male wasn't the type to answer to anyone, and it was her job to show him otherwise. It wasn't cowboys and angels up in Numen. The realm had skipped the Wild West phase of civilization.

"I think that because Senator Colbert's son has gone missing."

The director's gaze hardened from its normal granite to pure, glittering diamond. Yeah. She thought he'd know. The real question was why?

A muscle jumped in Bronx's jaw. "Did the senator show as much concern when her son's mate went missing?"

Tosca cocked her head. She didn't know Francois Colbert's history, but she didn't miss the sharp, silencing look Director Vale gave Bronx. "She's concerned about her son, not about a mate who abandoned the realm."

"Is that the story she's telling?" Bronx asked.

So the mate hadn't left willingly?

"Enforcer." The director might think he was distracting Tosca, but she noted everything Bronx had said. He didn't agree that the mate had abandoned the realm. Neither did the director. And these two had some insight into the case of the missing Francois and were likely meeting about it when Tosca had only been made aware an hour ago. "A missing party boy from the realm is your concern. If you think his absence is linked to the underworld, then it's my problem."

"How do you know he's a party boy?" Pampered, given what the senator had said.

Icicles formed on the director's cold words. "Because he likes to visit an oddly demon-free zone in Vegas. Almost no populated place on Earth is demon-free, just like almost no populated place is angel-free." She made the unspoken connection. Francois did what he wanted, and from the director's words, he wasn't using his time for humanitarian efforts. "So, yes. It's my job to find out why a senator's son gets to roam Earth with no oversight, especially after his mate goes missing and then, we assume, passes away."

She heard the air quotes around "passes away." What did he think had happened to Francois's mate? "You're accusing Senator Colbert of—"

"Nothing. It's something we're looking into, and when we have answers, we'll go to the senate. Like always."

The urge to cough *bullshit* was nearly overpowering. But professionalism was a powerful tool and she wielded it well. These two weren't going to give her answers, but she'd gotten enough.

They thought she was an unquestioning servant of the senate. She wasn't. There was something going on, and neither the warriors nor the senators were telling her the truth. She'd dogged the director long enough. Perhaps it was time to expand her investigation to the senators.

"All right. Keep me informed." She rose and skirted between the chairs, bumping her hip against Bronx's wing on purpose.

It was supposed to be an obnoxious move. Her one power play. But he curled the tip around her ankle like he wanted to trip her. As she walked, his feathers fell away. The quick exchange had been out of sight of the director.

She clenched her jaw. That male insisted on having the last word. He and the rest of his team were always one step ahead. One day, she would be on top—and not in the way Bronx was probably used to. She'd get to the heart of this mess before him. She'd do her job and do it well. And he'd be the one running behind. She'd make sure of it.

CHAPTER 19

$\mathcal{H}$arlowe wasn't going to be gone long, but
Sandeen couldn't resist roaming the Gloom.
Zanda couldn't hide forever. They had a deal.

All he needed was this one point of revenge. Something
to make him feel like he was worthy of his mother. She'd
died because of him, so it was fitting that the mate who
had sent her to her death would also die because of him.

A lithe form strode toward him. Determined walk.
Deadly wings full of spikes. Zanda.

"Do you have what I want?" he asked.

"Do you?" she countered.

"I'll give him to you when you show me the mate." Her
eyebrow cocked, but he pushed on before she asked for
details about how he was going to deliver Bryant Vale.
"I'm working on the director. I can get him to the exact
location you want—and he'll be alone. But I need to
know you have the mate. I only get one shot with the
director."

A smug gleam shone in Zanda's eyes. He'd been
worried she wouldn't believe him but her greed was too

large. She wanted to bag the director and move up the Daemon ladder.

"Follow me."

The Gloom nipped at his face as he trailed just behind Zanda's shoulder. She wouldn't allow him entirely at her back. Likewise, he wanted full view of her as well. He couldn't forget that she might have other ideas, like delivering him to his sire.

She walked for several minutes before she stopped. "Wait until I get into my host, then follow me in."

"In where?" He couldn't get a good sense of the place on the other side of the Gloom. A residence? A hotel room? He wanted to peek but wandering out of the Gloom into a populated area wasn't something he'd ever do.

But he didn't want Zanda to get the jump on him either. He edged forward as her eyes closed and she concentrated on overpowering her host.

Yes, a house. Spacious. He couldn't sense any movement from the other side. He didn't know which room the host was in. They didn't need to be that specific when traveling through the Gloom. So he didn't wait for Zanda. He stepped in, peering around.

A faint sound trailed after him. Zanda. Had she said something? Was it a warning? Laughter?

The place was large. An open-concept home—no. A mansion. One room stretched into another. There was a second floor somewhere, but in this main area, the ceiling soared overhead.

He kept his ears tuned for movement. Zanda should be inhabiting her host and coming to find him, properly pissy that he hadn't waited.

The decorations had a classy feel. An old-world style. Statues of cherubs in the corners. Ornate columns with engravings. Sandeen glanced at one as he strode by. An outline of a harp caught his eye. He paused. Angels playing harps were carved into the marble from floor to ceiling. When his gaze touched on the ceiling, he raised a brow.

It was like the house's owner had hired Michelangelo himself. A vibrant blue sky stretched from wall to wall with puffy white clouds. But that wasn't what made him pause.

Nude angels. Male and female, in all forms of embrace.

So, the owner of the house had commissioned Caligula, not Michelangelo, to decorate his ceiling.

He shook his head and kept searching. The main floor was clear. His footsteps echoed through the place.

Where the fuck was Zanda?

He stepped into the Gloom and let the sour mist surround him. "Zanda, what the hell—"

She was nowhere to be seen.

A sense of foreboding sparked in his chest. He'd had no plans to hold up his end of the deal, but he'd thought she'd at least try. She was greedier than she was smart.

So why had she taken him to the mansion? Had she wanted to show him some human's odd sense of art?

He returned to the house, picking up where he'd left off. He ran up the circular staircase with the wrought-iron railing two steps at a time. When he hit the upper level, he went down the hallway that had the most closed doors. The place was too open. A closed door must mean something.

He opened the first one and stopped before crossing the threshold. "Shit."

Blood pooled on the floor beneath a man slumped in an office chair, an arm hanging down. Gravity helped the blood wind down the man's arm and drip off the tips of his fingers. There were a multitude of wounds, but a knife protruded from his side, at a downward angle that made him think the man had stabbed himself.

He clenched his jaws so hard the tips of his fangs bit into the inside of his mouth. She'd done this. Zanda had murdered the human as she possessed him. She'd forced him to endure multiple stabbings by his own hand, then she'd left him. She'd probably enjoyed the pain and his personal agony.

Sandeen backed out. There was one more closed door. He didn't want to know what other surprises were in store. One thing he knew for certain—Zanda hadn't planned on returning. She'd terminated her host.

He closed a fist around the last doorknob. It was probably made of crystal or some shit, but he didn't care. He wanted to leave this mansion far behind and forget about it, but right now he was a pawn in a game he no longer knew the rules for.

Pushing the door open, he didn't enter. A wave of metallic odor hit him as a pair of lifeless eyes stared at him. He inhaled, letting the stench of blood and death flow through him.

He didn't need to step inside to see the body. It was sprawled a few feet from the head. The body was encased in a robe that had once been white and pristine. Wings that must've been morphed in life had unfurled and pushed at the robe in death. The angel had followed that rule at least.

A male. What were the odds that this was Francois? That Zanda had hunted him down and killed him before Sandeen could extract an ounce of satisfaction from it?

But she'd be here to gloat.

Zanda wasn't this clever. She was setting him up. But why?

~

HARLOWE DESCENDED TO THE FARMHOUSE. She'd never looked forward to returning somewhere like she did here. It hadn't been apparent until the day she'd talked to her dad, the heavy steps she always took to the door of the home she'd grown up in.

Since they'd made minor repairs to the plumbing—neither of them could do a thing about the water pressure—and flipped the electricity on, she'd liked staying here. It was private and she could come and go as she pleased.

While she'd love to see what the town was like, she'd have to wait to procure a car. She didn't think Sandeen would try to go anywhere, but that'd make it seem like they were staying.

Inside the house, the silence was too familiar. "Sandeen?"

Where could he have gone— Of course. The Gloom. But why?

Did this mean he'd been sneaking back and forth while she'd been gone? Was he going somewhere else?

Her eyes narrowed as she recalled the day she'd returned and thought he was gone, only to find him in the bedroom. She should've known. She should've realized. He hadn't meditated and come to a peaceful conclusion about his mother. He had more honor than he wanted to admit. Which meant he wouldn't be satisfied hiding. He wouldn't be content with getting on with life while his mother's mate lived the free life Sandeen wanted.

And that mate was missing.

"Shit." She stomped outside, grabbing her phone from her pocket. She'd have to notify her team. First, she'd make sure Sandeen wasn't taking a nature walk. He wasn't a nature-walk type of male, but she wanted to have faith in him. She wanted to think he wouldn't throw her under the bus, let her flounder while he ran off and harmed an angel she'd pointed him toward.

A crow cawed in the distance and another crow answered. She tuned them out and roamed around the house.

She peeked into the little attached garage. Dust particles floated through the streams of sunlight that filtered through the gritty windows. No footprints other than the ones she and Sandeen had made looking for tools.

As she walked around the back door, searching the hill that led to the little pond, a crow cawed again. Certain Sandeen wasn't around, she took the stairs to the front door. One more check inside to make sure that he hadn't returned before she reported him.

Why hadn't he talked to her? Was he afraid that she wouldn't understand?

The thought that demons lived in fear was foreign to her. But she didn't need to empathize with demons, she just needed to understand the one. She needed him to understand himself.

Perhaps that was what he'd been trying to prove to her all along. She was looking for the good in him, rooting for it, and he'd repeatedly told her he had no wish to embrace his angelic half. The thought of an angelic mother and what he'd lost drove him. He could've had a life like Sierra; instead, he'd gotten a life in hell.

She opened the door and almost went inside but a cacophony in the trees broke through her thoughts. Crows were cawing at each other like they were having a lovers' quarrel.

The crows from the cabin. They'd warned Sandeen about her.

She palmed her dagger as a whoosh in the air made her spin.

A hard thump hit her shoulder a second before searing pain exploded through her body. A pale-oak-colored arrow stuck out from her torso. She grimaced and snapped the end off, wrenching the portion that was wedged in her muscle and bone.

Another whoosh. She tried to stumble backward into the house, but the second arrow hit her thigh.

Her heel caught on the threshold and she pitched backward. The wrench on her leg made her thigh scream, but she twisted and rolled inside far enough to kick the door shut with her good foot.

"Fuck, fuck, fuck." She swiveled on her ass to the side of the door. She took the shaft of the arrow in both hands and snapped most of the length off. Then using the wall, she pressed her back against it, needing the leverage to get on her feet.

Her shoulder screamed and her thigh protested nearly as much now that she was on her feet.

How many were out there?

She flipped the dagger in her hand to a slash-and-stab position, grateful she hadn't dropped the phone from her other hand. Only her breath could be heard as she hit the emergency number Sierra had programmed into all of their phones.

"Ambush at the farmhouse." She didn't have time to tuck the phone back into her pocket. It clattered to the floor as the window to her left shattered. A slim figure dove inside.

The small female spun and drew a matte-black gun. Camo paint covered her face, matching the faded fatigues she wore.

Harlowe paused long enough to register that the woman was possessed before she launched her dagger. The woman didn't have time to react and the hilt of the knife hit her arm. A nonlethal blow that did what it was supposed to. Gunfire blasted through the cabin and wood splinters exploded from the wall next to Harlowe, but the shot had gone wide.

Harlowe pushed off the wall to tackle the human. If she could get the demon into the Mist, she could bury another knife in its neck and dissolve it with angel fire. Then go to Numen and recover.

The door slammed open behind her. Harlowe tried to put on a burst of speed to tackle the human and leave the realm, but her leg hindered her. A heavy form hit her from behind. Before she hit the floor, sour droplets spattered her face.

The Gloom.

Claws impaled the backs of her legs, but she twisted, reaching for the vial of angel fire in her belt. Her fingers grazed the cool crystal just as something heavy slammed into her head. The world went dark.

Blinding pain yanked Harlowe out of unconsciousness.

"This is the one my spawn has formed an attachment to?" a deep voice rasped.

She slitted her eyes ever so slightly. She ached like she'd been stuck through and roasted on a spit, and she smelled like she was bathing in spoiled milk.

"The very one." Zanda.

"Yes, she'll do nicely."

Cold fear pierced Harlowe worse than the arrows had. The voice was deeper than Sandeen's, more garbled. His sire. Zadren. Big Z. And the bitch demon. Had she staked out the house, just waiting for Harlowe?

They'd thought they were safe. Harlowe's team had known where the farmhouse was but had never been there. Sandeen's sire was the only other one. And they'd thought he was done with the place. Until Zanda.

Harlowe had walked right into a trap. She should've listened to the crows.

"Yes." A sharp foot kicked into the small of her back but

she remained limp. "Her hips are nicely flared. She should bear my young well."

She held back the choking sound in her throat. No fucking way. She was in the Gloom. If she could get on her feet, maybe even roll away, she could get back to her realm. Couldn't she? Sandeen had dragged her in and out the last time she'd been here.

She had to try something.

She took stock of herself. Her shoulder throbbed to the rapid beat of her heart. Her thigh felt like it was three times its normal size. Both arrow tips were likely still in her. She could also assume that the rest of her weapons had been stripped from her.

She should get back the vial of angel fire, but since it was just her, she had to get to safety. She couldn't fill out a damn report about a missing vial of angel fire if she was dead.

And she'd die long before that demon would touch her with anything phallic.

"Stake her down," Big Z growled.

Harlowe flared her eyes wide, ignoring the burn of the Gloom. A craggy demon towered over her on one side, Zanda on the other. Harlowe kicked her bad leg out, her lips pulling back from the agony. The demon fell, but Zanda's foot slammed into her head. She wasn't knocked unconscious, but her vision blurred. She was too slow to avoid another blow to her ribs.

Her dizzy gaze landed on a hulking demon nearly seven feet tall. He was nude, with a giant cock-like object hardening between his legs.

His bloodred lips were pulled back in a sneer as his lewd yellow gaze drank her in.

"Yes," he said. "This should prove fun."

~

SANDEEN'S THOUGHTS churned as he wandered out of the
Gloom and into the farmhouse's bedroom. That demoness
was trying to screw him over. He might've been doing the
same thing, but he wasn't planning to hurt anyone—other
than his mother's mate. But Zanda . . .

A crow's caw sounded closer than expected. He popped
his head up and charged through the house. The crow had
sounded closer because the front door was hanging off its
hinges and one of the living room windows was nothing
but a pile of glass.

Fresh blood was smeared along the wall by the door
until the drips suddenly stopped, as if the source of those
blood droplets had suddenly vanished. A gunshot had left a
hole in the wall by the door, and more blood spots had
dried on the hardwood. The drape over the couch had
caught the worst of the splatter.

He stepped onto the porch, scanning his
surroundings. Nothing but green trees and green grass
greeted him. A crow was perched on the branch of a
cottonwood. It stretched its wings as if to tell him there
was nothing to see out there, but that there had been
quite a show inside.

This was what Zanda had been after. She'd duped him.
Not only that, since he hadn't thought Zanda was capable
of such cunning, he'd left Harlowe vulnerable to attack.
Some of that blood had to be hers.

The human attackers that had been hosts had fled.
Where was Harlowe? Had she gotten Zanda to the Mist
and killed her? Had there been more than one intruder?
How had Zanda known about this place?

So many fucking questions and no damn answers.

In the house, he found Harlowe's phone behind the

door. The screen was shattered, but it blinked on when he pushed the button. Missed calls from Bronx and Urban.

Shit. He tried to envision the fight. Had they been waiting for her? She might have been in the house. They'd have busted in. The door and the window supported that theory.

How the fuck had Zanda known about this place—

His sire.

Dread swept through him like a tsunami. Zanda had anticipated that Sandeen wouldn't deliver and she'd gone right to his sire. And Big Z wanted Harlowe, if only because Sandeen cared about her.

He threw his head back and roared. His hands fisted until he thought the phone might shatter, but he didn't care.

He was about to enter the Gloom and dismantle that damn realm drop by drop to find Harlowe when the phone rang. He could barely tap the answer button without punching a hole through the phone.

Sandeen could only growl. Bronx didn't wait for a greeting. "Where the fuck is she? We haven't been able to reach her since she called to report an attack."

Sandeen bared his fangs. "I just came from Vegas, where I was supposed to deal with the selfish mate that fed my mother to the underworld. He had already been slaughtered."

"Francois? He's dead?"

"Francois lost his damn head, yes. It was a setup, and when I got back to the farm, Harlowe was gone. I've got to find her—" He hissed.

A searing pain tore through his wrist. An odd mark appeared in a spot that had previously been unblemished. He didn't believe in coincidences. He'd been complacent about his heritage long enough. Before he stormed the

Gloom, he asked, "Is a mark suddenly appearing on my wrist some sort of angel bullshit I need to know about?" He wanted nothing in his way when he hunted for his warrior.

"No fucking way. A sync brand?"

"A what?" Sandeen squinted at it. The outline of a wing was clear. Why the hell would he spontaneously develop a tattoo of half a wing?

"A sync brand. We get them when we mate."

"I'm not mated." Stating the obvious didn't help him understand what was happening.

"Or we get them when we're in trouble, when we're close to death and need healing." Bronx's tone grew excited, hopeful. "Go."

"Where? To who?"

"Idiot. It has to be Harlowe and she's in a fuck ton of trouble." Worry curdled his blood until Bronx added, "The brand will help you find her. Usually the warrior transcends to their mate. But you can go to her. The brand will guide you. Bring her back to the safe house. *Go.*"

Sandeen threw the phone down and was in the Gloom before it hit the floor. The little brand's subtle throb grew stronger. Fuck. There went the hope that she'd jumped Zanda into the Mist.

He stalked through the realm, increasing his pace to a run, trusting Bronx's word. This brand, whatever it was, would help him find her. Sylphs skittered out of his way. He ran over a symaster that wasn't fast enough. Sandeen would mow down anything in his way. He uncapped the vial as he went, holding it as steadily as possible as he ran.

"Bitch!"

Sandeen recognized his father's roar as the outline of the male's hulking form materialized. His sire was bent over, flanked by two other demons, Zanda and some archmaster Sandeen only knew as an annoying fuck. Downy gray feathers littered the ground.

Sandeen rushed his sire. He didn't have time to sneak up. With a snarl, Zadren spun, a claw-tipped wing flaring out. Sandeen ducked, nearly losing hold of the vial, but he managed to dump it as he barreled into his sire, shoving him away from the mess that must be Harlowe on the ground.

Sandeen leaped away as Zadren's howl pierced his eardrums. The male fell in a heap, writhing over the angel fire eating away at his leg.

"Master!" The archmaster staggered away from the thrashing heap at his feet toward the burning demon.

Zanda bared her fangs and lunged for Sandeen. He willed himself to ignore the bloodied mess on the ground and drew his dagger. He'd fought Zanda with his bare hands before, but he hadn't been trying to kill her.

Today, she would die.

He grabbed one of her wings and twisted. She stabbed her claw into him, but he braced himself against the pain and impaled the dagger in her chest. He gave it a twist as he yanked it out. She was out of reach before he could stab her again. The look she gave him was full of glee as she backed away to plan another assault. He'd known the wound wouldn't kill her, but it would slow her down. He had to fight as smart as he fought dirty.

"I always wanted to fight you to the death." They circled each other. "It brings me great pleasure to kill you now that I know you're one of them."

The words "I'm not one of them" didn't clamor on his tongue this time. The truth of this moment was that it was either Harlowe or Zanda. He launched at the demon.

Zanda grinned and twisted to impale him with a spike on her wing.

He knocked it out of the way and stabbed at her with the knife. She pounded at him with her fists and wings. The thorny tips shanked him repeatedly, but the blows affected him as much as biting gnats.

Adrenaline poured through his veins. He didn't relish beating her to death. But he didn't like the idea of death by a thousand cuts for him either.

The decision was taken from him. Harlowe surged to her feet behind Zanda. Blood streamed from every opening on her face. Her eyes were so swollen he couldn't believe she could see a thing.

He tossed her the knife. She snapped it out of the air. "Wanna see how *you* like being held down?"

That was what he thought she said anyway. Her words were garbled, like she was chewing on her own teeth. With a roar, she barreled into Zanda.

They were too close for him to jump in and be of any help. He was helpless to stand and watch. Harlowe favored her left side. Broken ribs. Maybe a broken arm. But she continued to fight. All he could do was make sure no one tried to hurt Harlowe.

His sire was gone. The archmaster must've dragged him to Daemon.

Harlowe managed to flip Zanda, pinning the demon's wings between them. She sliced the knife across the demon's throat. Using the same move Sandeen had when they'd fought in the Gloom before, she hugged her arms around Zanda's head and yanked. She continued pulling and twisting. Zanda flailed, but she didn't have Harlowe's rage to propel her.

A final scream ripped out of Harlowe as she twisted Zanda's head and used her knees to shove the body away. Rage gave her power, enough to rip Zanda's head off the rest of the way.

The demoness was dead.

Harlowe swayed. Sandeen jumped forward, catching his angel before she hit the ground. He eased her down the rest of the way to assess the damage.

She came up swinging. Her fist flailed and went wide. She tried thrashing with her wings, but they were crumpled at odd angles. She had fought with them and it must've been agony.

Sandeen caught her hand in the gentlest of grasps. Bones crunched under his skin. "Hey, it's me."

Blood leaked out of her mouth as she barked out a hoarse cry.

"Hey, hey," he murmured. "It's me. I'm getting you out of here."

She sagged but coughed more blood up. Her shirt was ripped open, one breast exposed. Her pants were ripped too and blood seeped through the material still attached to her body. Blood dripped onto the ground, staining the lowest droplets of mist red.

So much blood.

He had to get her somewhere before she bled out. They were immortal, but they weren't indestructible.

"M-my mate," she gasped, trying to roll to her side like she was going to rise, but her arms gave out and her face hit the dirt. "Coming."

The brand.

"That's me, angel." He didn't know where to touch her. There wasn't a place on her that wasn't bloody. The smooth skin on her face was hash. Blood leaked from her nose, from her eyes. From her mouth. She'd fought, and she'd been ready to fight to the death.

"No, no," she sighed out the words. "Need healing."

"How do I heal you?"

"M-mate heals." She slumped on her side, her head on the ground.

"I've got the brand thing."

She managed enough of an expression to frown.

He lifted his wrist for her to see. "It's how I found you."

Her eyes rolled back and she went slack.

"Harlowe." He nudged her ribs and she jerked. "Tell me what we need to do."

"Wings," she mumbled.

He couldn't waste more time. Other demons would find them. "I have to lift you. It's going to hurt."

He did so as nimbly as possible, but she cried out, the sound piercing his heart. He didn't want to hurt her, but he had to get her to safety.

Cradling her broken body to him, he walked through the Gloom until he sensed the safe house. Bronx and Urban were waiting for him, holding their arms out to take Harlowe.

As if he'd give her up. "Tell me what to do."

Bronx and Urban stepped back in unison.

"Lay her down," Bronx ordered.

She moaned when Sandeen laid her on the tile floor. He'd rather put her somewhere soft, but he didn't want her to suffer any longer.

"Cover her with your wings."

Sandeen didn't take his eyes off her as he did as he was ordered. "Now what?"

"I dunno," Bronx replied. "Just, like, think healing thoughts." Sandeen glared at him and Bronx shrugged. "It's not like I've done it. I haven't even seen it done. It's just what they say happens."

The nebulous "they" should've been more specific.

Sandeen rested his forehead on hers and willed her to heal. For the first time since he'd learned about his mother, he wished he was more in tune with his angel half. He wished he knew that side well enough to save this female.

He refused to let her down because he hadn't embraced that part of him. This once, he wouldn't be selfish. She wouldn't suffer any more because of him.

Warmth infused his body, flooding out to his wings. Something had to be working but he couldn't tell under all the blood. He just had to stay still and think about how much this angel had come to mean to him, and what he was going to do about it.

CHAPTER 21

Harlowe peeled her eyes open. The room came into view. It was the plain bedroom at the safe house. White walls. Taupe accordion blinds covering the windows. An end table with nothing but a lamp. Her body ached like she'd been run over by a semi and the semi had stopped and backed up to do it again.

Memories of the attack washed over her. She sat up with a gasp and shoved away the soft, dark wing that covered her. She palpated the shoulder the first arrow had gone in. Smooth skin.

She was naked.

Had Zadren . . . She closed her eyes and tried to remember everything. The fighting. The flailing. She'd released her wings and fought with them. The agony. Blows to her skull and kicks to her gut. She'd endured a lot, but not Zadren forcing himself on her.

She shuddered and her gaze landed on hooded blue eyes. Sandeen watched her, gauging her reaction.

She was naked, in bed with him, and he'd been covering

her with his wings. Her gaze drifted over the dark wing lying across her lap. The feathers along the edge of her wings mingled with his.

She was in the human realm with her wings loose. She should panic, but she'd been through a lot. So no panic. Just assessment. And acceptance.

An important question tugged at the edge of her mind. How had she gotten from there to here? Sandeen had rushed in to save her, but with her injuries, she should've been stuck in a healing coma, one she might never have come out of, her body too broken and battered to ever heal.

She twined her fingers together, trying to remember. As she twisted one hand, a shadowed symbol caught her eye.

A sync brand.

And Sandeen had found her.

The magnitude of what that meant loomed bigger than all three realms put together. The connection shorted her brain. So she wouldn't think about it.

She trailed her hand over the place where their feathers pressed against each other. The brand on her wrist showed, but she didn't look at it. She looked at the wings.

"I woke up like this once before. In the motel." But she hadn't been naked. At some point, she'd been run through the shower. Her hair had been loosened from its standard braid and brushed out. More logistics she refused to think about. So she'd think about how good this male made her feel. How safe she felt with him. How much she really needed both right now. "I want to finish what I was doing then."

"Harlowe, are you—"

She rolled and laid a finger across his full lips,

stretching out the rest of the way next to him. His beard tickled the palm of her hand and she abandoned his lips to stroke the fine hairs. How could a burly guy like him have such a soft beard?

She lifted herself onto her other elbow and dropped a kiss to a defined pec. His muscle twitched under her lips.

"Harlowe."

"I like it when you call me Lowe. Or angel. Even warrior." She was Harlowe to everyone else. It was who she was. But this half demon made her feel special.

"I don't want you to have regrets, angel."

"I regretted not being able to finish exploring your body."

His brows lifted. She'd spoken the truth. She could tell herself all sorts of lies. Like she'd wished she'd never done it. Or that she hadn't been upset when Zanda had burst in.

Zanda wouldn't be bothering them again. And Harlowe could admit that she had liked kissing him, and she'd been pissed to have been interrupted.

She swung her leg over his waist and straddled him. The wing that had draped over her fell away, tickling along her back as it did. She arranged hers behind her along his legs. Did he like how her feathers felt stroking his skin?

The blown pupils and the heat radiating from his eyes said he liked something. It could be the way his thick erection was wedged between them. A few swings of her hips to coat him with the wetness waking up naked with him had caused and she could have him inside. But she wanted to wait.

It was time to explore.

Splaying her hands across his chest, she let herself roam. Hard muscles under searing-hot skin. Dips and planes she bent to explore with her tongue. His breaths came in rough, hard draws, and the coiled power under her was intoxicating.

"You're a beautiful male." She rocked her hips ever so slightly. She felt every inch of his length under her, quivering as if it were only staying still on his command. As if he'd threatened dire consequences if his cock interrupted her lazy perusal.

Her hair was loose, her scalp blissfully tension-free. Maybe it wouldn't hurt to loosen up her braid a little. The way her silken strands brushed along her back, over her shoulder, made her feel . . . free.

All her bindings and restrictions were gone. They waited outside the door of this bedroom. Within these four walls, it was just him and her.

He placed his hand on her thigh. "I wanted to see you like this."

She didn't have to ask what he saw. He was seeing her as she was seeing herself. Unbound. Unconstrained. Her wings were out. She liked her wings. She loved flying. She'd love to fly with him, but fantasizing about that would invite responsibilities and obligations to impede on her time with him.

She blocked all things that weren't them, that weren't about finding pleasure with this male, and about the ecstasy she knew he could give her.

A low moan left her as she ran her fingers over his abs and down to where she sat on him. Her head tipped back and she swiveled her hips. Should she use her fingers on herself? Or on him?

"Angel," he rumbled. "Get on your back."

She opened her eyes to find the hungriest male she'd ever seen. The tips of his fangs peeked out from a snarl, and he looked ready to tear into her in all the best ways.

She'd wanted to explore, and she had, but the promise

in his ocean-blue eyes told her that she'd like what he had in mind better.

The change in position took seconds. As soon as she shifted to the side, he had her flipped and was between her legs. Her knees were spread wide and pushed to her chest a moment before his tongue licked through her slit and settled on her clit in a punishing rhythm.

She barked out a cry that was smothered by his hand.

Right. It was just them within these four walls, but they might not be alone in the house. She didn't need her team to burst through the door this time.

He lapped, he circled, he licked down to attack her opening, then up to tongue the tight bud begging for release. Tears leaked from the corners of her eyes as she tried to stay quiet. Her body was strung tighter than a bowstring, and when she shattered, she shook her head to keep from biting him.

Her throat was raw from holding back her cries. She gasped and released his head from between her knees.

He reared up and growled low, just for her ears. "That, angel, was the most beautiful thing I've ever seen." His cock jutted out, pulsing, the tip proudly glistening. "You want to ride me, don't you?"

Her gaze dipped to his erection and she nodded.

How he avoided the tangle of wings and feathers as he flipped her around again, this time on top of him, she didn't know. He was adept at fighting. Brutal, ruthless, and efficient. Perhaps he was finally using his skills the way he really wanted.

He settled her on top of him. "I knew it. Your wings are beautiful. A soft gray, like a thunderstorm fading against the sun."

She brushed a hand along his cheek before she sank down onto his thick length, loving the way his crown penetrated her and how her walls clamped around him. All the way down, she sank until he was buried deep inside of her. Until she didn't know where she ended and he began.

Until he bucked his hips up. Then she felt every inch of him. The long slide out and him slamming back in. She braced herself on his stomach and let him take over. This had started as her journey, but he had taken over, and she reveled in it. She didn't have to think, just feel. She didn't have to worry.

"I'm safe with you," she murmured, hitching her hips and using some of her own muscles to ride him, liking that he didn't fight her when she wanted to take over. They worked in sync. They weren't officially mated, but he was hers and she was his and that was all she wanted to dwell on.

"I would've torn everyone and everything apart to get to you, Lowe." His voice was gritty, rough, just like his fingertips at her waist.

"You did."

She rode him faster, but the effort was only half hers.

"Sandeen." She dragged her hand over his face, stroked his lips with her thumb, raked her fingers down his chest. Pressure built inside of her, coiling tighter as she slammed down onto him over and over, trying to find release.

He surged upward, his hips jacking up. The change in angle propelled her over the edge, but Sandeen was there for her. He wrapped an arm around her waist, his wings around them, and captured her cries with his mouth.

She shook apart in his arms, clutching him to her, her hands buried in his downy wings.

He stiffened under her, his arms locked around her. He pulsed inside of her and heat spread through her. His lips worked against hers, like he was struggling to keep from roaring and drawing the attention of the entire neighborhood.

She peppered kisses along his forehead and brushed her lips across the bend of one horn. His hair tickled her lips as she touched another kiss to his scalp. "Demon," she whispered. "I don't want you to let me go."

SANDEEN LAY on his back in bed. His angel rested in his arms. They were still nude. Her spring-storm scent surrounded him. They'd had a couple more rounds of not-so-quiet sex before she'd collapsed in his embrace.

She'd been exhausted. He hadn't slept a wink.

His body vibrated with the rightness of being with her. The brand on his wrist tingled and it hadn't escaped his notice that she hadn't mentioned it. She'd been branded and he'd been the one to show up. Therefore, they were mates.

He couldn't blame her. He had some of the same questions that she was probably stuck on.

What now?

How would they live?

What would she tell her family and friends? *Yeah, I was in this ferocious battle and my brand appeared and it was this guy—that you've never met or heard of.*

He couldn't go to her world. He didn't want to. It wasn't that he thought his demon side would bring trouble to Numen. Numen did that itself. It was that he had enough trouble between Daemon and Earth that he didn't need to add another realm to his issues. But Numen was her home.

It wasn't like they could live on Earth problem-free. She was an honorable warrior, and trying to do her job and stay on the right side of her people wasn't compatible with mating him and living in hiding.

Bronx had said he and Harlowe wouldn't be fully bonded until they went through a mating ceremony. Sandeen doubted anyone qualified to do that would be willing.

And yet, those weren't the only issues.

Gerzon wasn't his problem for a while. The demon would be pissed Zanda had been eradicated. He'd need to replace her and it wouldn't be too hard to find another ambitious demon that thought with more than the primal parts of its brain. But whatever his plan had been, it had been disrupted and it'd take him some time to regroup.

Zadren. His sire.

That male was a problem.

It was possible that the male would lie low, nursing his angel fire wounds in the mines where most of the realm were afraid to go. It was more likely that once he recovered enough for vengeance, he'd start hunting Sandeen. No, he'd hunt what mattered most to Sandeen. If he couldn't reach Harlowe, he'd go after her team, or even Alma. He'd find the farmstead and burn it down.

His sire would live to make his life hell. Sandeen couldn't allow that.

Nor could he allow Harlowe to get involved. Before he could think about a future with her, he'd have to deal with his sire. Because one thing was certain: he wanted a future with his angel. He wanted it more than he wanted to be left alone by all the powers in his life. And if his sire had taught him one thing, it was to be ruthless in getting what he wanted.

Voices traveled up the stairs to the bedroom.

He frowned as Harlowe blinked her eyes open and sat up. A female voice drifted up the stairs, firm and demanding. He couldn't hear Bronx's response, but he sounded like he was arguing.

Harlowe morphed her wings. They folded and disappeared in a blink, leaving nothing but a smooth, shapely back. She was pushing her hair back as she scooted off the bed. "Do you know who's here?"

"No," he said as he rolled out of bed. He didn't add that he'd like to rip out the throat of whoever had disturbed his morning cuddling his angel.

The voices drew closer to the bottom of the stairs. Harlowe dove into a dresser drawer, pulling out a white oversized T-shirt and pajama bottoms.

Sandeen didn't have clothing, and this wasn't the bedroom he'd been sleeping in when he'd stayed here. But he wasn't worried. He stopped next to Harlowe and murmured, "Go on down. I'll take care of myself."

"Whoever it is shouldn't be coming up here."

His gaze drifted to the closed door. They shouldn't be, but from Bronx's "What the hell do you think you're doing?" their visitor planned to barge right in.

"Go," he said softly.

She tied her hair back on itself in a sloppy knot at the base of her neck. "Yeah. I'd better find out what's going on. I'll keep them from coming in."

He tipped his head toward the bathroom. He'd cleaned himself and Harlowe in there, and it still looked like a slaughterhouse. "I'll be in there."

She nodded and her gaze dropped to his wrist. She swallowed.

"We'll talk about this later, okay?" He didn't like the conflict raging in her violet eyes. He'd had time to ponder the subject. She hadn't. He pressed a kiss to her forehead. A sweet move that was startling, but natural nonetheless. "You have something more pressing to take care of."

The voices approached.

"Go." Sandeen slipped into the bathroom. While Harlowe figured out what was going on, he would start by wiping down the bloodbath in the tub. Then he had another messy task to take care of.

CHAPTER 22

Sandeen's wings concealed his statue-worthy ass as he closed the bathroom door. She stared at where he'd disappeared. He'd been his usual frustrating calm, but it was obvious he was planning something. She'd like to think it was her intuition telling her so, but it was just Sandeen. He was part demon. He was always planning something.

Intent had been buried deep in his blue eyes, but she'd seen it. She didn't have time to think about what it meant, because the unwanted visitor and Bronx had reached the top of the stairs.

Harlowe's life had imploded and any time she had to figure out what the hell to do had been snatched away by the nuisance outside the door.

She secured a hair band around her wrist to hide the brand and flung open the bedroom door, her unangelic thoughts streaming across her face. The brows of the female popped and her eyes widened. So she hadn't expected an angry warrior with bed head in her face.

Tosca Smith. What was an enforcer doing on Earth?

Tosca had morphed her wings but was wearing her usual work attire, which matched the warriors'. Harlowe hadn't heard about the enforcer coming to Earth. Apparently the female had leveled up in her interference.

Harlowe's patience snapped. "Can't a warrior get some healing rest after a big battle?" She propped a hand on her hip. She had been friendly with Tosca, but she was fine burning that bridge if it meant keeping her from learning about Sandeen. "What the hell are you doing here? Don't enforcers like to party when they're on Earth? You're not dressed for it." She cocked her head to the left. "The nearest mall is that way."

Tosca's pink lips flattened. Bronx didn't bother hiding his snort.

The other female was a few inches shorter than Harlowe. At least five inches shorter than Bronx. But she squared her shoulders and stared Harlowe in the eyes. "I'm here on official business."

"Your official business is—"

"In the realm." Tosca rolled her eyes. "Yada, yada, yada. Warriors like to use that excuse when they're hiding something. I have clearance to continue my investigation into this realm. I have permission to inspect all the safe houses associated with your team."

"It wouldn't be clearance granted by a certain senator who has a son we think might be trafficking angels? Tell Senator Colbert that she looks guilty as hell butting into our work."

Tosca's expression flickered. That was news to her. "Senator Colbert's son was found decapitated last night."

The air leaked out of Harlowe. Had Sandeen killed the male? She wouldn't begrudge him the act, but it'd add another crime to his list. Another act that made it impossible for them to be together.

"We're the ones who'll find his murderer," Bronx pointed out.

Tosca leveled a cool gaze on him. "Who said it happened outside of Numen?"

Chagrin flickered in Bronx's brown eyes. "Why else would you be here? You think we did it instead of bringing him to face justice like we've done with every other criminal."

Harlowe crossed her arms. "Like we've done with our own. So call us confused that, somehow, you think we're all hiding something."

"You are," Tosca said flatly. "Director Vale is using you as his own personal team of vigilantes and he's hiding his actions or, at the very least, the true motivations behind them. One of his team falls, and now, conveniently, all fallen are protected. His mate's sister is now a senator and his own personal point of contact. And he has the rest of you doing his bidding on Earth. Following orders that the senate knows nothing about."

"Those are a lot of ignorant accusations." Technically. Tosca didn't have proof. That didn't mean they were false, dammit. It was exactly how things were working under the director.

The enforcer's expression turned smug. "If you have nothing to hide, then why can't I have a look around?"

The muscles in Bronx's jaws flared. They had so much to hide.

Harlowe twisted and shoved the bedroom door open. The light in the bathroom was off and Harlowe didn't sense movement. Had Sandeen heard that they were entering the room? "Go ahead," she said louder than necessary.

Tosca strode in, her gaze narrowed as she inspected

each corner. She squatted and looked under the bed. When she rose, her gaze roamed over the messy sheets.

Harlowe forced herself not to fidget. She'd been so very naughty in here. All night long. If Tosca thought Director Vale was hiding something, she'd be stupefied over Harlowe's secret.

Tosca's gaze hardened as she glanced back and forth between Harlowe and Bronx.

Bronx glared right back, but when Tosca turned toward the door, he shot an amused glance at Harlowe.

Harlowe gave a slight shake of her head. Not funny. It was convenient that Tosca thought she was messing around with Bronx, but Tosca had turned her attention to the closed bathroom door.

The enforcer marched to the door.

Sandeen could disappear into the Gloom, but nothing but pain and death awaited him anywhere his sire could reach him. She'd seen what happened.

Tosca flung open the door of the bathroom and flipped on the light.

Bronx tensed, then relaxed. Sandeen wasn't there. Harlowe's heart twisted. He'd chosen physical danger to himself over explaining why he had wings and horns and fangs—all on Earth—to Tosca. He'd done that for Harlowe.

Not only that, he'd cleaned a fair portion of the blood.

"What the hell happened?" Tosca asked as she evaluated the pile of bloody towels in the corner.

"Like I said, I was in a fight. Three demons." And she'd been losing terribly. Until Sandeen had arrived. "I've been healing since I returned."

"What demons?"

"Would you know them by name, enforcer?" The animosity between warriors and enforcers was serving her well right now. She didn't have anything against Tosca. No doubt the female thought she was doing the right thing, but she was too naïve to know that the senator who'd tasked her with this job was taking advantage of her.

That wasn't Harlowe's problem right now. She wanted Sandeen to come back to the realm. She wanted him safe. She wanted him with her.

She wanted him.

That was her answer about their sync bond. Her kind could reject a mate. No harm, no foul. Just hurt feelings and a heavy dose of resentment. But she didn't want to. Being with Sandeen felt right. She didn't care that he'd been born in Daemon, raised by a nasty sire, and done awful things. He'd had his reasons. He'd tried to fight against that side of him when he'd had no support or encouragement to do so.

He was a good male. And without him, they wouldn't have been able to save Sierra. They wouldn't have learned about what had been happening under their nose for a century. Harlowe wouldn't have learned that she had a sister, or what had really happened to her mother. Sandeen had contributed more to her kind than a lot of other angels. That wasn't nothing. Not at all.

"This blood from your fight?" Tosca asked. Her nose twitched from the metallic tang in the air. Harlowe detected the hint of pine and cedar underneath, but Tosca wouldn't know what that was from, or who it was from.

The enforcer continued wandering through the bathroom, inspecting the walls, the floors, and the heap of towels and washcloths in a corner. Sandeen had cleaned the worst. He'd done enough that it looked like Harlowe had showered while trying to heal, had attempted to clean the mess, said fuck it, and gone to sleep for a while instead. The mess looked like what one injured person would generate.

Not an angel who'd been close to death from complete blood loss in addition to a half angel who'd been covered in the gore of a couple of demons along with his own blood.

Bronx must've taken care of the mess from when Sandeen had first brought her to the safe house. She faintly recalled being on the kitchen floor.

Tosca's lips drew tight. "I know you guys are hiding something."

Bronx scoffed. "You should be saying that to the senator you work for."

"I work for all the senators."

"You sure?" Bronx smacked his lips. "You might want to double-check that."

Harlowe turned away as the two bickered. She needed to eat. A day of healing and sex had made her ravenous, but more importantly, the task of finding some food would distract her from wondering if Sandeen was okay and when he'd be back.

"I don't need to. Just like I don't need to double-check the security camera at Francois Colbert's place."

Dread crawled up Harlowe's back and she spun to face Tosca.

The female's expression wasn't a gotcha one. It was grim. "But I do have questions about the male with wings like an angel and horns like a demon who was walking around the place after Francois Colbert was killed."

Sandeen didn't have a stitch of clothing on as he ripped through Daemon. Symasters and archmasters alike cowered behind rocks and outcroppings. Word of how he'd saved an angel, injured his sire, and killed Zanda had spread. They figured he was here for his sire and they didn't want to get mowed down in the process.

He swept past his place, his feet crunching over the rock.

He didn't miss going barefoot. He enjoyed having a barrier between his skin and whatever soft, disgusting thing he stepped in. But that didn't matter today.

Today, he was facing his sire.

He strode through the realm to a place where more skeletons lined the path. A sulfuric haze filled the air. He continued deeper into the realm. To the mines. The angel-fire fountain was in the middle of Numen; the mines were the center of Daemon. In Numen, the senate controlled the angel fire. His sire controlled this section, Gerzon another. The mines equaled power, but not many demons planned ahead as to how they were actually going to refine the metal into a usable source. It took massive amounts of self-discipline to sling a hammer over a blazing fire when they could find a host to possess and enjoy a vacation in Cancun or the Maldives instead.

With the promise of angel fire, powerful archmasters like his sire and Gerzon could force an army to both mine ore and refine weapons. A promise that never came to fruition.

And angels claimed demons were dishonest.

He approached a cave. This place. He'd promised himself he'd never return to this house of pain. Big Z had turned this hill into his own hub of power. He lived in one of the connecting caves, kept prisoners in adjoining caves for his pleasure, and used the larger center circle to conduct his business—fighting, feeding, and fornicating.

Following Big Z gave the less powerful demons something to do. They weren't massing together to take on larger demons, and they weren't being recruited—or hounded—by other demons like Zadren. Fighting and the stench of blood, adrenaline, and death whipped the lesser demons into a frenzy. Entertainment and culling in one shot.

Sandeen had moved away as soon as he'd gotten old enough to fight his way beyond this part of the realm.

Three wide, burly demons blocked the entrance to the cave. Blunt horns dotted their heads and their wings were as small as a pixie's, if pixies had been real. The trio were related somehow, but Sandeen didn't want to guess at how their bloodline crisscrossed.

"Move," he growled. He wasn't worried about losing against the three. He didn't fear them ganging up on him. He just hated to waste the fucking time.

The middle one shook her head. He doubted they spoke. For as long as he remembered, the three had kept demons in or out, depending on what his sire's orders were. He'd fought them when he'd left that last time, but he hadn't killed them. His idealistic self had thought it might earn him respect.

"I can either fight you all. Or you can see if your boss is still up to being king of the hill." Not even his sire could've snuck back unnoticed with his injuries. The uncommon loyalty these three had shown toward Zadren would fight against their natural instinct to let only the strong survive. They couldn't protect their master after Sandeen had just called him out. It was the only form of honor in the underworld, to be able to defend one's self.

The demon on the left bumped the arm of the one in the middle. They both waited until the one on the right did the same thing. The middle one hesitated, then stepped aside.

"Make him suffer," she grumbled as he swept past them.

Light from sconces danced along the walls. The flames

burned without fuel. If they could do this, could they achieve something more complex—like plumbing?

His eyes adjusted to the darkness. Sylphs stuck to the shadows, their bodies shaking. They weren't allowed to leave. It was like having cattle roam around the yard. Whenever his sire wanted a burger, he gutted a sylph.

As long as they stayed out of Sandeen's way, he didn't care. Chains rattled as prisoners peered out the openings of their side caves. He didn't recognize any, and a few were unrecognizable. Zadren loved his cruelty.

"Zadren!" he roared and stood in the middle. "I challenge you."

The archmaster who had helped his sire escape the Gloom was nowhere to be seen. Sandeen had expected to fight through him, but it made sense that he was gone. Zadren had probably eaten him, caught the archmaster when he least expected it and ripped out a jugular. Easy, unsuspecting prey that provided energy to heal and a show of dominance. Zadren wasn't beyond fighting dirty. But if he ate one of his prisoners and floundered, that'd do his reputation more harm than good, and he'd find a passel of demons at the door ready to challenge him.

Murmurings came from all around him. The light flickered as if a wind blew through the dank caves.

Gravel scraped as his sire's voice cut through the dank air. "You think I'm weak and you can finally take me, whelp?"

"I think it's past time you die."

Zadren appeared in the opening. He tried not to make it look like he was leaning on the wall, but his shoulder was a little too close. His skin was freshly healed. Patches of gray and pink covered half his body. He hadn't been hit with the full vial of angel fire. It had been enough to rescue Harlowe, but Sandeen still wished it had killed the demon.

"Your angel tasted sweet. Just like your mother."

Sandeen's blood boiled. "You didn't get to taste my angel. She was too strong for you."

Snickers sounded from the caves. Zadren's head cut to the side. The sound died, but the presence of the prisoners swelled. They believed Sandeen.

"And as for my mother"—Sandeen flared his wings out as if to showcase how different his were from the rest of his kind—"you'll pay for what you did to her."

Zadren's grim smile was full of smug menace. "They said it couldn't be done. That our kinds couldn't mate. You're a disappointment but . . . I broke each and every one of those angels and it was *divine*. I'm going to have your angel—and you'll have to watch."

Sandeen rushed his sire. This wasn't about pride. He'd come here to do one thing—and if fighting dirty like his sire had taught him was the only way to win, he could live with the cosmic irony of it.

Zadren wasn't caught off guard the way Sandeen would've preferred. He doubled over, made his spikey wings into a dome, and aimed his horns at Sandeen.

Sandeen barreled into him, using his horns to ram his sire's. Pain blasted through his skull, but if he felt it, so did Zadren.

The male snarled, but Sandeen took advantage of his momentum. They tumbled backward. Sandeen flung himself away before Zadren could stab him with his claws. Searing pain exploded through his torso.

His father was brandishing a fucking dagger. The shady bastard probably had them hidden all over. Sandeen had spent too much of his energy ducking and weaving. As he moved and spun, he kept an eye out for more hidden weapons.

Zadren lashed out with his blade, but Sandeen caught

his father's wrist and twisted. The male roared but didn't drop the weapon. He whipped a wing out. The talon swiped across Sandeen's cheek. He stumbled back. Zadren dove in and buried the knife to the hilt in Sandeen's gut.

He cried out and went down, his sire not letting go. The male tried to rip the knife out, but Sandeen held it still. He was half propped on a large boulder his sire used as furniture. A pile of fresh bones was at the side, a femur piercing him in the side.

Fire raced through his belly. The stab had done maximum damage, and wrestling his sire for the blade still buried in his flesh wasn't helping.

Sandeen planted a hand on the cool rock to brace himself. He kneed, then headbutted his sire, but his strength dwindled. It was draining out of him with every drop of blood.

Instead of fighting his sire off, he changed tactics. He freed one hand from the fight for the knife and hugged his sire to him, buried his head in the crook of Zadren's neck, and sank his fangs in as far as they could go.

Zadren refused to give up trying to gut him with the dagger. His hands twisted at the hilt of the blade, his claws digging into Sandeen's abdomen. Sandeen released his first mouthful and bit down. Over and over. Until Zadren tried to pull away. Until his energy faded. Until he went limp and Sandeen pushed him away.

He couldn't rise. Too much time. Too much energy. He used what he had left to grip the slippery handle protruding from his gut and pulled.

Zadren tried to press on the flowing wound at his throat as he rolled to his back, his wings crumpled under him. "You think," he wheezed. "You think they will ever accept you?"

"I only need one to accept me."

Zadren flashed his bloodied fangs. One had loosened during their battle. "She will never forsake her people for you, Demon."

"Not a demon. Half angel."

Sandeen crawled on his hands and knees to his sire's head—and sawed it off.

CHAPTER 23

The warm grass under his feet was a welcome change from the stinging mist of the Gloom. Taking down Zadren, injured or not, had sent tides of fear through the realm. Sandeen had freed the prisoners and the sylphs, then made a deal with the three brutes guarding the mines.

Sandeen hadn't been the only one who remembered leaving them alive when he escaped. They agreed to continue to guard the mines. In return, Sandeen would bring them sweets. The demons had rarely left the realm and were unable to possess humans, thanks to the emotional link between the three of them. So they'd demanded pie and pastries. Sandeen had also promised a cooler full of unmelted chocolate if they recruited five other demons to secure the mine—and kill all those who tried to fuck with it. The mines weren't just power in the underworld, and Sandeen needed them.

He wove across the lawn, barely able to hold up his battered body. His gaze locked on Harlowe as her long body leaped from the top of the steps on the porch and raced for him. Why wasn't she at the safe house?

Behind her, Bronx stared, slack-jawed. Sandeen stumbled a few steps before his brain registered Bronx's presence. His plans for a happy reunion with his angel and a long shower faded. Harlowe was beside him now, her fingers tracing over his wounds as she murmured to him. The words were probably important, but he couldn't rip his gaze away from the door.

What the fuck was everyone else doing at his farmhouse?

The director followed a much shorter angel out. Sandeen hadn't seen her before. She was dressed like a warrior expecting a fight.

Sandeen might not have much of an issue with Bronx's presence, but the director and some stranger who stared at him like she clearly knew what he was? That changed things.

And his secret was officially out. What shitty timing.

"They know?" he rasped. His fangs still throbbed from ripping his sire's throat out and his tongue was swollen. Those issues were barely noticeable, since he was literally holding his entrails in.

"They know about you. About your mother." Harlowe feathered her fingers across his face, too tentative to touch anywhere else.

The words she didn't say echoed between them.

They didn't know about *her* mother. They didn't know about Sierra. The warriors would protect their own.

He wasn't a part of the team. He was her mate, yes, but this other female was here. The way the others kept their distance told him she wasn't part of their team, and she wasn't welcome. And that meant others had learned about him and were getting involved.

He'd barely survived Daemon politics. Coming out of the other side of Numen political machinations with his head still attached seemed far harder.

"How?" he managed to get out. He'd only wanted to come back, lie on his bed, then destroy his ruined mattress later, when he was recovered. Then he'd wanted to find Harlowe. He might've fantasized that she'd find him and he'd wake up beside her.

Instead, he'd been turned in.

"Security cameras at Francois's place."

His eyelids drifted shut. He summoned what little strength he had left to force them open. Stupid. He'd been foolish. Zanda had probably known the place was monitored. She'd made sure to leave the body lying around with the wings out, and she'd made sure he'd walked clear through the damn house, looking like he did.

The only sense of relief he felt was that Harlowe hadn't turned on him. But it passed quickly.

He was in deep shit. Aside from his injuries, Numen knew the truth about him. Did they know he and Harlowe were mates too? What would they do to her? To him?

The other angels approached behind Harlowe. The stranger scanned the place in front and behind her, caution igniting her gaze.

"He needs to hide his wings," the female said. "He can't be out here like this."

He didn't care about her fear. His wings were on display and he wasn't going to attempt a morph for anyone. He definitely wasn't going to attempt a morph until the bones in his wings mended. And he'd regenerated some blood. He'd be light-headed, but the fiery pain lacing his body kept him grounded.

"He needs to heal," Harlowe said testily. "So move the hell out of the way and let me get him to the house."

"But you can't—"

A low growl escaped his chest. He didn't want to deal with this drama. He wanted to hold his mate while his guts mended together.

Harlowe shot the female a quelling glare and urged him to walk. His legs trembled, but fuck if he was going to fall in front of everyone.

The tiny crowd parted for them.

He couldn't summon the energy to keep his wings from dragging on the ground. Harlowe supported him up the stairs to the house and led him inside. He winced at the mess he was leaving with each step.

This house was supposed to be his safe place, but he'd brought his filth here once again.

He was about to veer toward the bathroom but Harlowe steered him to the bed.

"You can clean up later. You need to heal."

There was no bending with his gut wound. He fell back onto the bed, his wings spread beneath him to avoid putting weight on the broken bones, his legs hanging off the side. "I'm going to ruin the bed."

"I wish that was the worst of our problems," she said softly and went to shut the door.

Sandeen kept his eyes closed as Harlowe spoke to the other female who'd followed them into the house. "He needs to heal."

"I can't entrust him to you. This is—"

"He's been entrusted to me for weeks. And he's been entrusted to me for . . . eternity."

He cracked an eye open. Harlowe was holding up her wrist. The director towered behind the short female. He didn't look surprised, but he shook his head anyway. So he'd been told, but seeing was believing. The other female, though . . .

Her mouth dropped open and her face paled. "Impossible."

"Apparently not." Harlowe slammed the bedroom door in their faces and locked it. As if a flimsy flip lock would keep any of them out, even the short one. "Okay, let's get to healing you."

"He won't come after you again."

She stopped at the foot of the bed. "Who?"

"Zadren. He's dead."

Her gaze dipped to his gut, and she crawled next to him, careful not to jostle the bed too much.

He put a hand to her back. "Don't."

"I need to heal you."

"Don't release your wings. Don't risk it."

"The door's shut. I'll be fine."

His little rule follower would go renegade for him. But she was in deep shit with him now that the secret of their mating was out beyond the rest of the team. "I'm not dead. I'm not dying." He was in bad shape, but he'd recovered from worse. He was away from the underworld. Never had to go back.

Sure, there was a lot to figure out. But he'd gotten what he wanted. He was here, with his angel. He'd mend. Things should only get better from here.

Harlowe pulled her shirt over her head.

"Lowe, no," he pleaded.

She stretched her neck as she released her wings. "I'm gonna go ahead and listen as well as you do." She leaned over him, draping her wings across his body.

He didn't deserve his angel. But he could spend the rest of his life trying to.

~

"We might need to terminate him," Senator Colbert announced. "You all do realize that?"

The senators assigned to handle the Sandeen situation were settled around Director Vale's office. Harlowe refused to entertain any of them at the farmhouse, and surprisingly, Tosca hadn't revealed the location. Senator Colbert had a frantic look in her eyes, and while she was dressed in a pristine white robe that reached to the floor, her hair was a touch wild and her gaze jerked everywhere. Was the female usually this shifty, or was the death of her son and the allegations lodged against her mate the cause?

Her mate, Jean Luc Colbert, had been taken into custody. The male had broken down after learning of the death of his son and had confessed that he'd known about Sandissa. Then he'd proclaimed his son's innocence when it'd come to the other angels and spouted a few details only the person who'd trafficked the angels could know.

Senator Colbert should've been removed from Sandeen's case entirely, but she'd blustered her way in. Senator Nassim was here as well. She was an avid supporter of Director Vale and his team, as well as an old family friend of Odessa's. Conflict of interest wasn't important to the senate unless it was convenient.

Harlowe had expected the rest of the senators to complain and throw their power around, but Felicia, also in the office, had said enough senators had a morbid fascination with the idea of a halfling to overrule those who'd wanted to pretend it wasn't possible and never would be. There were also plenty of older senators who'd shown no surprise. They'd been around long enough and had figured it was an eventuality.

There would be an official hearing, but Harlowe had been summoned. She'd nearly refused to leave Sandeen's side, but ignoring the director was different than ignoring several senators.

She yearned to be at the farmhouse, but Sandeen was in the sleeping phase of his recovery. It'd been two days since his belly had mended and she'd wrestled him into the shower. She'd changed the bedding as he'd sat under the spray and let the caked blood soften enough to scrub off and wash down the drain. She'd gotten him to drink broth, milk, and water, but for now, all she could do was wait and get a sense of how Sandeen's chances with her kind fared.

With *his* kind.

Now that she was here, among the senators who wanted to interview him—interrogate him—she still wasn't sure. Tosca was the only enforcer attending and it was likely because she knew about Sandeen already. The senate wanted to keep the news from spreading until they decided what to do with him. Felicia and Senator Nassim would be more likely to support Sandeen's existence. Senator Colbert had a lot of emotional baggage around her decision. Thus her "sudden" realization that Sandeen might need to be killed.

Harlowe stopped chewing on a fingernail long enough to say, "Anyone who tries to get to him has to go through me."

Senator Nassim lifted her chin. "He's still half angel. We can't hold him accountable for the circumstances of his birth, but we can for how he conducted himself afterward."

Senator Colbert sniffed. "He was born and raised in Daemon. Any spark of good would've been suffocated there."

Harlowe's patience snapped. "Just like all sparks of evil should've been suffocated in your son, and your mate, just because they were raised in Numen?"

The female's eyes watered. Perhaps in her fraught mind

she thought that if Sandeen turned out to be a horrible creature, her mate's and son's actions would be justified. She'd lost one and was desperate not to lose the other.

Harlowe hated to commiserate with her. She'd lived years hearing a different story about someone she'd loved. Only in her case, her mother's truth had been tragic. Honorable, but horrific. For Senator Colbert, she'd learned the ones she'd loved the most were the ones causing harm.

Her pain didn't give her cause to execute Sandeen.

Senator Colbert blinked back her tears. "Human corruption is a real threat for those who work so closely with them. It's why I don't trust warriors to handle this delicate situation."

Harlowe had heard that excuse before. Tosca's gaze flicked from the senator to the rest of the room. Did she believe it? Harlowe had wanted to like the female, respect her at the very least, but Tosca had endangered her mate. She'd been doing her job. But that wasn't good enough. Harlowe was so dedicated to Director Vale, even if he did some work off the books, because he strived to determine right and wrong beyond what they'd grown up being told. He didn't have the personality to get embroiled in senate politics. He was a male of action.

Senator Colbert raked her gaze over Harlowe. "I can't believe you think you could mate . . . that."

"You want to talk mates?" Harlowe glared at the female. Even Tosca raised her brows. The senator waffled between playing the victim and demanding vengeance with Sandeen as her target.

Senator Colbert hunched back into herself.

Harlowe rose. She'd learned what she needed to know. Sandeen would have some support. Only some. "I'll go see how he's doing."

"I think Tosca should go." Senator Colbert was down, but not out. "Someone the senate trusts."

"I trust Harlowe." Felicia bounced her leg. She was dressed like she used to before becoming a senator: workout shorts and a fitted athletic top in an obnoxiously bright color. "I trusted her with my life and my sister's. My mate trusted her to have his back."

"An enforcer should accompany—"

"If you keep pushing this, I will push back," Harlowe snapped. "And trust me, you won't like it."

The room went quiet. Threatening senators wasn't a good idea. They held her wings in their hands. Harlowe hadn't violated any laws, but the senate *made* those laws. Sandeen was a gray area, and if they decided against him, Harlowe could lose her wings too. Telling Senator Colbert that she would beat her scrawny ass if the senator didn't shut her mouth would only expedite things.

"Be cautious, warrior," the senator intoned. "You seem a little too attached to a male we find a threat."

They knew Sandeen couldn't morph his wings. They also knew he couldn't cross into the Mist on his own—like other demons. He couldn't get into Numen, but the Gloom and Daemon were open to him. The biggest threat to him, besides existing, was exactly what she had feared when he'd first roamed the realm on his own: he couldn't blend in.

SANDEEN GROANED AND ROLLED OVER. His angel was sitting on the side of the bed. She twisted to look over her shoulder.

"Hey, you're awake." She put her leg up on the bed to face him better. "How are you feeling?"

"Like I got gutted by my sire."

Concern was carved into her features and he sensed it wasn't just about his injuries. He was mended. Zadren and Zanda were gone. Gerzon was still an issue, but if it wasn't him, it'd be another demon. Wasn't there a human saying about the enemy you knew being better than the one you didn't?

"What's wrong, angel?" His voice was rough. He sat up, grabbed the glass of water on the side of the bed, and downed it in one swallow. A cup of broth was next to it. He'd rather have a nice slab of medium rare filet, but the lukewarm broth hit the spot for a minute.

"After you eat, we need to face the senate."

He had figured that was an eventuality. "All of them?"

Her braid slipped off her shoulder as she tilted her head. He'd often wished that she'd let down her hair more, mostly because he wanted to run his fingers through the silky strands. He hadn't gotten to touch such softness for much of his life. But his warrior *was* her morphed wings and braided hair and he wouldn't change her.

"There's a committee, if you want to call it that."

He scooted until his back was against the old wooden headboard. Kelly's dad had made it as a wedding gift for his wife. It was one reason why Sandeen had never cleared the house of furniture. "A firing squad, you mean."

Her gaze was solemn. "The senate allowed Senator Colbert on the committee."

"Interesting choice." A furrow formed between her brows. He leaned forward and brushed a thumb down it. "You're worried, angel."

"The committee will only advise the senate on their thoughts. The senate as a whole is supposed to make the decision, but there are always a couple of older senators that lead the rest."

Then it was hard to say whose hands his fate was in.

"I don't know what they're going to do to you, but I'm certain they won't be able to leave you alone."

He could take care of himself like he always had, but it was no longer about him. It was about them. This female was tied to him and she hadn't decided to be. At first, she'd called it her duty. Then she couldn't resist helping him. Then the mating bond. They weren't synced yet, but it wasn't like they could elope and tell the world to go fuck itself.

No, the senate wouldn't leave him alone. And that meant they wouldn't leave Harlowe alone either.

"Tell me the worst-case scenario and be honest." His voice was gruff. "What could happen to you?"

"Senator Colbert wants you dead. She hasn't made that a secret. She blames you for her mate being in jail and her son's death."

He didn't give a shit about that senator but the female might have more power than he realized. He knew nothing about her. But that wasn't what he was concerned about. "What about you?"

"What do you mean?"

"If the worst happens to me, what will you do?"

She frowned and the furrow was back. "Fight it." Exactly what he was worried about. "You don't deserve the worst. And I'm not the only one who thinks so. Bronx will speak for you. Urban too."

Aaaand now it wasn't only Harlowe he had to worry about. "What would the repercussions be for speaking for me? Worst case?"

He read it in her eyes. The warriors would lose their credibility and the trust of the realm if they championed him. Harlowe would fare worse. If she completed the mating, then what? Would she lose those wings she was so careful with?

"Hey," she said softly and scooted across the bed to him. "It'll be fine. This isn't Daemon. You have us."

The words left a melting pile of goo in his chest. He had people. Just like that. No deals struck. No bargains he didn't plan on holding up.

He couldn't speak. Conflict raged inside of him. He hadn't thought he was an honorable being. He'd been fine just not being as evil as his sire. Then he'd done a few good deeds and maybe he'd liked how it hadn't left him with the slick, oily sickness that being bad did.

So he was faced with the senate and whether he wanted them deciding his future. He was faced with fighting to be with Harlowe, or letting her go for her own good. He'd be hunted, but thanks to the Gloom, he could hide. If he stayed and let others decide his destiny, would he be any better off than when he was in Daemon?

He tugged Harlowe onto his lap. His thoughts were getting crowded out by her proximity. Blood was leaving his brain.

She straddled him, fully clothed. He wanted her nude, but he doubted they were alone. "Is the door locked?"

"Yes." She cupped his face, still too much worry in her eyes for his taste. The weight of the senate's decision was on her mind.

He wanted her to think of other things, and he had an ideal way to distract her.

He didn't go for her mouth, but wrapped his arms around her and pressed his lips to her neck. She shivered in his embrace. He increased the pressure, opening enough to lick his tongue out.

"Sandeen," she whispered and wriggled on his lap.

He scraped the tip of a fang against her skin, eliciting a low moan from her.

He slipped her shirt free of her waistband and brushed his hands up her torso. Losing himself in her soft curves, he massaged and squeezed and licked until she was writhing on his erection. The solid barrier of her clothing was between them, but this wasn't about his pleasure. It was about enjoying this moment, about not worrying about their future.

He flipped open the button on her pants and unzipped them far enough to slide his hand inside. Heat enveloped his hand. He used his other hand to lift her shirt high enough to bare her breasts. Burying his face in her round globes, he slicked a finger through her seam, coating the tip, and stopping on top of her swollen clit.

He didn't have to move his hand. Her breath hitched and she swiveled her hips. Rocking back and forth, she buried her nose in his hair. Her hands were at his face, around his neck, stroking him. She reached between them and gripped him.

"You don't have to—"

"Shh." Her hot breath washed over his horns.

The tight fist around his cock made him close his eyes. They were too close together for him to move much, but she did all the work. Her hips circled. Her arm pumped. He'd started this with her pleasure in mind, but now he had to switch to not coming before she did.

"God, angel." He tipped his head back. He had to see how beautiful she was. Once they left this room, this was it. Their relationship was no longer their own business. She wasn't like him. She couldn't be torn between two kinds. She wasn't half demon. She was all angel and she was supposed to be his. But maybe he hadn't earned her. Maybe the people of her senate would see that he wasn't enough. That his sire had been right. He could do nothing that would've made his mother proud.

"Demon," she whispered and gripped one horn as she blew apart against his hand.

He waited a moment, holding his own explosion back by sheer force of will as she bucked and bit her lip to keep from crying out.

Beautiful. All his.

Her phone buzzed in her back pocket. It was probably someone from her team, wondering if he was awake and when the hell he would face the senate. It was the only slap of reality that could yank him from this moment.

The way she trusted him with her body had cemented his decision.

He wasn't like her. He wasn't one of them. But he was himself and he could bargain.

CHAPTER 24

Harlowe stood rigid. She'd let her wings out and kept them flared. Her back was straight and her expression was nothing but business. Facing the mass of the senate, she couldn't afford to look less than confident.

They'll never accept me, angel, Sandeen had said as he'd pressed a kiss to her forehead. *But I have an idea. Trust me.* Then he'd stepped back and been gone.

Just like that.

Senator Thomas scrutinized her. "And he just left?"

"Yes."

This senator had centuries on Senator Colbert. And when Harlowe had ascended to Director Vale's office and told him Sandeen was gone for an unknown amount of time and an unknown reason, Senator Thomas had been the one to calm Senator Colbert down. The female had stormed into the senate demanding punishment for Harlowe, the director, and the entire team. Then she'd focused on Harlowe, ordering imprisonment.

Tosca hadn't jumped to arrest Harlowe. She had

deferred to Senator Thomas. Colbert's explosive reaction and orders for immediate punishment seemed to have bothered the enforcer.

Harlowe had gone willingly to give her team time to figure out what the hell to do now that they had no demon-angel hybrid to present to the senate and no way to go after him. The sync bond hadn't been completed, so Harlowe couldn't find him based on her own mate intuition. All she had to show for her time with him was the brand, and without him, it was nothing but a blemish.

Trust me.

He hadn't bargained. He hadn't made her a promise. He'd just asked her to trust him. She'd hung on to that as Tosca had taken her to a holding cell.

She'd sat in that cell for a full day before she'd been summoned for a hearing. Had she been in the same cell as Sierra? Harlowe's outlook was a lot better than her sister's, but it was possible that Harlowe might soon be seeking her sister for advice on how to be a fallen.

And Sierra would be there to help her. Her fear of that outcome no longer drove her as hard as it had. If Harlowe lost her wings, her sister and Boone would scour the earth to find out where she had been dumped. Because that was what family did.

What would happen to her father?

She hadn't spent her time in her cell terrified over what might happen to her or worrying about what Sandeen was up to. Well, maybe a little. No, she'd regretted not visiting her father more. Getting him to talk, to *really* talk. He was full of life but he didn't know how to live on his own. Was it all that different from her workaholic lifestyle? They'd each avoided the realities of their world.

Sandeen had had to kill his sire. So whether she fell or

not, she was going to find a way to reach hers, to make sure they didn't waste their time together.

"Tell us again why you think he left, but try to be more specific," Senator Nassim said. She'd been the calmest of the seven senators sent for Sandeen's interrogation.

"She could've stopped him," Senator Colbert sneered. "She already admitted to following him into the Gloom."

It would look bad for Harlowe to argue, but she'd already explained how that had happened and it was going to be hard to hide her irritated tone as she reviewed it a second time.

"She already explained why," Senator Nassim interjected, her tone even.

"I think he has a plan," Harlowe repeated again. She didn't know why he hadn't told her. Had he even known what his plan was when he'd left?

"His plan is one of destruction and death." Senator Colbert searched the rest of the senate. Some nodded their heads. "He's a demon. Plain and simple."

Harlowe shook her head so hard, her braid flung around. "He cares about me. Do you understand that? He *cares*. Daemon don't care. But he does. Because he's not solely a demon. And because of the conscience he carries, the same conscience he got from his mother, he cares. He asked what would happen to me. Would I be able to continue my work? Would my team? My work is important to me. He knows that. My team is important to me. He knows that too. He's coming up with a plan."

"If he cared, he'd be here," Senator Colbert spat.

Grumbles ran through the senate. One hundred angels sat in the ornate marble auditorium. In the middle, next to where she stood, was the slab of stone that Winger used when he carved wings from angels' backs.

"His chance at living our life was taken from him before

he was even born. Safety. Security. Support. He grew up in Daemon, yet despite that, he's been an ally." Most of the time. She'd use the director's tactics about what not to say to the senate. "He's compassionate. He's witty. He likes to cook."

Senator Colbert's mouth opened, but her brow furrowed and she snapped her mouth shut again. The cooking thing took them all by surprise.

"He's not a demon. He's so much more. And he shouldn't be. He should be a bitter, hardened bastard who hates our realm for acting as if his mother's disappearance was inconsequential. He should want retribution." She shrugged. "Actually, he never got it. He might've killed Francois had he gotten the chance. But in the end he didn't even kill his sire for revenge. He did it to keep me safe."

And he'd done the entire realm of Numen a service. But where the hell was he?

Murmurs rippled through the crowd. She scanned the senators in their pristine white robes. Her own father wasn't here. He couldn't be told about what was happening. There were a lot of angels in this auditorium, but the information would stay here.

She met Director Vale's gaze. His lips flattened. He wasn't getting a good vibe from the crowd.

The ancient senator spoke. "I appreciate what you say, warrior. I can hear the conviction in your voice. You believe the truth of what you say. You believe in him." He let out a breath and she heard the *but* coming. "But . . . he's a being who can continue to travel to Daemon. Who was raised by a monster. A male who's grown and developed, yes, but raised a demon all the same. His concern that we would find his appearance a risk we're unwilling to tolerate is valid. He is an issue. I think we're in agreement over that. What we need to decide is how we're going to handle him."

Felicia had mentioned that many members of the senate had worked together so long they knew what the others thought or would say without a physical vote. The older senators knew when their mindset outnumbered the others. Was this one of those times? Were there no others who could support her mate?

"Death," Senator Colbert suggested as if it was a foregone conclusion. "It's the only way."

Harlowe was shaking her head as Senator Nassim broke into the murmurings. "Perhaps removing his wings is an option."

Harlowe's stomach clenched. Not those gorgeous obsidian wings.

"And the horns?" Director Vale's amber eyes blazed. "You gonna carve off everything you don't like about the bloke and call it good? I feel like recent events have shown us that removing angels' wings doesn't do us a damn bit of good if we're going to ignore the bigger problem. And make no mistake, Sandeen is of Numen."

Senator Colbert yanked at the collar of her robe like she wanted to shred something, anything. "And by our standards, he should've had his wings removed already."

Senator Thomas shot Harlowe a sympathetic look. "Death or imprisonment are our only options, and I'm afraid he's already proved extremely intelligent. Imprisonment may lead to the trouble we're hoping to avoid."

Harlowe shot out of her seat. "He's not a rabid dog!"

The director also rose, speaking on top of her. "You can't kill a male just because it's easier."

The old senator put his wrinkled hands up to quiet the crowd. "We won't make this decision lightly."

"You kill him, you might as well take my wings too." The words left Harlowe's mouth without thought, but that made them no less true. "Not only would I quit, not only would you lose a trained warrior, but I'd shun the realm. My people aren't going to destroy my sync mate, the male I love." Stunned silence fell over the crowd. "You heard me. I love him and I don't give a shit about who his sire is or was, or how Sandeen was raised. You destroy him, I'm done with Numen. Take my wings and let me live on my own, away from here."

A CROW CAWED OVERHEAD. Soaring pines shifted above him in the wind, and the scent of soil surrounded him. All else was quiet, but Sandeen knew better. He wasn't alone.

"I didn't come to cause trouble."

"You'll have to excuse me," said a male voice from deep in the trees. Boone had found him. Since he was human, he must have cameras all over to know Sandeen had entered his property. "But when you're around, there's usually trouble."

"That probably won't change, but this time I'm running into it instead of away from it."

Boone's voice drew closer. "Is that why you're hiding?" he asked wryly.

The next person to speak wasn't him or Boone. "You've rejected your bond, then?" Sierra asked.

"News travels quickly."

"I don't need to sit and have tea and wait for the gossip to get juicy. All the messages I've been tapping into say that you abandoned Harlowe."

Shit. He'd had to go to Daemon before he'd come here and the trip had taken longer than he'd wanted. A lot of demons liked the idea of him being able to shuttle creature comforts between the realms.

"Have they taken it out on her?" That had been his biggest worry, but he needed to arrange a few things before he faced the senate.

"She spoke for you and the senate is deliberating her fate, as well as yours, as we speak. I honestly don't know what's going to happen."

He blew out a gusty breath. "I need to get back to her, but I also need a little help."

Sierra wandered out of the trees in faded camp pants and a shit-brown top. She wasn't known for her style. "I'm intrigued, but I can't reveal my own heritage. I have Arik to protect. The senate can't know about me until he's as big as you and as much of a pain in the ass to them. How do you think I'll be able to help you?"

"Actually, I need your father's help. How can I find him?"

Another day had passed while they deliberated Sandeen's fate. Her fate. She was back in the auditorium after a sleepless but determined night. Her mind hadn't changed.

Half the senators argued in her favor. The other half was more than happy to hang her out to dry. Even Winger had had a few choice words to say. "I've removed an innocent angel's wings before and I don't care to do it again."

Director Vale had blanched at that. The innocent angel had been him, and he'd been the recipient of a little known loophole. One that required a mate, and that was where Harlowe fell short. If she lost her wings and didn't have a mate to heal them back on in less than twenty-four hours, they'd be gone permanently.

She didn't know where Sandeen was and she hated to admit her trust was wavering. But she'd always been an angel of principle. Punishing him for deeds against their kind when he'd just been surviving as a demon was a low blow. And killing him was despicable.

Senator Thomas's brow crinkled. "I think we're ready."

An ominous boom sounded from outside the auditorium doors. Voices chattered, growing in volume.

Bronx's raised over the din. "Let him the fuck through."

The heavy doors squeaked open and a handsome man strode through.

That wasn't right. No humans were allowed.

The male wasn't just handsome. He was devastating and familiar.

"Sandeen?"

He glanced at her and winked as he strode through the crowd in an expensive suit. "The dog does tricks," he said to the old senator. His gaze hardened as it skipped over Senator Colbert. He didn't have to know who she was. The rage radiating from her was better than a label stuck to her robe that read *Hi, My Name Is* . . .

His beard had been trimmed, but that was the most minor change. His wings were gone. Morphed? His horns —also gone. And when he smiled, the white tips of his fangs were no longer there.

But aside from all that—

"How the hell are you here?" Director Vale asked her incredulous question for her.

Sandeen stopped beside her and snaked an arm around her waist, his pine-and-cedar scent surrounding her. "Here's the thing. I'm part angel and part demon, one who's been told his entire life he couldn't get into Numen. Thus I never tried getting into the realm before, nor have I had reason to. But I heard a story of a fallen who'd been able to cross to save the one he loved. So when I got my head out of my ass and realized that, like most angels, I want to be with my mate, well, hello." Out of the corner of his mouth, he whispered, "Ransom taught me how to ascend, among other things, you know, since he has experience with someone like me. Let's hope I can descend."

"Why?" What had happened to his horns? She ran her fingers through his hair and he winced. "*No.* You burned them off?" The loss of his horns made panic well in her gut. No. He needed them back. She needed to stroke them one last time. The thought of their smooth, warm texture echoed across the sensitive nerve endings of her lips.

His smile was bittersweet.

"The fangs too?" Tears gathered in her eyes. She ignored the senate and faced him. "Why?"

"Because they were going to be a hard limit for them." He nodded at the senators surrounding them. "I'm here to show them that I'll do whatever it takes to be with you."

Even if it meant making himself look more angel than demon. "I don't want you to have to do this."

"It's done, angel." He arched his back. "I didn't think I was going to nail the morph. I don't know how you can stand it. It's like stuffing my body into a fanny pack."

He'd done this so they could be together. She wouldn't let it go to waste. If he could blend, they could go anywhere on Earth. They could live on the run.

Senator Thomas was the only one unfazed, the other senators alternating between staring at him and muttering to each other. "I'm afraid your impressive display doesn't change anything. While it's clear you've managed the appearance problem, we still have concerns, especially now that it's confirmed you can enter the realm."

"I'm not surprised your minds aren't changed even though I've proved that I'm willing to work with your expectations." Sandeen's voice held a hint of a taunt.

He was up to something. She tried not to smile.

The ancient senator gave him a placating smile. "We have an entire realm to protect."

"And you're willing to do what it takes, right? Good. Then you'll understand that *I'm* willing to do what it takes."

"Are you making threats, demon?" Senator Colbert's eyes bugged.

Harlowe's lips peeled back. The way the female said *demon* sounded like Harlowe had not too long ago, but she'd changed. So much had changed. And she wished she could stuff that tone down the senator's throat until she gagged.

"Is telling the truth considered making threats?" Sandeen asked innocently. The old senator's brows dropped as Sandeen pinned his blue gaze on the other male. "There were a few benefits to being Zadren's son. I heard about the deals."

Harlowe peered up at her male. What was he talking about?

"I haven't told my own mate." He gave her an apologetic look before turning to Senator Thomas again. "Since I know what you do when you don't want a secret to get out. Like the one that will get out if you make any other decisions that don't include letting me stay on Earth with my warrior."

Whispers rippled through the crowd. How many knew what Sandeen was referring to? The director's brows had dropped; he was just as confused as she was.

Senator Colbert's gaze wasn't confused. It was shifty as she took in the other senators and swallowed. She was losing ground. What the hell was this secret?

"But in case you doubt my intention, you'll find all those personal inboxes you keep, be it computer or phone or what have you, have an example of the message that will be released if I'm not there to ensure it doesn't get sent."

A couple at the back of the auditorium took out their

phones. Senator Thomas glanced at them. One nodded, his face pale.

Sandeen grinned. "It's all there. At least the deals you reneged on with my sire."

Harlowe's eyes widened. Deals?

"I also included how several females were trafficked and how weak the investigation into them was. But I saved most of the space for the angel-fire deal struck centuries ago. You remember?" This time he was speaking directly to Senator Thomas. "I heard your name several times. Not many demons are left who remember your part of the deal. You made sure of that."

Senator Thomas's expression hardened, giving everyone a hint of what lengths the male might go to.

"What deal?" Director Vale asked what everyone else not involved wanted to know.

"Your steel." Sandeen gestured to the director's knife strapped on his belt. "Ever wonder where it came from?"

"It's innate to our realm," a young senator answered. Felicia nodded. She wasn't the only young senator with a confused expression.

"Is it?" Sandeen tilted his head. He reached into his pocket and pulled out a chunk of soft, grayish metal. He tossed it up and caught it. Senator Thomas sat forward. "Would you like to answer that? Or would you like to tell them about how my sire mined a shitload of Daemon ore in return for angel fire? Angel fire that we never got?"

"We couldn't give our fire to Daemon," Senator Thomas scoffed. If anyone hadn't thought Sandeen was telling the truth, they did now.

"But you were willing to have them do your work. You've made so many deals with the demons, it's ridiculous. No one will fault you for not living up to your end. No one wants a demon to have access to angel fire.

But what about the other deals? Like getting more ore in exchange for some of your females?"

Senator Thomas rose. A rare display from him. "We did no such thing."

"*You* may not have. But your failed angel-fire deal gave others some ideas. Regardless, the end message is the same—senators do business with Daemon. Always have. Always will. And if the people knew, they'd question their entire existence, including why the hell they have a senate in the first place. And there goes your power."

"We are not proud of that time in our existence," the old senator wheezed.

The "we" he referred to was self-evident. It would be too easy to walk through the ranks and pick out who was involved. The guilt was written into their expressions and the way they hunched in on themselves, as if trying to disappear.

"But you did it. Angels have died for it. And you'll do it again. Because the metal doesn't last forever."

Another veteran senator spoke up. "You might have uncovered some unsavory parts of our past, but we won't do it again. You're wrong about that."

"False. Human metal just can't compare to ours, can it? And I'm guessing that due to your recent conflicts with demons, your stash is going down."

Harlowe gave her head a stunned shake. They had to track their weapons. Andy had gotten a stockpile and ruined it when the club had burned down. The director was trying to figure out how to get it back, but that much evidence disappearing from some Vegas police precinct was problematic. But warriors had always been instructed to be careful and file a report. Their stock was replenished, but she'd never really wondered from where. None of them had. The senators had taken care of it.

Sandeen tossed his little hunk in the air and caught it, watching Senator Thomas's reaction. "Now that you know what will happen if you renege on *this* demon, I happen to have found myself in control of a mine."

The senator lifted his chin, his gaze shrewd.

Sandeen grinned. "I pay my demons in Twinkies and gummy bears, so no need to worry I'll ask for the same payment as my sire. You leave me and Harlowe alone, and I'll provide some fresh material for those weapon stores you're worried are getting real low."

Senator Thomas's fingers tapped his knee. "We must still discuss this."

"By all means." Sandeen crooked his elbow out. Harlowe curled her hand around it. It didn't matter what he did next. She was with him regardless. "The director can pass along your decision. If I see anyone but him or my mate's other teammates near my home, then that mine dries up."

As they turned to walk out, Harlowe whispered, "That's a hell of a bargain."

"It's one I plan to uphold, angel."

"What if they don't?"

He grinned as they exited the senate auditorium. "We always have that stash of fallen blood to threaten them with. I know a lot of demons who'd love to test what it can do."

She smothered her gasp. "You're so naughty."

"You like me that way."

Sandeen stretched his neck from side to side. He was getting better at keeping his wings morphed for long periods, but his muscles protested. His gaze landed on the pan in front of him. "Shit."

Harlowe swung her legs on the counter. "It's fine."

"I almost burned the shrimp," he grumbled as he took the pan off the stove and put it on the other side of Harlowe. She stopped swinging her feet to keep from kicking him in the groin.

She'd done enough to his dick this morning. All the best things, but still. It'd feel a tap from her bare little toes. And hurt would be the last thing on his brain if she touched any spot near his cock.

He was perpetually hard around her.

The whole bond thing was pretty cool. Director Vale had completed the sync. Sandeen wasn't sure if it enhanced sex or if it was all the emotions the angel brought out in him, but each time he was with Harlowe was better than the last.

"*Almost* burned," she reiterated. "Not burned. Besides, I think you could stomp on the shrimp and she wouldn't care."

"Alma flew all the way to Michigan to see me. I'm not getting footprints or char on her food."

Harlowe grinned at him. She loved him in the kitchen.

Since the senate had met and told Director Vale to notify Sandeen that they were graciously allowing him to remain on Earth and to mate one of their warriors, he'd been on probation.

If probation was what they called a sorry attempt at a power play, then fine. Sandeen would play along as long as he was left alone in this little farmhouse with his mate.

The director's personal team had taken a hit in the hearing. They weren't suspended, but Bryant was negotiating for his own warriors to be assigned as needed, and that those warriors be Harlowe, Bronx, Urban, Jagger,

Dionna, and Ransom. The director had been prepared with a litany of reasons to have warriors not already assigned to missions at his disposal, ones he trusted implicitly. According to Bronx, who'd almost collapsed from laughing so hard while he told the story, the director had a way of making it sound like if he wasn't allowed to keep his team, it must mean the senate was still shady and hiding shit.

He'd done more than insinuate. He'd said it out loud.

So Harlowe wasn't out of a job. The director had said that between his personal missions, they could still continue working as warriors like normal. Sierra and Boone would still lie low. Her secret was safe, but it was best to be cautious. Dionna was still on personal leave, and Jagger spent his time off in Numen with Felicia.

The doorbell rang.

"It's open," Harlowe called as she hopped down.

Bronx swaggered in. "Long story short, I hope you made extra. Urban heard you were cooking."

Sandeen grinned. This place had become a gathering spot for the rest of Harlowe's team.

"I always make extra," he said the same time Harlowe said, "He always makes extra."

"Ugh." Bronx shuddered. "If you two become *that* couple, I'm going to quit being your friend."

Sandeen ignored Bronx's good-natured teasing and went to the little old lady Urban was helping up the walk.

Alma glanced up and beamed. "My demon." She stopped and held her arms out.

Sandeen went right to them, folding himself into her embrace. He'd hated possessing people for his own gain, but it'd been his only escape from the underworld. Yet taking over Alma had been the best thing he'd ever done.

She wrapped her skinny arms around him and hugged with more force than he'd thought her body could manage.

He held her carefully, afraid he'd crush a rib or something. But damn. He was glad to see her.

Harlowe was teaching him how to transcend between places on Earth. She'd forbidden him from using the Mist like he used the Gloom, claiming only warriors should do it, and only when necessary. Watchers could do it too, but humans couldn't see them.

He'd follow the rules, for her. The only place he wanted to transcend was to Alma's house anyway.

"It's good to see you, Alma." He hugged her as long as she held him.

"It's so good to see you. I never thought we'd be able to visit like this." She pulled back but kept her hands on his shoulders, barely able to reach that far. "I'm proud of you." She rose to her tiptoes and patted his face.

An unfamiliar sensation stung the backs of his eyes. She smiled, her soft cheeks crinkling, and shuffled into the house. "Ooh, I smell something good."

She was proud of him.

Alma had lived longer than his mother. She'd seen a lot in her time. She'd known him when he'd been nothing but a demon, and she knew him now. A mated male. Half angel.

And she was proud of him.

He turned to the door. The others were already inside, but Harlowe leaned against the closed door. "I think they're going to start without us."

Her violet gaze brushed over him. She skipped over his head and his back. She'd said before that she missed seeing his wings. She missed his horns and his fangs too—and what those could do to her. But he didn't.

The other day when he was in town, a little boy had asked him about his beard. Asked if only tall men could grow them. It was the first time Sandeen had talked to a child. Their innocence blew his mind. They spoke more frankly than symasters tattling on each other. And the lady he bought milk and eggs from liked to tease him about how she was going to load the beat-up old truck he and Harlowe had purchased with chicks so he could learn to raise his own egg layers.

He went through a lot of eggs.

Losing his horns and fangs had given him the freedom to be with Harlowe. It'd always be worth it. Worth it to walk around the realm in his own body, in front of anyone. Sure, he and Harlowe would have to move every generation or so to keep people from wondering why he and his mate stayed so youthful looking. But there were a lot of other farmhouses. A lot of other small towns with kids who had questions about beards.

He went up the stairs and dropped a kiss on his mate's lips. During their time together, he'd learned that she wanted to fly with him. His mate would never fly on Earth, but he had a plan. "What do you say tomorrow night, we sneak into Numen and go for a little night flight? Maybe visit your father?"

Her eyes brightened. She'd gone to see her father a couple of times, for no other reason than to talk. She'd told him about her new mate, telling him Sandeen had been raised away from the realm and that his work was on Earth and it kept him busy. The worry that her father would sink further into depression watching his daughter fall in love while he'd lost his mate passed quickly. He'd livened up, said it was good to see her have interests outside of work, and asked her all about "Sander" and where they were staying. After the last visit, her father had told her he enjoyed their time together, and that if Sander was too shy to enter Numen, he could just come to the house. Said he wouldn't tell anyone.

Harlowe had practically floated home. "Demon, I like that plan."

He slipped an arm around her and led her into the house. "Then it's a good thing I have plans for you for the rest of my life."

CHAPTER 26

"Please, call me Juliette." Senator Colbert took a sip of her wine. The green bottle was on the end table between them, covered in cobwebs and dust. Or was that mold? The senator had said something about cellars and aging and mold and quality, but it could've been a foreign language.

Since there were no vineyards in Numen, much less cellars full of seventy-year-old wine, Tosca pondered how the senator had gotten it. Did she belong to an old-wine-of-the-month club? When would she have had time to go to Earth and get a bottle between defending her mate and mourning her son? Maybe she'd stolen it.

Tosca tried to retrieve the thought as soon as it slipped through her mind. The senator wasn't a thief. She refused to even joke like that about Senator Colbert, a female who'd championed her rise through the ranks of the enforcers. A senator Tosca considered her mentor. The mentor she'd confided in about wanting to become a senator herself one day.

Juliette Colbert wasn't a thief.

Tosca's gaze strayed to the bottle. She'd been to the senator's place before. Had dined with the female and her mate. Jean Luc wasn't around too often. He and Francois had been close.

Close partiers.

Stop it. Tosca lifted her gaze to the senator's. The female watched her expectantly.

"Uh, I'm sorry. I didn't catch that."

The senator's gaze darkened before friendliness returned. This time Tosca hadn't imagined it. Senator Colbert had been under a lot of pressure. That had to be why she was short-tempered.

"I said to call me Juliette. After all, we're going to be spending a lot of time together." Her eyes misted over and she winced, lowering her gaze to the floor. "Since Jean Luc no longer wishes to return to the realm."

Despite his initial tear-filled confession, one filled with details supposedly only the trafficker could know, Jean Luc had been declared innocent, the entire blame put on their son, Francois. At some point Jean Luc had admitted he'd been distraught and had wanted to protect Francois's legacy when he'd learned of what had happened to the boy. Hence the since-retracted confession.

And the senate believed him.

How terribly convenient. If Tosca hadn't witnessed the fallout in the senate herself, she would've been suspicious. But she couldn't imagine more shady deals getting made after Sandeen and all his threats.

The information he'd revealed had been shocking.

It should've been *staggering*, but apparently her time as an enforcer had made her jaded. Enforcers took their oath of silence seriously. They were exposed to the worst of their kind, the worst of angels who thought they were above the sins of humanity.

"I can imagine he doesn't feel safe here," Tosca said. She wanted to support Senator Colbert—Juliette. Weird calling the senator by her first name. Tosca wasn't one with a lot of friends.

"No. Not at all. The way they used his grief against him . . ." She took a long sip and poured more into her glass. "Don't you care for the wine?"

It all tasted like juice splashed in rubbing alcohol. Either that or Tosca had been on the right side of the law for so long she had a hard time indulging in anything that resembled her old life. "It's decadent, thank you."

Juliette waved her hand and took another sip. "Absolutely welcome. What would I do without my personal enforcer?"

Whenever the senator said that, it put Tosca's teeth on edge. *This is how friends treat each other*. Tosca was rustier than she'd thought at peopling.

"Anyway, I could use your help."

Disappointment settled around her shoulders. Juliette Colbert was a busy female. She couldn't be making social calls during the day. Tosca was off today, but that didn't mean she wasn't ready to serve her realm. She set her wineglass down. She didn't want to hold it when she was talking about her job. "I'm happy to be of service. Do I need to make a formal report?"

Juliette's smile was wide. Had the wine stained her lips bloodred? Her even, white teeth shone the same way the Big Bad Wolf's must've for Little Red Riding Hood. She gave her head a shake. The few sips Tosca had must've been stronger than she'd thought.

"No, that's not necessary. I've been thinking." Her gaze dipped to the glass of wine. "Are you sure you don't want more? It's such a rare wine. Practically invaluable. I'd hate to waste it."

The pout prompted Tosca to lift the glass. She steeled herself for another sip, taking a large enough one that she could finish the glass quickly, but not gag. "No, it's great."

Ugh. There were a few ounces left, but she didn't want to disappoint Juliette. No one served Tosca their finest of anything. That'd take getting invited somewhere first. She forced another gulp down.

The senator sat back with a pleased smirk. "As I was saying, I've been thinking that I need to do something to get back in the good graces of the senate. They seem leery of me."

The scandal with Jean Luc was pretty bad. How had her mate gotten off so easily anyway? He'd known so many details that a male who claimed to be innocent shouldn't have.

"I want my good standing back," Juliette continued.

Tosca blinked and stared into the liquid. There was an ounce left. She chugged it, managing her gag reflex as Juliette prattled on.

"As you know, there's nothing more important to me than the work I do in the senate."

There wasn't much more important than being a senator to most senators.

Tosca, knock it off.

She didn't want to be the jaded, lost girl anymore. She was an enforcer. She had a purpose in life now.

Her head spun and she blinked. She needed to get to sleep earlier. Getting to bed on time was fine. It wasn't like she had a full social calendar. It was dreams of a certain warrior that got under her skin. Images out of nowhere. Of him. And her. Entangled.

Her cheeks blazed.

She wasn't a prude. She had experience. But ever since she'd cleaned up her life, she'd decided to put more thought into who she shared a bed with. If all the eligible males of Numen lined up for her perusal, Bronx would be her last choice. He was everything she'd left behind.

She stifled a yawn. What the heck was going on with her?

She blinked again, her eyelids heavy. With more effort than necessary, she looked at the senator.

Juliette watched her, a gleam circling her blue irises. "Tosca? How was the wine?" She practically purred the last part.

Long-silent alarms rose in her brain. Something was wrong.

"Julgubegoodch . . ." Her tongue quit working and she canted to the side. Her wings hung like they were lined with lead feathers.

What the hell?

"Tosca, my dear," the senator's chiding words were the last she heard as she struggled to remain conscious, "you really shouldn't have over-imbibed."

Tosca succumbed to the darkness. She'd trusted the wrong person. Again.

––––––––––

ANGELS SHOULDN'T BE FRAMED for murder, but Tosca is. When she goes on the run, Bronx is sent to hunt her down. The real question is, what is he going to do when he finds her in Corrupt Fire?

. . .

THANK you so much for reading. I'd love to know what you thought. Please consider leaving a review of Warrior Fire.

FOR NEW RELEASE UPDATES, chapter sneak peeks, and exclusive quarterly short stories, sign up for Marie's newsletter and receive a download link for three short stories of characters from the series.

ABOUT THE AUTHOR

Marie Johnston lives in the upper-Midwest with her husband, four kids, and an old cat. Deciding to trade in her lab coat for a laptop, she's writing down all the tales she's been making up in her head for years. An avid reader of paranormal romance, these are the stories hanging out and waiting to be told between the demands of work, home, and the endless chauffeuring that comes with children.